Apocalypse Party
Art Direction by B.R. Yeager
Layout by Mike Corrao

Paperback: 978-1-954899-34-6

THE SAME THINGS KEEP HAPPENING

Your son is thirty and still can't take care of himself. He faked it long enough to secure a wife, but it gave out sometime after the second year. He goes days without bathing, nursing bacteria-caked pits and crotch. Always congested. Scratching hot spots into his flesh, staining bedsheets with blood and snot. Your daughter-in-law tells you that six months ago she resigned herself to the couch. She can't look at him without crying.

Your son lost his job. Your son went back to community college and dropped out. Your son won't look up.

Your son still jerks off seventeen times a day. Lets his seed just drip and crisp on the sheets that once also belonged to his partner, or seep and stiffen the fibers of his jeans. He never washes his clothes—just cycling and re-cycling through three distinct piles of filthed garment, cultivated into volcanic islands atop the carpet. Every shirt he owns streaked with dried soup, either red or pus-colored.

The last time you saw him, he smiled but there wasn't anything behind his eyes.

Your daughter-in-law tells you she is frightened of him. She says she can count on one hand the words he says in a day. She tells you that several months ago they adopted a puppy, but she had to give it away because your son would never feed or walk it while she was at work.

Your daughter-in-law buys all the groceries. Your son never leaves the apartment. He refuses water when offered.

Your son is still a liar, and you still can't quite be sure you're safe because he still dreams of you each night. He dreams of you in ways you could never begin to imagine. And no one knows this, but your son is watching you right now. He is standing in his bathroom in his worn-elastic boxers and sweated-out sneakers, the laces untied and flailed against the freckled tiling. His eyes are wide open, aimed just above the mirror on the medicine cabinet, and when he focuses hard—so hard his eyes go blurry and his temples ache—he can see you, awake and pacing the hardwood miles away. And if he could speak to you, he would say he was the face in the light of the moon. He'd tell you his teeth are made of ice and grit, his breath a frozen spear. And if he could, he'd breathe all over your world, turning it cold and gaseous. He would watch your skin and your hair starve gray. And he would smile at how surprised your mouth curled and eyes widened. He'd smile at how that expression would be locked on your face forever. You would be so surprised because even though you couldn't see him—you have no way of knowing it's his breath raining down from the moon up high—you would feel his familiarity. And he would look down on you from the sun's reflected light, knowing your last memory is of you fixing his tiny, eight-year-old frame in a bed shaped like a race car, silently praying he'd still be safe and okay when you came to wake him the next day.

Any precious thing can lose meaning. Anything. It's only a matter of repetition. That old cliché—repeat a word enough times and it'll become nonsensical. Transform into noise. Nothing. Everyone knows this. Cliché beyond cliché—knowledge so common you get marked a fool for even mentioning it.

A man answers the phone. "Hello?"

"Good morning," I say. "My name is Chelle Pleasant, I'm calling on behalf of the Massachusetts Department of Public Health."

Beep beep. The man hangs up. Gone.

So repeat. Call a different number. Listen to the tones, wait for someone to pick up, to say *hello*, and repeat the words. "Hello, my name is Chelle Pleasant, and I'm calling on behalf of the Massachusetts Department of Public Health. How are you this morning?" *Beep beep.* Gone.

Repeat. Dial the numbers. Speak the words. Repeat them, like a machine, like hands on a machine. It's a sound, a tone, vibrations in your throat, and eventually there's nothing else behind it. Say it over and over, until it makes no sense and there's nothing there.

This job used to mean something to me: self-sufficiency—a baseline at the very least. I knew the work was bullshit and didn't accomplish anything (even with the best intentions, a public health survey will only ever amount to a bureaucratic check mark), but it still enabled food and shelter and the occasional night out (when we still went out). And it still is that, objectively. It just doesn't feel that way anymore.

Repeat. Repeat the motor functions until your fingers go numb. Repeat the words until they're just ugly syllables. Say "I love you" each day until it's only hiss. Barely discernible from wind at the windows, power humming in the walls. Hold him until he feels like humid summer air. It's something that should hurt, that maybe used to but no longer aches. We pretend it doesn't matter but we should be grieving.

✦

Tony sits at the kitchen table, his headset plugged into his phone, repeating the same lines as me. "Hey, my name is Anthony Rossi. I'm calling on behalf of the Massachusetts Department of Public Health." His voice overlapping mine, at times in sync but mostly drifting in and out. Competing.

It's supposed to be a blessing that we can work from home. But now every aspect of living just feels like work, regardless of whether we're clocked in or not. No matter what we're doing.

Dial the number. Wait for an answer. Recite the script. "Hello, my name is Chelle Pleasant, and I'm calling on behalf of the Massachusetts Department of Public Health." Wait a beat for the sound of the respondent clicking off. The *beep beep*. But it doesn't come. Instead, just crackle and mouth breathing. So continue. "We're conducting a general health study of Massachusetts residents. It will only take ten to fifteen minutes. Can I confirm that I am speaking to someone who lives in this household and is over eighteen years of age?"

I wait again for the click, the *beep beep*. But instead, a ragged voice sizzles through. "Yes. You are."

⌒

"Generally, I am not very worried about my health. Would you say you strongly agree, somewhat agree, somewhat disagree, or strongly disagree?"

"Agree."

"Would you say you strongly agree or somewhat agree?"

"Somewhat agree."

"I have many friends I like to exercise with."

"I dunno."

"Is there an answer on the scale that aligns with that statement?"

"What scale?"

"Strongly agree, somewhat agree, somewhat disagree, or strongly disagree."

"Somewhat disagree."

"Thank you. My friends and family tell me I seem healthy."

"Agree."

"Would that be strongly agree or somewhat agree?"

"Somewhat agree."

I ask if she's been pregnant in the past three years. I ask if the pregnancy resulted in a live birth. I ask about major surgeries, medications, and whether she's been raped in the previous six months. And there—that's when she hangs up. *Beep beep.* Nothing else. It's over. The interview will be marked as incomplete and the data will be discarded.

✦

Tony brings in the mail. He cracks open an envelope and unfolds the insides. "Did you pay the electric?"

"Yeah." I don't look up from my phone, scrolling through text and images. "I mean, I'm going to."

"Isn't it overdue?"

"I know. I'm sorry. I'm taking care of it."

"Like, right now?"

Text and images, unrolling down and down. Jokes by people I've never met, will never meet, will never speak to. A video of human beings falling from a parade float. "I will. Today."

"It's just —" he starts. "It's just that —" A sentence begins and aborts, catching in his delicate throat until he snags an opening and rides it out. "I don't think it's fair for me to have to pay half the late fees when it's not my fault they're late."

An image of a tapir with squinting eyes and bared teeth, face frozen in a sneer. "*You* can always pay it." My stomach, my mouth, the back of my throat all sour. "If you feel that strongly about it."

He tosses the bill on the table. "I do a lot, I think." Small and sweaty. "I pay the internet. I wash your dishes half the time."

"Alright then." A cartoon of a woman shrieking at a bearded man. "I'll pay it this evening."

"I take the trash out every week."

I place the phone on the table and press the heels of my palms into my eyes. Text and image behind my eyelids now, scrolling down and down. "I'll take care of it."

"You don't even know where the bins are. I know you don't. You have no clue."

⌃

We prepare our dinners separately—fusilli with shitty meat sauce for me, yellow rice and canned beans for him. We eat separately. Separate places and separate times—him at the kitchen table at 4:35, me on the couch at 6:00. When I'm finished, I dunk my dishes in the sink and head back toward the living room, but terminate mid-step, and return to the sink, twisting on the water, picking up the sponge.

Tony sidles up, nudging into my side. "If you give me the account number I'll pay it."

Don't say anything. Focus on the bowl. The cheese that won't scrub off.

"Okay? Does that sound good?"

"Yeah." I keep low, scrubbing the dish. "Sure. That's good. Thanks."

⌃

Our house doesn't belong to us. I mean it's not our house. A small house on a tobacco farm, rented from a farmer who lives enough acres away it mostly feels like we're on our own. A tiny house, almost not a house at all—just a bedroom, a half-kitchen/half-living room, a bathroom. A dirt floor basement beneath our feet.

Night turns the sky hard purple and rust red—UMass

light pollution sooting the true night. No moon, switching the landscape off to black. We sit outside at the top of the driveway, pointed out toward the road. I pack a bowl, take a hit and pass it to Tony. "Sometimes it feels like if I walked right there —" I point out toward where the road's supposed to be, but it's just a black hole. "— I'd walk straight off the edge of the Earth."

Tony takes a hit, silent.

"Like I'd just fall off. Probably just die immediately. Just fall into space and die."

Tony hands the bowl back to me. "But it isn't a ledge. It's a road. There is no edge."

I hit the bowl and exhale pale plumes. "I'm saying it feels like there's nothing in front of me. Nothing. Like I don't have anything in front of me. That's it. That's all."

Tony looks out at the black hole. "Okay."

⌁

I'm on the couch reading about eastern spadefoot toads when Tony comes out of the bathroom, scrunching his face like he might cry or has been crying. "You should do a tick check," he says.

"Yeah?"

"Just pulled one out of my asshole."

"Are you okay?"

"Yeah. I mean, I will be."

⌁

In bed I tuck myself behind his back, rubbing his deltoid and spine with my nipples. Reaching down and tracing my fingers beneath the band of his underwear, then further, brushing fingers through pubic hair, taking hold of his soft penis. He groans. I stroke it, but it stays limp, refusing to fill with blood. He groans again and bats at my arm. "I'm exhausted," he says, flipping onto his stomach.

I touch myself but it isn't what I want, not alone. I don't want me. So I go to sleep, or try to.

⌃

We call strangers, we speak words, we make noises, and they hang up on us.

But not my fifty-seventh call. I get through the intro script and the respondent is actually happy to talk. "Now's a perfect time," she says.

So we get into it. She tells me her name: Cherise Flint. A sixty-three-year-old cancer survivor with three grown children, who doesn't exercise but feels healthy, and has never been raped. We talk for twenty-seven minutes and reach the final section. "Thank you for taking the time to complete this survey. I now just need to ask a few de-mographic questions." And right there she clicks off. *Beep beep.*

The interview will be marked as an incomplete and the data will be discarded. All of it, meaning nothing. I grasp my knees and squeeze, as though to pull them from their sockets.

The phone buzzes. Work's number. I pick up, shaking.

"Hey, Michelle?" A nasal masculine voice. Familiar. One of my supervisors. We've never met but we've spoken before, maybe. "I monitored that last incomplete. Now a good time for feedback?"

"Yeah, sure. Just a sec." Almost crying. So stupid. I put the laptop on the coffee table and head toward the bedroom. Tony looks up and mouths *you got this*. I close the door behind me, locking it. "Hey."

"So close!" the voice says.

"I know."

"Don't worry about it. Nothing you could do. It happens. Anyway, I don't have much here. So good work answering her questions about medications. But on Q24, I think it was on the nebulizer part?"

"Yes, totally. I know the one. I know what you mean."

"Right… It seemed like you may have guided her a little too much there. No big deal, just something to watch out for. So all in all, I'm giving you a ninety. Does that sound good?"

"Yeah, sure. I mean, thanks."

"No problem. And I just need to record your acknowledgement that I, Dennis McKean, on July 17th 2021, delivered supervisory feedback on an incomplete with Michelle Pleasant."

"I acknowledge."

"Great. Cool. I'll submit that now."

"Great."

"One last thing." The voice changes; constricts. Like a gentle hand on his throat. "I hope this doesn't come off sketch or anything. But I actually just moved to Massachusetts, and I saw that you actually live just a town away from me. And —"

Back in the living room, Tony asks how it went.

"Fine." Trying to recollect, to pull together what just

happened, what was actually going on. "That guy, though. The supervisor. Have you ever had—Dennis I think?"

"I have no clue."

"Doesn't matter. Anyway, after the feedback and everything, he tells me he just moved to the area, to Hadley, and he doesn't know anyone around here, but he saw that I lived in the area."

"Whoa." A frown creases.

"Yeah, right?"

"Why does he know where we live?"

"Right? And that's the thing—he asks me if I want to get together sometime or something."

"Yeah?"

"Yeah, like he says he just moved to the area, he doesn't know anyone, and wanted to know if I'd want to meet up."

He sneers. "Well, that's really fucking presumptuous."

"Right?"

"That's like, definitely crossing a boundary. Like, professionally and all sorts of other levels."

"*Right?* Like, why does he have access to my address? He shouldn't have access to my address."

"What did you tell him?"

"I told him, I told him, I'm real busy. You know. I didn't want to piss him off. But I'm not fucking meeting up with him. That's for sure."

"Good. That's so fucking weird."

⌣

We go on Facebook and type in *Dennis McKean*. Little circles with photos inside pour down the screen. All these faces: An old man with an old woman. A young man with a beard, a chocolate lab's head beneath his chin. Two cats staring out a window. We click, skimming profiles then returning to the list. An elderly man in a recliner. A man and a woman and baby.

But there: A smiling face, flat and angular, an ugly curled cowlick atop the head. White, clean hairless skin, outside in the sun. Click, open his profile, and scan. "I don't know," I say. "It says St. Louis, Missouri." But something else. "Wait, he works for MSC Data Capture."

"He said he just moved here, right?"

"Yeah. That's right. It's got to be him." Switch over to his timeline. All the posts are from months ago. Open the gallery. A photo of Dennis leaning against a Buick LaCrosse. Dennis holding up a beer, one eyebrow raised. Dennis soy-facing, pointing to a pirate mini-golf course. "Woof."

"How old is he?"

"Let's see. Whoa, thirty-eight. Yuck."

"I'm so fucking mad this guy lives around here now."

Scroll further. There are maybe a hundred pictures. Nobody else in them, only him. Dennis at a Starbucks. Dennis drinking beer, outside, in the dark. Dennis at a public pool, alone. A broad, lycanthrope grin. "What a creep." I close the laptop. "I don't even want to think about him."

⌁

I'm cooking stir fry for myself when Tony yells from the couch. "Holy shit!"

"*What?*"

"You've got to see this."

"Just a second."

"What? No, come on, you got to see this." His voice

like hands wringing me out from the inside.

Inhale. Pull inward. Exhale. I take the pan off the heat, twist off the burner, and meet Tony at the couch. "What is it?"

He pats the cushion next to him. "Look."

I sit down and look at the screen. A map covered in red dots. "Why are you on the sex offender registry?"

"Forget that. Look." He points to a headshot in the sidebar.

A flat face. Jagged-edged. A small flat nose. Unkempt hair. A long slit of a mouth. "Wait. Is that the guy?"

"It's absolutely the guy."

"Oh. Oh no."

"Our fucking supervisor."

"Oh no."

"He touches kids."

"Oh no." I look over the map. "Where is this?"

He leans into me, wild eyes. "Fucking St. Louis. Right?"

The pieces snap together. It pulls all the air from my lungs. "Okay, so he moves here. And, and it's like he's trying to start over here or something?"

"That's it."

"Jesus. Like, he doesn't have a rep here, so he figures he can start fresh." Leaning into the screen, focusing on the picture, the pixels constructing his face. His skin looks different from the pics on Facebook. Scarred, pockmarked. A ring of days-old stubble around his mouth. "Are you sure it's him?"

Tony wobbles his head side to side, sucking teeth—the face he makes every time he thinks I've said something dumb. "Of course it is. Look at him." He pulls up Dennis's Facebook profile and puts it side by side with the sex offender registry. "Same name, same eyes. It's fucking him. In fact —" He clicks open another tab. It's the web page for our work, the Hadley branch, the staff directory. He scrolls to a photo and bio. Dennis McKean. The face there looks more like the one on Facebook than the one in the sex offender registry. But I guess it looks like that one too.

I think of his voice. Evoking foul moisture. Shake it away. "What are we going to do?"

Tony doesn't say anything. He pulls up the registry website again and just stares at the headshot.

"Should we tell work? Like maybe they don't know? Should we go to the cops?"

Nothing.

"What are we going to do?"

He closes his eyes and shakes his head. "I don't know. I don't know. I don't know I don't know I don't know."

⌒

I finish up the stir fry and watch a program about Alaskan-Yukon moose. Lumbering, tearing their velvet open on tree branches and bark. Tony never looks up from the computer. At 10:00 I ask if he's coming to bed.

"In a little while."

I fall asleep alone.

⌒

"*Hey.*" A single hushed syllable. A hand at my shoulder.

Twisting awake, eyes snapping open. A blurry shape over me.

"Hey." Tony's voice. Tony's face. Hovering in the dark. "Are you awake?"

∾

I curl inside his armpit. Kneading my fingers. Making them pop.

"It's just an idea," he says. "We can stop talking about it."

"I didn't say I didn't want to talk about it."

"Well, will you say something?" Tracing his fingers along the ridges of my belly. "I just think we need to be doing something right now. Something we can focus on."

"Yeah. I know. You're right."

∾

My psychiatrist stares empty at me through the laptop screen. "Are you still doing yoga before bed?" she asks. "Meditation?"

"I've been jogging during the day. I haven't touched caffeine. I just can't get to sleep."

"What about screen time? Are you on your phone before bed?"

Ahead of me, behind the computer, Tony paces, gnawing his knuckles. Watching me.

I shake my head. "I don't look at any screens after dinner," I lie. "Not even TV."

"Have you ever tried melatonin or magnesium? Or an over-the-counter sleep aid? CBD can help."

"I'm doing all that," I snap. Tony is nodding at me, mouthing *yes*. "Nothing's working. I need something."

She stares at me, through the screen, through me.

"Okay. I can write you a script. You can pick it up from Jeanne at the office."

A smile breaks on Tony's face. Silent, he pumps his fists. He places his palms together and gently bows.

⌔

We order rope, chain, bungee cords. Handcuffs and zip ties. Two-day shipping on Amazon. We dig a metal folding chair out of the closet and take turns tying each other up, seeing if we can break free.

⌔

The number feels wet as I dial it. Five rings.

"Hello?" The voice says.

"Hey. Is this Dennis?"

"Yeah. Is this Michelle?"

"Yeah. It's Chelle."

⌔

He arrives early. Tony answers the door. "Hey! You found it!" he says, maybe too enthusiastic. Almost certainly.

"Yeah, man." Dennis steps through the door. That flat broad face. Small nose. Clean pale skin. "Not too hard to find." He looks exactly like the photos. Maybe. I can't remember. Maybe a little heavier. Or thinner—thinner arms, narrower eyes. Different hair. He looks at me. "You must be Chelle."

"Hey." My voice creaks out like sliced paper. I barely meet his eyes. "What's good?"

"You know. Everything." Dennis scans the living room. "Nice place! I'd love to have me a place like this someday."

I head toward the kitchen. "I'll get drinks."

"Word'em up. I'll take whatever."

A sack of ice, margarita mix, a bottle of Pepe Lopez on the counter. Three glasses with cartoons painted on them: a Snoopy, a Grimace, and a generic clown. I blend up the drinks and open a drawer, removing a bag of crushed powder, sprinkling a thimbleful into the clown glass.

⌃

"So how're you liking Mass?" Tony's knee bobs up and down, sloshing his drink onto his pants.

"It's cool, it's cool," Dennis says. "I actually went to school out here. Like, way back."

"Yeah? Where?"

That wide, wolfen smile rises between his lips. "Brandeis. Yeah, I know, I know. Like, initially I thought I'd major in acting or something but ended up doing business instead. Figure I could learn art and philosophy on my own or whatever. Might as well do something viable, fiscally, while I'm there, right? You know. But man, I do miss college." He gulps his drink, licking the salt-less rim. He points a pair of fingers at the two of us. "How long you been a thing?"

Tony inhales, eyeing me. "It's been?"

"Seven years," I say.

Dennis coughs, nearly spilling his drink. "You're kidding. How old are you?"

"Twenty-two."

"Twenty-three," Tony says.

"High school sweethearts, yeah? Damn, that's really sweet. That's really lucky, man." He downs the last of his drink, smacking his lips, and points to the empty glass. "Delicious. Delicious juice."

I ask if he wants another. "Yes and please," he says, head wobbling on its stem, eyes becoming slits. A mannequin. A toy.

⌒

"I mean, no one wants to admit it, and I get why no one wants to admit it—I don't even like to admit—but it's just the way it is. It's just a matter of cultural homogeny. That's it. Like—and I know, I don't like this either, I think this sucks, I think it's a bummer—but really the only reason those places can pull off safety nets like that is because they're, like, intensely homogenous."

I bring Dennis his fifth drink. Acting natural is easier than I thought it would be. He makes it easy. He's the only one who's ever talking. He's only ever aware of himself.

"Ah, mazel." He takes the glass and immediately slurps at it. Greedy bloated infant. "Man, if you knew me maybe two years ago, this would be a completely different situation. Like, I used to get bad when I drank. Like, *really bad*. Like, me and this guy Seth—like my best bud from the last place I was staying—when we'd drink we'd get into just the shittiest most malicious shit. For no reason at all. I mean, real dark shit."

"What do you mean?" Tony says.

"You know. Fights and waking up not knowing where you been and shit. You know. But that's fucking history. You know. Getting a new life together." A big sloppy sip.

"New town, new life."

A simmer in Tony's eye. He leers forward. "So where exactly are you from?"

Dennis pulls his lips off the glass and raises a brow. It hits me with déjà vu. There it is. Recognition.

"Where are you from? Originally?"

Dennis shrugs. "Nowhere specifically. Traveled lots. Army brat stuff."

"Where were you before here?"

"Aberdeen. Aberdeen, Washington. Had a gig there, you know, with this start-up that hooked restaurants up with LLCs and whatever. But then like, everything happened and they laid off the noobs."

I clasp the back of Tony's neck and squeeze gently. He eyes me from the side, sweaty, shaken, then looks back at Dennis. "You ever live in Missouri?"

Dennis pauses. Stares into space, like he's been switched off. Then, snapping back, he meets Tony's eyes and shakes his head. "Can't say I have."

"Really?"

I touch Tony's forearm. "Don't."

"Nah, man." Dennis rolls his eyes back, like he's looking for something just over his head. "Never lived in Missouri. You got family there or something?"

"Yeah. My mom's from there."

"Tight." Dennis kills his drink, belches and stands. "I must apologize," he says, mocking British English. "I must once again make use of your facilities." Stepping forward, he sways immediately, knees buckling. "Whoa." Another broken step, bracing. "*That's* a drink." He falls into the wall. "Oh shit." Dark piss revealing across his khaki shorts. "Oh *God*," he whimpers. "I'm so sorry." And slumps to the floor.

Tony comes to bed naked. Crawling in beside me, penis hard, tip already glazed, pressed to the small of my back. Right hand wrapping me, caressing that dip at the bottom of my belly, just above my pubic hairs. He kisses my shoulder, my neck, and breathes gently in my ear. Wind through a wasps' nest.

I close my eyes. Dennis's skin, hanging loose in slumber. Loose flesh cuffed and chained in the basement. Do I recognize him? Is it the same face?

I jolt. I pull away.

"What's wrong?" Tony asks.

"Nothing," I say. "I'm sorry. Just too in my head."

He sighs. A ruptured beach ball. His hand comes off me as he rolls onto his back. "It's okay. Understandable."

"I think I just need to sleep."

"Yeah, totally." He rolls away from me. "Tomorrow's gonna be crazy."

"Yeah. Totally." And it's just us breathing, peepers yelping outside. "Goodnight."

"Goodnight."

Lying there, eyes closed, trying to remember. Conjuring the face I saw online, the face I saw in our basement, trying to overlay them in my head, trying to make them overlap. Make them identical.

The bed rocks. Just slightly. A rubbing. Tony rubbing his cock beneath the sheets. Stifling moans, holding his breath. I lie still, waiting until he stops and wipes his mess on the side of the mattress topper. I wait until he starts snoring to sneak down to the basement.

Dennis. Skin and muscles loose in sleep, strapped to the chair with handcuffs, bungee cords, zip ties and chain. Heaving breaths through his nostrils, and the space between his lips and the tennis ball taped into his mouth. Like an apple in a dead pig's jaw.

I hold up my phone, one eye on Dennis, one eye on the screen. Looking at the photo on the sex offender registry, holding it side by side with his real face, looking for the similarity. Looking back and forth, at screen, at skin, at screen, at skin, waiting for certainty to click into place.

⌣

Tony wakes me, or I let him think he does. He hugs me from behind and I flinch, pulling away. He frowns.

"Sorry," I say, shifting back towards him.

"Are you excited?" he says, the smile returned. "I'm excited."

I nod. We both get dressed in silence and head downstairs.

Dennis is still bound, still asleep. Heavy snores blowing snot down his lip, over the tennis ball. The basement reeks of him, his piss and sweat and gas.

Tony steps forward, dipping his face toward Dennis's. "Hey."

Dennis doesn't respond, slumped forward and to the side.

"*Hey*." He claps his hands.

Dennis doesn't wake. Tony steps closer and slaps him hard on the temple. Finally, he stirs. His body slowly growing rigid, as though filling with air. His eyes creak open.

"Finally, you piece of shit," Tony says, stepping back toward me and pulling me close, kissing my forehead, but keeping his eyes on Dennis the whole time.

Dennis groans and bucks clumsily in the chair, against his bindings, and at first I think he's trying to break free. But instead, he wretches, face clenched. Watery yellow fluid spitting from between his lips and the tennis ball.

"He's puking," I say, pulling away from Tony. "He's gonna choke." The vomit smells like milk on hot asphalt.

"Shit." Tony reaches out and tears the duct tape from Dennis's cheek. The tennis ball falls from Dennis's lips, rolls off his chest and plunks to the dirt. His face tips forward, spewing hot viscous yellow into his crotch. He hacks and blubs.

Tony wipes his hand on his jeans and slips around behind me, running his left hand over my belly, pulling me into him. His erection pressed into the top of my ass. Resting his chin in the crook of my neck, he removes an Xacto knife from his pocket. Uncapping it, he places it in my right hand, folding his fingers over mine.

Dennis's head lolls. Eyes widening weakly. "Whu—Whus goan on?"

Tony's hand around mine around the knife. He points it right at the flat bloated face, guiding it like a paintbrush.

"Whus happing?"

The face we saw on the screen. Flickering in my memory. I close my eyes to see it clearer, and open to compare. Screen and skin, screen and skin.

I let go of the knife. It falls to the dirt on its side.

Tony lets go of me. "You dropped it."

"Can I talk to him?"

He stares dumbly.

"I want to talk to him."

"Yeah," he pouts. "I guess." He picks up the Xacto knife and points it at Dennis's chest, drawing a circle in the air. "Scream and I'll cut your fucking heart out."

"Whus—whus—" Dennis mumbles, then a long ragged groan.

Tony looks back at me and tosses his hands. "So you want to talk?"

I step toward the bound soiled man. "Where did you live before coming here?"

Dennis just looks at me and sighs.

"Dude," Tony says. "We know who you fucking are. We looked you up."

"Stop," I say.

"Three fucking kids."

"Stop. Please." And now I'm crying, turning from both of them, running up the stairs. Tony's voice calling out, chasing after with an alien, frightened fury. At the top, in the kitchen, he catches me, grabbing my shoulder, spinning me around.

"Hey hey hey," he says. "What the fuck."

"It isn't him." Pressing my face into his chest.

"I don't know what that means."

"It isn't him. I don't think it's him."

He steps away. A tremor mounting. "Are you *fucking* kidding me?" He throws the Xacto knife at the wall. It bounces off and skitters across the counter, clattering into the sink. "You saw him on the fucking registry. You *saw* him."

"I don't think it's him."

"Who else would it be?"

"I think we made a mistake."

"Okay." Pacing. Pressing his palms into his temples. "Let me get this straight. Okay. Okay? So, because you can't trust your own two eyes, because you can't trust your basic fucking cognitive faculties, you're going to—*fuck*." He punches the wall, denting the plaster.

"I—I don't know."

"That's fucking wonderful. That's spectacular. You know, you know, it would've been nice if you'd expressed this uncertainty, you know, pretty much any time before right now, you know? I mean, *God*. Any fucking time. I mean, *Jesus Christ*."

"I don't know what you want me to tell you."

He bends toward me, bringing his face to my height, meeting my eyes precisely. "I want you to say 'Yes Anthony. That's the kiddie toucher we saw on the sex offender registry.' I want you to say 'Yes Anthony, you were right.'"

I lift my fist and strike him in the chest. It's like hitting an empty box. I go to our room and slam the door.

ᐱ

I imagine a life, a new life moving on. A life without him. Lying to the cops, telling them it was all his idea, that he threatened to kill me if I didn't comply. I testify in court and my fiction satisfies all relevant parties. He goes to jail forever and I sell half my belongings and move into a single-room apartment in a sprawling, tucked away complex in Florence, or Greenfield, or Easthampton. I probably don't keep my job, or maybe I do if Dennis leaves to a new career, maybe in a new state, where this can all happen to him once again.

I go out—to shows, to dance nights, to karaoke, trying to pick up boys and maybe girls, but I've forgotten how to converse, or even engage. The ones who approach me initially, thinking my face or body is cute, they cringe when I speak, retreating from my wilted syntax. Or maybe there's someone who waits it out till we're both too drunk to understand what's happening, and the next thing I know I'm on a strange mattress with things stuffed inside me. Sneaking out the next morning before he or she wakes, getting brunch by myself—waffles with peaches and whipped cream on top, home fries on the side. Considering hobbies I could adopt, ukulele or edgy needlepoint. Then the headache—the bitch from the night before, the drilling of it—turns everything so insurmountable and I put my forehead on the table and puke in my lap.

Stepping over the ledge. Seeing if anything's beneath me.

⌣

We hear him scream from the basement. Sometimes words but mostly just sound. Tony stomps downstairs and is gone for five, ten minutes, then back up again. You can still hear the screams, just muffled now. Easier to pretend like they aren't there.

⌣

When you're young, you think of love as something tangible. Like it's an actual thing—an energy, or even an object, like a physical property binding you to another person. And that's why love fails, usually. Real love isn't a thing. It's an action; it's a verb. It's what you do with that energy that matters, and what you do to preserve it. It's work. It's so much work. It's so fucking hard and that's one reason it fails too.

✧

It's not the screaming, because eventually Dennis stops screaming, but I don't sleep. I'm already up, sitting at the kitchen table in my underwear when Tony wakes on the couch. Rising, squinting through puffy eyes.

"Hey," I say.

He winces in surprise, finding me. "Hey."

"Hey," I repeat. "Can we talk?"

"Yeah. Sure." He gets up, reaching into his underwear, flipping his hard-on under the waistband so it won't show as much.

"Come." I hold out my arms, hands dangling on weak wrists. "Come here." He comes and I hug him around the waist, my ear pressed to his stomach. His belly gurgles. "I think you're right."

"Hmm?" He rubs my hair in his palm.

"It's him. He's the pedo. You were right."

He looks down at me. "Yeah?"

I nod. Force a wet smile. "Yeah."

Tension unwinds from his frame. A small sleepy grin. "Okay. Alright."

I stand, snaking my arms over his back. Tucking my forehead beneath his chin. "You want to go downstairs?"

He squeezes me tight. "Yeah. I think I do."

"Alright." I step back. Inhaling deep. Exhaling every alternate future. "I want to get high first."

✧

Smoke. Breathe in. Exhale. Tell myself till I believe it.

∿

Dennis lies on his side, on the ground, in the dirt, still trapped in the chair. He either sees us or hears us because he starts screaming through the ball again, or trying to— his voice is blown, it's just a rasp, like a draft. We grab him by elbow and head and it takes three heaves to pull him upright. He cries and farts and his skin feels slimy and not even human.

Tony cups around my belly, slipping fingertips beneath the band of my sweatpants, and reaches out to Dennis with his other hand. The Xacto knife flashes in the light. Dennis bucks in the chair, trying to scream.

∿

Tell myself till I believe it. Focus on the children. Children I could never know but I know they exist, still alive, forever ruined by him. I don't even need to close my eyes to see their faces. They hover in front of me. Spinning globs. Eyes, noses, ears, and mouths. Composites of children I've seen, in person, on TV, online. I see the children more than I see Dennis. But really there's nothing there.

∿

The blade draws a curl into his forehead. Red lines poured into a red eye. A failed red scream. I touch Tony's thighs and press back into him, my forehead beneath his chin, a hard-on atop my ass.

⌄

The sun in the sky, the core of the Earth. The sweat. My body and his and his.

⌄

The blade reaches out into Dennis's shoulder and pulls down through his arm. Flesh parts like a curtain, revealing alien fauna, red yellow and white. The body attached tremors and squirms.

⌄

Tony laps his tongue at mine, at my lips, at my teeth. Holding my breast, circling the areola with his thumb. Catching on the bumps. He pinches it between thumb and forefinger, tugging gently, slowly pulling it farther and farther. I grab his hip and gasp into his mouth.

⌄

Slice the skin between his fingers, beneath his fingernails. He rocks, he bucks. Clamp his nipples and pull till they tear. Light his balls on fire. Break his wrists. Crush his kneecaps. Shave off his nose. Cry like he made them cry. Sweat and red, sweat and red.

⌄

Sliding a finger inside him, pressing his prostate. He moans and his cock pulses, lifting in my other hand, the tip already glossy. Slipping my lips over it, sipping salty gel, sucking my cheeks in and out. He cries out and laughs, running fingers through my hair, behind my ear, over the back of my neck.

᷁

Unspool his mouth into petals. An orchid, candy apple and beige. Cut lips and gums to swollen anther cap.

᷁

He slips inside me like a trap. Rocking above me, his eyes and nose and lips, his hair and skin. He looks like a teen-ager. Smiling, he tells me something, lowering his face to mine, sucking my lips and licking my teeth. I whisper something back.

᷁

Press the blade to the corner of his eye. Press just so it clicks against bone. A rusty tear. Tilt the blade back, scooping. Pry out his eyeball. Another eyeball squishes out from behind, right into socket. Pry it out. It falls, and another eyeball, seven, thirteen eyeballs spill out. A hundred, thousands of eyeballs spilling out, filling the basement, rising above our ankles.

Blood draws down past his body, past the chair, dangling into dirt, a wine rope toward Hell. It hardens to a spear, plunging into earth, planting, spreading roots, fouling soil like salt. Years forward the crops will rot, the farm will be in ruins, and we will be somewhere else.

❧

I breathe I gasp I scream.

❧

We fuck again in the shower—arms lifting me, floating me in the fake rain, to be speared against the wall—and again in bed. On our backs, crowns of our heads touching, we talk about each other and memories and a future we previously hadn't the capacity to envision. It all opens up before us. He holds me like we're conjoined and we sleep like wolf pups.

❧

He wakes before I do, kissing my shoulder. Stretching against his body, twining our limbs, I suck his neck, then chest, his nipples, crawling down his torso to his groin. Slipping his cock between my lips, swirling my tongue around the tip. Resting my pussy over his mouth. He laps and sucks, pushing his bottom lip against my clit. Making me shiver and gasp. I turn myself around and fall on his cock and ride until he bursts up through me. Laughing and kissing.

We wash in the kitchen. I pull out pancake mix, eggs, milk, butter. He slaps six strips of bacon in the skillet and throws on the Doobie Brothers, singing along. *Girl, don't you worry, I know where I stand.* I mix everything up in the bowl while he holds my hips. Then he helps me scoop the batter into the frying pan.

We sit side by side at the table, each of us eating with one hand, holding the other's thigh with the other. Then he washes all the dishes while I roll a joint, and we head back to the basement.

✧

Dennis doesn't move. He won't move. Slumped in the chair, tilted forward. Limbs ripped and still. His groin a blackened holocaust. No throb, only cold red drooling from ruined holes. The stink of old shit.

"Hey asshole," Tony says. It doesn't sound like a threat. The man chained to the chair does not reply. Tony reaches out a shaky hand and touches the burgundy chest. He looks back at me with wet eyes. His face explains everything.

The day has left us.

✧

Tony goes to the bathroom so that I won't see him, but I hear. His face pressed in a towel, a quiet muted weep.

✧

We take him out of the chains, duct tape, bungee cords and handcuffs. I lay down a tarp that we'd used years back—that time we tried camping, spiders and thunderstorms, once and never again. We pull him off the chair. He slushes to the floor, onto the tarp. We wrap the blue around him and roll him up.

I ask Tony what we're going to do. He exhales, and for a moment it looks like he's going to cry again. "We can dig a hole," he says. "A grave."

"Yeah." Wait. "That'll take a while, won't it? Isn't it like way harder to dig a grave than it sounds?"

"I don't know." He takes out his phone and types something in. He scrolls and taps. "Jesus Christ. It takes like ten hours."

"Oh."

He slips the phone back into his pocket and stares at tarp-wrapped Dennis. "Fuck."

I rest my head against his shoulder. "We can just leave him for now. We'll figure something out."

"Yeah?"

"Sure. Why not?"

∿

We shower separately. Washing off the filth, the filth and some of the future, the potential. Washing off the way he looked at me last night. Pulling soap through my hair and crying quiet.

∿

I open the door to take out the trash. And there it is. Dennis's Buick LaCrosse, sitting in our driveway, completely forgotten.

I look for where the garbage bins are kept—first in the garage, then by the basement. Finally, at the back of the house, I find them. I toss the bags in and get back inside quick.

I don't tell Tony about the car.

∿

We find each other on the couch. He sits, head back, staring at the ceiling. I lay my head on his lap. We stare at the ceiling together. "What now?" I ask.

"I guess we wait."

"For what?"

He gazes down into my eyes, and I see myself in the glass of his, and I look wrong, I don't look like myself, I don't look the way I remember being. He runs his fingers through my hair. "You know."

Twisting onto my side, facing his belly, I close my eyes. "What do you want to do tomorrow?"

"I've got a shift."

And right there the rest of the world comes back and I remember where I am and who I am. "I almost forgot work was a thing."

"Yeah, I know. Are you scheduled, too?"

"Yeah. Of course. Always."

"I guess that's what we're doing, then."

The evening passes and morning comes without sleep. We ignore odors. We listen for sounds, foreign footsteps, outside and within. Doors breaching. Siren's yelp. But nothing. We clock in. We dial numbers, we speak words, we ask questions, we speak, we make noises, together and apart, holding separate spaces in a single room. Gestures and sounds, repeating, repeating, and none of it means anything.

Where We Breathe

But that wasn't really us. That never really happened. It was a story she told herself. A dream, a passing thought (the way our memories and fictions exist in montage—summary—allowing us to, internally, traverse vast swaths of time in mere moments). This thought, this daydream, is what kept her from leaving me. That was a decade ago, and you'd need to ask her if things are better now.

A starved Labrador in a concrete landscape on the TV. The dog points snout toward a black hole broken out of a wall. The camera zooms in and when I squint I can almost make out the glint of twin yellow eyes deep within the dark. The commercial ends, smash cutting back to the show we were watching (*Monsieur LeBlanc's Premium Eaterinos*), and neither of us are sure what it means or what it's trying to sell.

Rochelle nuzzles into her corner of the couch, folding her arms over her chest. "I so hope I'm not pregnant."

"Why would you be pregnant?"

"I forgot my pill. Like a month ago. Just one day. I went right back on it, so it should be fine, but I feel all fucked up."

"I'm sorry." I spoon a pearly glob of yogurt into my mouth.

"I can't think of a worse time to get an abortion."

"You know I'll do whatever needs to be done."

She laughs. "You mean, like, get the coat hanger?"

"No, I mean, like, I'll help find kind and considerate professionals to take care of it."

She lifts herself up, slumping onto my lap. She smiles up at me and presses the side of her face into my belly. "You'll punch me in the stomach a couple times?"

The Shrill turns back on. This alien tinnitus, this whining tone like a laser shot through my skull. When it first started happening, I thought it was just me—an ailment, maybe real tinnitus—but she could hear it too. Not something inside me, but vibrating through the air. Outside, the dogs bark for blocks. At some point, we get up and make pancakes.

Our apartment is above a preschool, not on a farm (yet another daydream). A month ago, the children stopped coming, and all we'd hear was the teachers milling, their muffled speech. Then they stopped showing up, too. Now it really is only us.

We break into the downstairs, jamming my driver's license in the bolt until the doorknob twists. It's all melon walls, cardboard animals and cut-out numbers taped up. Heaps of wooden blocks. We fuck on a pile of green ragged beanbags, and kick apart dollhouses and aged plushies and shelves filled with slim books with titles like *It's Not Easy Being a Bunny*, *Don't Let the Pigeon Drive the Bus* and *There Was an Old Lady Who Swallowed a Fly*. Piling the wreckage into a corner, Rochelle says, "If our toilet stops working, we can always use this."

∿

I log into Zoom. My boss and co-workers appear across the screen in a grid of stuttering rectangles. Each rectangle a unique room—Samantha in a log cabin, Pauline on a porch, Hannah in a kitchen. All dressed nearly identical, button-up blouses and sports coats. Made up like they're going out. I've been telling them my webcam doesn't work, so I stay in my ragged t-shirt and boxers and socks. We talk about the projects that apply to me (only two now, since I've been reduced to a support role, which is fine, I don't care), and when the discussion moves on I mute myself. I work my dick out of my boxers and stroke and tug at the shaft but it won't get hard. The voices are too distracting, needling, and I don't find any of these people attractive, and my space no longer belongs to me, it's entirely futile.

Vic wraps up his updates for the final report on the aquifer study, and everyone says bye and drops out of the call. Still pawing at my groin, I find Rochelle in the living room, stretched across the couch in a tank top and bicycle shorts, tapping at her phone. I hop on top of her and we pull our clothes off and try to fuck but I still can't get hard, so we just lie there and listen to each other's breathing.

∿

There's so much noise. Not just the Shrill—its whistles from robins and blue jays, throaty screams from grackles and crows. The neighborhood dogs—a dumpy golden retriever, a ragged terrier, a rusted mutt that looks like a young Robert Redford—howling and yelping. Swole pickups dragging U-Haul trailers the fuck out of town. Blasts echoing off the mountain—thick, basso *poooohhms*. Fireworks, maybe. Probably. And then there's this clicking, like tapping on the inside of a wall, like an insect's mouth. This clicking. She hears it too. We trace the walls but can't find a source.

If I lie awake at night, after everything has quieted down, I can sometimes hear the neighbors thinking, I can hear their dreams, and I go tense with what I learn.

We'd been watching them—the neighbors—and they'd been watching us, through the windows, or when they were in the yard. A family of four in the house to our right—a man, a woman, a child and a baby. We never really met them because who meets their neighbors anymore? But we'd see them outside, the man raking the yard and the woman burning brush and the child building kingdoms of dirt, and when we looked down at them they looked up at us. Bleary eyes and dead frowns. Moving like sleepwalkers, but also a simmer somewhere deep in those faces. Some kind of fury.

We never saw the baby. The baby shrieked so loud you could hear it all the way over in our apartment. Like a rake against glass. All day and all night. Sometimes harmonizing with the Shrill.

At some point—maybe three weeks ago, maybe three months, maybe a year—they stopped going outside. We'd only ever see them in the windows. Looking at us through the glass, eyes sour and glazed. Rochelle would lean into me and we'd just stand there, taciturn, looking back at them, until we got bored and turned on a show or played video games or something. We'd check back every once in a while, and sometimes they'd still be staring at us.

Then we stopped seeing them altogether. Never in the windows, never outside. No sign. No trace, except for the baby. The baby still wailed invisibly through day and night, piercing caterwaul ringing through our glass and walls into our space, impossibly. Then, one day, it stopped too.

Nobody came for any of them.

✦

Out for a walk in the afternoon, it's soupy overcast, drizzling, grey, titanium. A plasticky, narcotic scent. Chalky dew coating my hands, face and neck. A buzz in the particles, like drugged mist.

I pass the other neighboring house. The one with people still alive inside. There are two of them. A man and a woman. Elderly—in their sixties or seventies. Maybe that isn't elderly, or it's almost elderly. It doesn't matter, I don't care. They stare at us—at me right now—through their window. Like the other neighbors before, they've long ceased going outside. Droopy wet wrinkled faces side-by-side, yellow and blue-ringed eyes. A weird, fiending starvation inside.

A man sings in my earbuds: *It's my favorite kind of day, filled with the things we fear, that find us where we sleep and fuck us where we breathe.* He shouts but sounds exhausted, like he's spent the year pushing his hands through skin and sap. Ugly, stupid and unacknowledged.

Empty sidewalks. No one on the roads. Geese cackling past a line of houses—a new prefab subdivision, but already most of the windows are boarded and vacant. Even the inhabited ones baring lawns gone to deep primordial hell. Quasi-reclaimed.

A skinny hand of lightning reaches down and touches the mountain ahead. The drug water falls sharper and harder, permeating my hoodie and jeans. Buzzes harder. I half-walk, half-run back home. Past the living neighbors, still at the window, eyes still following me, like a haunted painting, a real fucking hate creasing their brows.

Do they have guns?

Inside the apartment, Rochelle asks, "What's that smell?" That damp, plasticky reek. I shrug, strip off my clothes and snuggle up to her on the couch. Our skins break out in hives, hives on top of hives, until the entire lengths of our skins are just one big hive. We scratch each other bloody. The Shrill comes but this time it almost sounds like nothing.

⌁

The fog of war describes the doubt and precarity of decision making during military operations. In video games, you can see it rendered as a blurry black space beyond your characters' sight and memory. A lantern encircled by black smoke.

We turn on the TV and watch a video on how to make plastic explosives from bleach.

⌁

I heat up kimchi-flavored ramen and frozen Brussels sprouts. She cooks a stir fry. We watch a show about cartoon animals trying to break out of prison. An anteater shivs a basking shark, saying, "You gotta have teeth if you wanna make it in Animal Prison, bitch." I say that I think the voice is Ray Liotta's.

"I don't know who that is."

"He was in *Goodfellas*. And *Cop Land*. And *Corrina, Corrina*."

"Huh."

I pause the show. "Look it up."

She takes her phone from the side table and taps on the screen. "Yeah, it's Ray Liotta."

⌃

I go back out at night. There are a few feet of grass dividing the sidewalk from the road so it feels safe. No cars on the road anyway. Trees gnarled and hard like broken hands reaching for sky, spaced evenly.

Something squishes beneath my feet. Balancing on one foot, I look at the underside of my shoe but it's too dark to tell what it is. Probably dog shit. I try and scrape it off on the curb. A woman comes out of her house with her dog, looks at me, then goes back inside.

The mountain ahead stretches tall, black against black, lording over. A pyramid of stringed lights set atop the peak's pavilion. It wants me to climb, to reach its summit, to be away from the rest of the world, but instead I walk back home.

I take off my boots at the top of the stair. The rubber sole caked with wet red and white. Crushed dark green skin and bone. I let it drop to the shoe rack and go inside, to our room and wake up Rochelle.

⌃

Here's what really happens.

Hours before the sun pulses through the clouds in a grey glow, we drag garbage bags of old mail and clothes to the elderly neighbors' house. We siphon gasoline from their Buick LeSabre, and once it starts flowing we stuff the other end of the tube in one of the bags, then another, soaking the paper and cloth. The fumes turn our stomachs, turning the muggy air woozy, but we shrug it off. This is important.

We remove the paper and fabric from the bags, wad them into balls, and pack them around the house's foundation. It takes less time than you'd think. I take out one of those long-stemmed lighters, click it on, and touch the flame to the fabric.

It's like stepping out of a jail cell.

It's a while before it gets going, but the structure gradually lights up golden, pumpkin and brass, pissing an onyx tube of smoke toward heaven. We run out into the street and watch. The doors never open. No one gets out. Fire trucks never arrive. Rochelle leans into me and we wrap each other in gas-soaked arms. The space belonging to us expands—our neighbors' houses now another wall between us and the rest. Next week maybe we'll worry about the houses beyond, and take care of them too. Expanding the fortification. But right now, in this moment, I feel safe. I think she feels safe, too.

Burn You the Fuck Alive

B.R. Yeager

APOCALYPSE
PARTY

CONTENTS

You've dreamed about me. A face you thought was your own invention. But really it was me. I was there, and I saw you too.

You've let me worry you.

You'll be thinking about me for weeks. When your gums puff and swell, when you spit rust while you floss. You'll think of me, and won't ever be able to stop.

An asshole filled with nail clippings. I dreamed of great white maggots shaped like anal beads burrowed deep inside my feet. And now you've dreamed them too. Where does it come from? Light from icy blade moon down to your spine and mine also.

I killed your dad and married your other dad, so I'm your dad now too.

The joyous days are over. Thus says I.

No one's afraid anymore. But I can twist your leg into a spiral. I can make you forget you ever knew how to breathe. When you found the beaten red sack behind your home, was part of you excited? I mean, the look on your face.

The twenty-seventh time in your life you've realized there is still so much you haven't considered. It's almost enough to knock you flat, so hard you never get up.

Your waist buckles. Your lips pucker like a sweet milky anus. Ankles and rotator cuffs worn to ruin. I'm the breath that swallows this world. An inhalation sucking away the oxygen between each body.

You sucked face with your lover and sucked so deep your lover's lungs collapsed.

How about that?

My words stitched upon your trachea. You will never forget.

I ended the world just to get to you.

The truth is, I don't expect them to show up at all. I'm used to getting blown off. It's basic as hell—New Kid Blues, et cetera, et cetera. You arrive in town the same way you've arrived in the last six towns, mid-way through the semester—long enough for factions to solidify among the student body, but too late to find one for yourself. Split any group of kids into factions and overnight they'll hunger the blood of anyone beyond their circle. It's instinctual—a survival mechanism. Any new variable is a threat, and right now the variable is me.

So I'm wary when this lanky rat-faced kid approaches at lunch. Older, maybe even eighteen. And yeah, very rat-faced, especially with those mean little eyes and that dopy smirk—an archetypal outcast. But that goes for most kids at Los Suelos K-12, and sharing outcast traits isn't enough to make you kin. So forgive me for not exactly throwing myself out there when he sits down at my table, sucks a strand of mucus back up a narrow nostril and asks, "What's the haps?"

I ignore him, figuring he's talking to someone else or just trying to fuck with me.

"You talk, man?"

I look up. "Sometimes."

He smiles wide—sharp canines, like a coyote. "You're new, right? What brings you to Los Sueblows?"

I push away my lunch tray. "Get on with it. You gonna shake me down? Show me the hands? You want my food?"

"Damn, dude." Rat Face puts his hands up, palms open. "Who hurt you?"

I look back down at the tray filled with pink sludge and maybe eggs. "Never mind."

He introduces himself as Max, says his pop hauled him here like maybe ten years ago, and that he knows the deal with this place. He tells me he can get me anything I need.

"Okay," I say. "Cool."

Then he leans in real close—skin smelling like old yolks, breath like rotten cabbage—and asks if I've heard about the Buried Man.

I smile. I haven't heard of the Buried Man, but I know what it is. I'd been in this position before, in any number of bullshit towns, learning the mythos. Haunted bridges and murder houses. A Kansas cemetery might contain a gateway to hell, a New Hampshire hill town might house a Micah Witch, the Florida panhandle might have a skunk ape. Local legends. The details change, but it's all the same thing—an excuse to go out at night. Everything else is just regional flavor.

So Los Suelos has a Buried Man.

"No." I iron out my smile. "I don't know about the Buried Man."

Max leans in close, grin like a sickle. "Then you're in luck. This Saturday's a full moon."

"Yeah?"

"Yeah. You'll see."

Taptaptaptaptap. I jolt up from bed, my room filled with warm blue light. Mom snoring away in the room over. Then *taptaptaptaptap* on glass. I grope the side table for my glasses and slip them on, squinting at the window. *Taptaptaptaptap*. A grey shape moves behind it, then snaps clear. Max, contorting his face into evil grins. The tapping stops, replaced by hushed giggling.

I pull on my pants and slide over to the window. Shushing him, I reach the bottom of the window and gently pull it up. "Lemme get some clothes on," I say. There's another boy standing away from the trailer. He looks more my age, maybe fourteen or fifteen. Skinny, tall, in a black trench coat. I point to him. "Wait over there."

Max nods, still giggling, and walks to his friend. I pull on some slides and a shirt, then climb out the window and head over to meet them.

"Dude, what is good?" Max laughs. "This is so tight. Thought you were gonna bitch out for sure."

I almost say I didn't expect him to show either, but bite my tongue.

He slaps my shoulder and points ahead, past the trailer park fence. "Let's go. Up here."

We climb over the fence and jog to where the ground descends, down a gradual slope toward a long squat building, hard grey in the moonlight. Hunkered in the warehouse's shadow, Max pulls a pack of cigarettes and three warm beers from an old burned-out oil drum. He points to the other boy. "This is Raf."

Raf dips his head slowly, almost as a curtsy, eyes never leaving mine. His coat billowing in the wind like a cape.

"The pleasure is mine." A voice like chain dragged across stone. "So, what hellish turn of fate brings you to the Sue-los?"

Flares in my head. Mom's new boyfriend. Mom crying on the telephone. Packets of white. A gun in the dresser.

"New job," I say. "My mom got a new job."

Raf nods. "Of course."

"Come on," Max says, pointing ahead with his beer. "It's like a mile out."

We step from the shadow to rows of vacant lots, dust skittering over asphalt, a warm cottonmouth wind rising.

Crossing Cypress Ave to the outskirts, Los Suelos' lights diminish behind us and a full circle of moon, hung high above the Bolt Gun Hills, takes lead. Max and Raf talk and laugh, jokes relying on contexts I don't yet understand. I keep silent, watching the shrubs trembling in the breeze.

"Alright, it's coming up." Max points to a car-sized rock ringed by spiny blooms of thistle. "That's always how you can tell." Leading us past the landmark, a few yards down, we reach a small crater, diameter of maybe a hula hoop.

"Oh shit," Max says, pointing at the crater. "I've never seen it come up before." And just as he says that, there's a sound—a hiss. Air releasing. The sand within the crater shifts. A gurgle. The sand turns brown and begins filling with water.

"Man," Raf says. "That is beautiful."

I step toward the crater, now a small pool. "What is it?"

Max smiles wide. "It's the Buried Man."

"And what the hell is the Buried Man?"

Max squats and lets his ass fall into the sand. "You ready for a history lesson?"

I laugh. "Sure. What you got?"

"So like, around two hundred, one-fifty years ago, when white boys started taking over, this place was part of the California Gold Rush, and folks were setting up mines all over. People going crazy over the stuff. And sure, a lot of places had gold, but like ninety percent of the time, they found jack shit. Can you guess which category Los Suelos fell under?"

"Jack shit?"

"Smart. But before anyone knew that, this prospector, Joe Barnsey, bought out this land right here and hired up the locals to dig and sift for gold. Just over that ridge, maybe a hundred yards up from the river, you can still find the mine."

"So is that where we're heading?"

Max laughs. "*Fuck* no. Even in the daytime that place is suicide. I knew this one kid, thought he was hot shit, skipped class to go out there. Never found. Some folks are *still* looking for him.

"Anyway, one of the miners was this guy Francisco Muñoz. He had a deep history with this place—his lineage goes back before even the Spanish. Francisco had a small family out here—a wife, three kids, a dog, the whole deal. And he always told his children: never, ever go near the mine. He understood and even respected the adventurous nature of his children, but he also knew firsthand how supremely dangerous the mine was. Just that week he'd lost two buddies from a cavern collapse. All he wanted more than anything was to keep his family safe.

"Then one day, on his walk to the mine, he hears a noise. A crying. He must've been —" Max turns and points back toward the way we came. "— maybe a dozen yards that way. And the noise was right around here—like a little boy crying. So he runs toward the sound, but even as it gets louder, he can't see anyone. He calls out, 'Where are you? Let me bring you back to town.' But the voice doesn't respond. It just keeps weeping. And Francisco is a good man, he knows he can't let a child die out here, so he keeps following the sound, until he reaches —" He points toward me. "— right around there. And that's when he realizes, the sound's coming from *beneath* the ground." He pauses for some kind of reaction.

"So what?"

"So he starts digging. He figures a kid from town had gone into the mine and gotten lost. It never occurs to him that if that were the case, he wouldn't've been able to hear the cries from above ground. Like, times were different. People were dumb. Anyway, he digs and digs, and as he digs, the crying gets louder. And by the time he's waist-deep in the hole, he begins to recognize the voice. It's his youngest son Alejandro! Oh shit! So he starts digging like crazy now, praying for his son's safety but cursing him, too, for disobeying his instructions. He digs so deep, with no concern for how he'll get out of the hole. He digs until nightfall, until the hole is twice as tall as he. But here's the thing—he never reaches the source of the crying. The weeping always seems just below his feet. And as the shovel falls from his blistered hands, he looks up to find the moon, positioned perfecting over the hole, shining its silver light down on him." He stops.

"And so then what?"

Max shakes his head. "The hole caves in on him. He's buried alive. When he doesn't come home, his family goes out searching for him. Later on, his wife claimed she could hear him weeping beneath the dirt. And when they called out for him, this little pool gurgled to the surface. You see—it's Francisco's tears, from his ceaseless weeping. Because he knew he'd never see his family again."

Mulling it over, sifting the details through my head. I laugh. "Shut the fuck up, dude."

"It's true, man," Max says, but he's laughing too. "It's totally that dude's tears."

"This is so far from my first rodeo, man."

"It's *true*. Just ask anybody."

"Let me get this straight," I say, waving my hands like a professor. "So while Francisco was digging, there had to have been somebody with him, right?"

"Nope, he was all alone."

"So how the hell would anyone know what he heard? How would anyone know he got buried alive? He probably just got sick of mining and dealing with his family and dipped."

Max shakes his head. "You know how these things work, man. We just *know* it happened. Don't need any witnesses or shit."

"Okay, and why does he cry when it's a full moon? How does he even know that?"

He laughs again. "Who cares?"

I creep further toward the pool, blades of blue shimmering across its surface. "Really though. What is it?"

"So we actually have another reason for bringing you here."

I turn back to him.

"It's kind of an initiation thing." He dusts his hands on the sides of his pants. "If you wanna roll with us, you gotta drink the tears."

Raf starts laughing. Max restrains a smirk.

"Yeah?"

The two boys side-eye each other. "Yeah."

"Alright then." Creeping to the side of the pool, I crouch onto my knees. The water's skin ripples. Crystal clear, like a jellyfish. Cupping my hands, I reach in. Colder than I expected. Icy, almost. I lift a handful of water.

"*Wait wait wait.*" Raf's voice, now filled with panic.

I tilt my head back and raise the water to my lips.

"Dude it's a fucking joke!" Max shouts.

I drink it down. So cold. Like ice, or blades. A push inside my head—vertigo—swaying me off balance.

"You should make yourself hurl," Raf says. Neither of them are laughing anymore.

"It's just water," I say.

"No, for real—there is so much contamination around here. You should really make yourself throw up."

"Raf's right, dude." Max pushes himself to his feet. "You're not even really supposed to drink the tap water here."

Flashes in my mind—of lead, of arsenic, of birth defects, of a life of blindness.

I hold my belly with both hands, now swollen, even though it was only a sip. "Oh."

♪

Doubled over, stomach clenched, every muscle in my face flexing. Grunting dry. I put my finger in my mouth, trying to touch the back of my throat. Gaggy dry heaves, my limbs going to pins and needles, and a thick glob of saliva falling off my lips. But the water is still in me. My stomach gurgles and moves, like an eel's nest. Reaching my entire hand inside my mouth, I tap where my tongue becomes my throat. My guts clench and hot fluid rockets through my mouth, onto my hand, onto the ground.

"Whoa!" Max shouts.

"Damn, son," Raf says. "That was a heroic puke."

Buckled over, hands on my knees, spitting the taste out. Bile and beer and the mac and cheese with spaghetti sauce Mom made for dinner. And something else. Like a fire. Burning wood. No, burning plastic. Like a dollhouse on fire in my mouth, in my stomach.

Standing upright, the landscape blinks in quarter-seconds. It feels like a fever. I take a step and almost fall over.

"You alright?" Max runs to me, around the puddle of puke, and grabs my shoulder.

"I'm fine, probably." I step away from him, but the ground is unstable, like standing atop a mammoth water balloon. I feel myself falling and shift my weight to the other side.

"Hey!" Max grabs my shoulders, keeping me upright. "You gotta sit down."

"I'm fine. Can we just go home?"

"Dude, you're not going anywhere like this."

"Nah, man. It'll be fine." Leaning back against his hands. "Just hold me up like this and I can walk."

"I don't know, man."

Then I hear Raf. "I do need to get home."

Max groans and shakes his head. "Okay. Let's go."

It's only ten minutes before I feel stable again, and Max no longer needs to hold me up. My stomach still disturbed, but it's probably psychosomatic—a product of the atmosphere and Max's story. We cross back into town, past the warehouse, over the fence toward home. Approaching my trailer, Max taps my shoulder. "Hey man, we good?"

I smile. "Yeah, of course. This was tight."

He smiles back and points at my belly. "If you start feeling sick and shit, get that looked at."

Raf holds out his hand. I take it. "Godspeed, sir." And they both walk into the night.

I step to my window, slide it back open and pull myself up into the sweltering room. I strip off my clothes and fall into bed. The clock reads 4:44 AM.

Falling. No, floating. No, I'm sinking. Sinking in blue. A blue the shade of cosmos. A blue the size of the Earth.

Something ahead of me. No, below. The place I'm sinking toward. A plane as broad as everything I've ever known. Coming closer, closer. And then I land. My feet meet the ground—clay and sand. Bubbles erupt around my circumference.

Through the blue, the blue like night, I see the landmark. The rock, and the swaying thistles reaching out from it. And beneath me, I hear a quiet weeping.

I wake up wet. At first, I think it's sweat, but no, it's wetter than that. I'm soaked. *Oh shit oh shit oh shit*. I bolt upright and slide off the bed. This hasn't happened since I was little. My underwear, my sheets—fuck, my entire body. Even my fucking face and pillows, *Jesus Christ*. Gagging. How could I have pissed this much? Smelling my wrist. It's salty, but not like urine. Almost like the beach. I press down on the mattress. Fluid squeezes through the fibers.

God. All this fluid. Trickling down from lips, nostrils, tear ducts.

A knock at the door. "Dennis, you up yet?" The alarm clock reads 11:17. "I'm going for groceries, you want to come?"

"Hey Mom. I-I think I'm coming down with something."

"Oh no." The doorknob shakes. Locked, thankfully. "Let me see."

"I don't want you to catch it. I'm just gonna sleep it off." I can't stop sweating.

"Oh, okay." Exhaustion and some sadness tinting her voice. "Drink lots of water."

I listen for the front door to shut, for Mom's car's ignition to rumble, for the sound of dirt and gravel shifting beneath tires. Then I run to the bathroom and jump in the shower. The water stings, like it's tearing through my flesh.

I get out and towel myself down. Immediately, I'm dripping again. I unplug Mom's hair dryer and head back to my room. Strip the sheets, pillowcases and mattress cover. I press down on the mattress again. More salty liquid rises over the fibers. Completely saturated. I open the window and hang the mattress cover, pointing my fan toward it. I plug in the hair dryer and wave it over the mattress. I don't feel hot but I keep sweating. Tears keep pouring from my eyes, but I'm not crying.

Mom leaves me a plate of Italian mac and cheese at my door. When she goes to bed, I bring it in but don't eat. I sneak to the bathroom and pee for fifteen minutes straight.

I leave for school before Mom wakes, before the bus even comes. I leave a note, lying, saying I feel better, but today it's so much worse. Wet fills my mouth, and I keep swallowing, gagging on thin saliva. Sweating through my clothes the moment I put them on.

I need to find Max.

The sun doesn't dry me. The wet keeps coming out. Out my tear ducts. Out my mouth, out my skin. Leaving a trail behind me like a slug. My clothes cling to my thighs and armpits, rubbing them raw.

At school, Max is standing at the front entrance, playing hacky sack with himself. He sees me coming and smiles. "Hey, man." The smile vanishes. "You okay?"

"What did I drink?" The words glug out. A mouthful of drool falls from my lips with each syllable.

"What?" Then a flash of realization. "Oh, I don't know. Just buried water. Dude, you are not looking good."

"I'm not feeling good."

"You should go to the doctor, man. Or at least the nurse."

I shake my head, flicking wet off me like a dog. "Never mind, I have to get to class."

I jog down the hall to first period, geometry. All the other kids look at me, the sheer wetness of me, removing their eyes only once Mr. Cantillo arrives. He takes attendance and begins talking about transformed figures, rigid and non-rigid transformations. I look down at my desk and close my eyes. It isn't black in there but blue. An endless blue. Bubbles and shapes in the haze. The opposite of void—space filled completely, to the brim. It feels like portent.

My bladder expands.

"Dennis."

Pushes back up through my stomach.

"*Dennis.*" Mr. Cantillo's snarl.

I snap into the room. A hard-on swollen with fluid beneath my desk. I look up. "Can I go to the bathroom?"

"Dennis, we're just starting."

I open my mouth to speak again but it's only water that comes out. Salty and raw.

"Dennis, can you explain how —"

My bladder releases. Pee shoots against the front of my already soaked pants, all over my lap and down my leg. I jump out of my seat.

"Excuse me!" Mr. Cantillo shouts.

I cover my crotch. Everyone looking at me again, giggling. "I-I-I-I —"

"Sit the hell down!"

"I need to use the bathroom." And before he can respond, I just take off, through the door, down the hall, still pissing, leaving a trail of seawater piss on the linoleum. Shouldering into the bathroom, I yank my pants open. I pee. I pee for five minutes. Ten. Fifteen minutes. Twenty.

Thirty. The bell rings. Other students come into the bathroom and piss and shit in the unoccupied urinals and stalls. I keep pissing through it all. I can't stop.

The bell rings for the next period, and when I no longer hear commotion in the hall, I stuff myself back into my pants—still pissing, soaking already soaked pants and skin—and open the door. I run. I run to the front entrance, past a yelling hall monitor and administrator. I run to the outside, to the heat, to the dry, and I keep running.

⌁

I don't know where I am and it doesn't matter. All that matters is that it's dirt. The only thing that can dry me—it has to be. Pushing through the shrubs and brush, hunched over, groping the ground till I touch a long, thin rock—like a spade. I grasp it, falling to my knees. Water falling from my eyes in torrents, blinding me. Water falling off my skin in sheets. It all hits the ground and sinks through it. Becoming absorbed, becoming dry.

The rock slips in my hand. I lift it above my head and bring it down to the sand, scooping a tiny amount to the side. I spit out gallons of water onto the dry, and keep digging. Sweating, weeping, pissing water, shitting water, vomiting it. Scratching at the dirt with the rock, deepening the hole ever slightly. In hours, maybe an entire day, it will be deep enough for me to slip my body into. But even then, will it be enough? I will have to keep digging, until I'm far enough under, to the point that I can't climb out. It's all I have left. Dirt to dry me, absorb me. The only thing that can. It will plug and hold me until it's no longer able, and I will burst forth and flood the Earth.

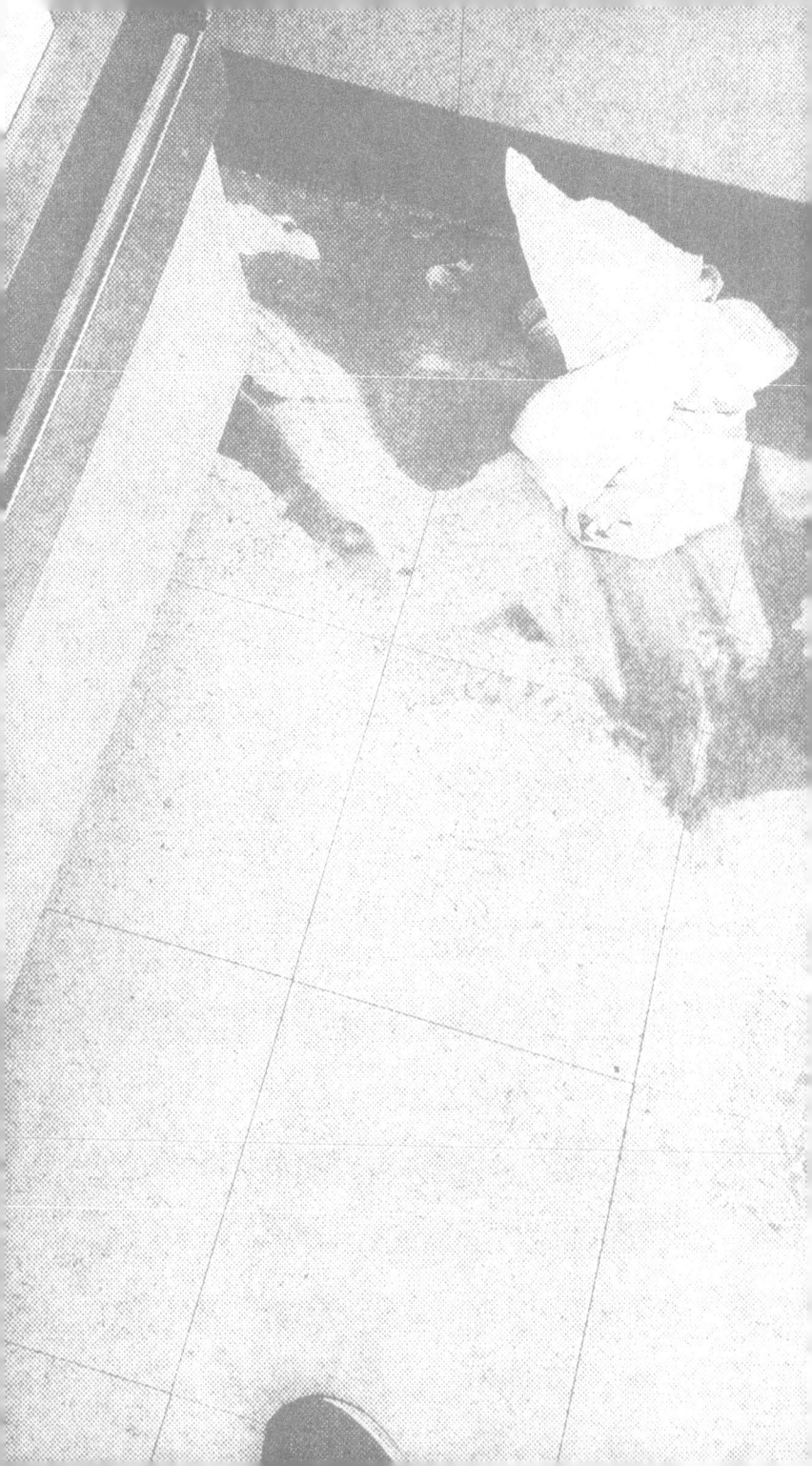

The
Autocastrato

It was the only thing he ever wanted to do, and once it was done, he could never do it again.

Arcade

Of those offered, the knife seemed the most practical object. But now you're regretting it. By your thirtieth mile in the city, the bike has more appeal.

Live with your decisions.

You reach Davis and Nicholson Ave, which your friend in data security recommended, but it's all empty storefronts. Scattered dough body toughs, in their customary black slacks and bare tops, roaming the sidewalks, grilling you. Begging you to make your move.

The one posted across the street: just muscle and bulk, scalp buzzed into a bullet, naked floppy breasts hanging to belly. You didn't expect the hunger in these people's eyes. You'd thought they'd be beaten down. A stupid assumption. They've been waiting for someone like you.

You move on, stopping at the next intersection to take a picture. A burnt orange sunset behind boarded-up complexes. Post it to your feed and wait for notifications, but none of your friends or followers even look at it.

Ditch down Nicholson to Balsam Lane. Not a single window lit, leering black and emptied. But it only feels that way. Feigning death. The buildings are filled and angry and that makes you ten-thousand times outnumbered.

Walk on. Search for something, any opening, any activity. But it's just brown and grey façades and paper blown across concrete.

Four hours in, still grasping for a starting point. The hummingbirds buzz overhead, capturing footage, but it's nothing anyone will have any use for.

⌁

Follow a path over the hill and arrive at a superior vantage point. Neighborhoods unfold below like a Christmas gift. A centipede of single-floor public housing units surrounding a courtyard. A small gathering there. BBQ. Families of dough bodies. Dough body children.

Slide down the grass to the complex and creep along the outermost building. Not everyone could be at the BBQ—maybe someone stayed behind. Maybe someone was left behind. A child—a rebellious teen pouting in their room. You could probably overpower that. Maybe an elder, or another sort of debilitant, or a baby—somebody with mobility issues. That'd make an okay start.

Loping along, you peek through windows, scanning for movement, but the rooms are darkened. All you find is your reflection. So head to the courtyard.

Stilted laughter around a grill. About fourteen mister and lady dough bodies. Nine children. Turning their heads as you approach, like they knew you were coming.

"Yo," you say to the bodies, pointing at the grill. "Can I grab that lighter?"

The burger-flipping mister dough body puts his hands up. Shakes his head. "We're just trying to have a good time, man."

"I know." Put your hands up too. Try to ingratiate. "I'm just looking to light a cigarette. Can I have that?"

The mister takes the lighter, glances it over and tosses it toward your feet. Pick it up.

You point at the bag beside the grill. "Let me get some coals too. And that fluid."

The mister narrows his eyes. "Why?"

"I want to BBQ too."

He says something to another dough body—you can't make out the words and you understand that's intentional—before picking up the bag of coals and the lighter fluid and walking them over to you, dropping them about a yard from your feet. "Look man," he says. "Please don't do anything here. Just go someplace else."

It's a reasonable, polite request. You'll consent, because you need to start somewhere less populated anyway. Plus these buildings are made of brick—they won't catch easy. "Yeah," you say. "Maybe." You like the fear in their eyes.

Drop the lighter and fluid in the coal bag and toss it over your shoulder, and book out of the complex, down a few blocks into an old perished suburb where the houses are made of wood. Pick a yellow house to make your own. An ideal set up—a wooden porch, with a wooden chair sat atop. Hop up the steps and drop the coal bag, then grab the chair and shove the top rail beneath the front door's knob (a financier friend who'd weekended here had offered this tip). Pour the charcoal at the foot of the door, spray lighter fluid all over, and light it up. Run to the middle of the street to watch the rest unfold.

There's pounding behind the front door, but the chair holds. A window breaks open and an arm, then a lady's face and shoulders, then her whole dough body scrambles out, slicing skin on the shards. Kicking out the remaining glass, she pulls a little boy and young mister dough body out by their collars. They run toward the street, but catch you hovering with your knife and halt, keeping to the sidewalk. A second lady springs from behind the house, gripping a large metal pot, running up the steps, pouring the pot, dousing the flames while the first lady kicks coals into the yard. Once the fire's all the way out, the family just stares at you, a quake in their stance. Hummingbirds crisscross the lower sky, capturing it all. More footage that will not be shared, for there's nothing of note to impart.

There's nothing else to do here so you leave.

∿

Here and there, it's the same story. Bodies keep to groups; the only loners stacked with muscle and brandishing death wish. No simple prey. Your closest brush with action is a massacre long completed—corpses split, marshmallows bubbled up through incisions and dried; hard cakes and candies crusted to breathless lips.

You've never felt so out of shape. And you remember your Wall Street friend bragging how he trained half a year prepping for his trip. High-repetition heavy lifting, count-less miles of running. A diet of fish, eggs, avocado and pow-ders. By the end, he said he could tear a body in half.

Think about the emeralds you've wasted—fifty-thou-sand, scrounged coordinating arms sales for low-lev-el startups. Or remember what your IT friend had said about how you really need to spend a week here to get your money's worth.

Think about filing a lawsuit. Taking the cocksuckers for all they're worth. But you have nothing to back it up. You signed the agreements. It's on record. It's your own fault you're dissatisfied.

It hurts but it builds character. That nothing is truly as good as advertised. That there is no true freedom left in the world. That God, government and natural law are indifferent to your desires. You don't feel sad (you lack the capacity), but a knot ties inside you and grows dense with mass, almost dragging you to the ground. But you keep walking, because your money's gone and you may as well see everything they have to offer.

There it is. Finally, your first lead. A flyer stapled to a line-less telephone pole on Rainier Boulevard. A big-eyed clipart lamb grinning dumbly from eggshell paper. Text sheared into its coat:

LOBE UP!!!

MAD DYNAMIC CALF CHECK

WIN REWARDS | EARN A CUTE SURPRISE

495 WELLINGTON ROAD

Your masseuse had mentioned the Calf Checks before. "A lot of folks skip them, but they can be worth it. I got my first gun that way. Plus it toughens you the fuck up. After mine, I felt like I could do anything."

Check your map and make the trek, past collapsed

homes and burnt trees strung with intestines and hanged cats. Hop onto Wellington and cross the bridge over slow whirlpools sucking bubbles into murk. Arrive on the other side surrounded by hollow beige buildings.

It's night now, and arrows made of Christmas lights hang from oil drums and dead cars, guiding you through metal and mortar corridors. You spill into a courtyard clogged with pink and blue buses with naked glitter-doused women and men dancing atop to no music. A line of entrants curls around one of the warehouses. A caterpillar. Join at the end of the queue, watching them try and trade their starting objects.

A woman walks along, handing out branded nylon bags. You take the bag and tell her they should have done a better job advertising. That you've wasted all day drifting around like an asshole looking for something to do. That it's bullshit, that you're entitled to at least a partial refund. But the woman only smiles and presses down the line, distributing the remaining bags to horny kids who look exactly like you.

You open your bag and peer inside. A box cutter, a flare, and a blue and pink mouth guard.

⌃

Staff have you fill out some forms before ushering you into a white room where you sit alone with a woman in a lab coat asking you questions. "Have you participated in a Calf Check in the past six months?"

"No."

"How did you learn about tonight's Calf Check?"

"A flyer. Out by the suburbs." Quietly: "You really

should advertise it better."

"Many have said that the search is part of the experience. Which starting object did you select?"

"The knife." You remove it from your pocket, unfold it, and lightly stab the air.

"Good. You should have no problem then." Beckoning you to the doorway, she leads you through to a second white room. Two men—one bald, one with greasy, shoulder-length hair—stand beside a young brown cow, neck and torso and legs wrapped in wide rubber straps connected to the wall. Just overhead, a hummingbird flits, capturing footage.

"Did Allie tell you everything?" the bald man says.

Nod. "I really get a gun if I win this?"

"Is that what the flyer said?"

"Yes." Though now you're unsure.

He scowls. "Then why would you think otherwise?"

You consider grabbing him and driving the blade up through his chin into the roof of his mouth, but assault on staff carries heavy penalties. You'd never get out. They'd make a dough body out of you.

"Alright, you ready?"

You nod.

"Great. You've got five minutes, starting…now!"

A buzzer blares and you run at the shackled animal, plunging the knife tip into its eye. The cow moos deep, a pained roar, resonating off the walls, beating at your eardrums. You want to drop the knife, to cover your ears, but you waited in line too long for this. Your fist stays around the knife and you stab again, breaking through hide and glancing off the skull. The cow tries to struggle away, but the straps draw tighter, holding her in place.

"Try the throat," the greasy-haired man yells.

Allie makes like she's going to hit him, but stops herself. "You're free to do whatever you want," she shouts.

Take the advice. Go for the throat. The knife sinks in just beside the jawbone. The cow moos. Pull downward through flesh and fat, severing esophagus, milk bulbs. Yank the blade downward till it escapes the bottom, opening neck. A flush of milk. It must be milk because that's what comes out of cows. A torrent of merlot-milk washing down ragged drapes, pooling at your feet. The straps pull the animal to the ground, refusing her death throes.

The buzzer rings out.

Allie appears by your side. "Excellent. You qualify. Congratulations." No emotion in her voice. She hands you an Abject Dynamix-branded towel and heads for the door. Just before exiting, she points to the bald man. "He'll get you to where you need to go."

The floor opens beneath the bovine carcass, and the straps drag it to a concrete grave.

"Don't get arrogant," the bald man says. "It's a design flaw. The only ones who pass are the ones who picked the knife. They always make it through, while everyone who picks the rope or bicycle—they never do. So it's all arbitrary. No skill." He takes a long pull from his vape. "They tried to fix it, giving everyone box cutters, but the blade's too short." Exhales a ghost. "And on the other end, five minutes is way too long to give you. You should have to kill that thing real fast." Shaking his head. "Anyway, come on. This way."

⌃

A cavernous loading area, decommissioned and stripped to concrete floor and steel pillars. Two other entrants—a boy and a girl—sit in folding chairs, dressed almost exactly as you are. The girl scrolls through her device, her elbow on her thigh and chin in her hand. The boy—a teen in an eyepatch—sits back, hands in his lap, cradling his knife. Hummingbirds flit overhead, recording.

The bald lab coat man presses the nub in his ear. "Entrant three just arrived. Yeah, this is all we're going to have."

The girl looks up. "After this we get the taser, no?"

"Sure," the man says. He begins explaining the rules.

Your body shakes. "Wait, what?" you say, indignant.

The bald man prickles. "Yes?"

"I'm supposed to get a gun."

He shakes his head. "We ran out of guns three nights ago. We've got tasers though."

"No no *no*." You punch your fists into the tops of your thighs. "I've been waiting here all fucking night. Do you know how much fucking money I've spent on this?"

"Of course I do."

"Jesus Christ."

"Look." He points to the other entrants. "A lot of folks like the taser." Tonguing inside his mouth, reaching deep in one pocket. "It's pretty fun." An alarm buzzes. "Okay? You ready?"

Neither you nor the other entrants reply.

The bald man taps his ear nub. "They're ready. Let's lift. Three, two, one, *go*."

Ancient gears press against one another, and the steel door at the end of the room begins to rise. Terrible sounds pressing out behind it—moans, gurgles, strained whining.

So much of it. The sound of a world being wounded.

The door is three-quarters raised and the bodies begin to spill. Bodies, bodies, dough bodies, spasming, crawling, whining, naked or almost. Chocolate-streaked, vomited, inflamed candy, marshmallow pustules, starved grey. Bodies spilling and spill. Dozens. Fifty dough bodies spilling to the floor. A hundred. Swollen grape bruises, bone splintered and protruding, sliced Achilles. Twitching, frail thrashing, movement deprived of mobility—superficial action.

Rush upon them.

Grabbing hair, dragging blade across throat. Rotten geyser of hot soda. Knife tip punching ribcage, cracking through, scraping plums, breaching neck, reaching throat, rendering irrelevant. Carved mouth popcorn erupting. Bodies pulled off bodies, reaching new bodies, reaching, splitting, rancid corn syrup releasing, spritzing, smelling off. Stuffing released. Bodies still spilling, writhing live replacing the inert, replacing the floor. Crawl across, crawl with your knife, popping balloons. Plastic hummingbirds clicking overheard, recording, tallying.

The eyepatch boy does something else.

Watch him shove the girl. Twisting her ankle in the soft floor of bodies. She falls backward to the tangle of them. Falling atop her, the boy plunges. Two brief stabs. The neck and the chest.

The bald man shouts something.

The hummingbirds flit over the boy, clicking and whirring. *Snip snip.* Two darts fired, pinning the boy's neck. He clutches, staggers, crumples to the writhing pile.

The alarm stabs out, evolves into a whine, a rumble, vibrating the walls, shaking your eardrums, churning your guts. You feel like you're going to vomit, and then you do.

⌣

They put you in a white room. Distinct from the first two. This one feels like a cell. Allie reviews the NDA you'd signed upon registering, explaining the penalties upon breaching with the vaguest of terminology. She finishes and places her palms flat on the table, flashing teeth. "So with all the boring stuff out of the way, the good news. Because Elaine was eliminated, and Russell forfeited by violating policy, you qualify for the final round by default."

"I still get the taser, right?"

"You will if you complete the final round."

Boil. Seethe. "Nope. *That* was the final round."

"Nope, that was the second qualifying check."

Shake your head. You know you're right. "You know that isn't true."

Her smile smooths to smear. "I know nothing." She stands and heads for the door. "You'll get it after this. Some guy will be by to tell you the rest."

⌣

A man—winking, familiar to you but not from here—introduces himself and leads you upstairs into open air. A narrow walkway slashed ahead between two massive holes torn in the roof, each filled with piled dough bodies. Twin writhing humped breasts. Crews in blue and pink hazmat suits waving flamethrowers at the piles for reasons you can't decipher. A crane stretches overhead, swinging nets filled with more twitching bodies, pouring them on the piles.

The man laughs. "Fucking wild, right?" He leads you across the remaining walkway toward the helipad. "They need to bring you off-site for this one." Enunciating slowly, as though to a child. "It's special."

Follow him up the steps, into the copter. Where do you know him from? Did you dream of him? Did he die in your dream? He touches the pilot's shoulder and you lift into the air.

The man reaches into a vest pocket and pulls out a baggy filled with yellow powder. "You're going to want to take this. You can mix it into your water. That's probably what I'd do."

Wave it away. "I'm good."

"I'm not asking. You can take it or we can drop you off right here." The pilot chuckles at this. "I'd recommend mixing it into your water."

You do so. It's chalky, also familiar, like a medicine that'd been forced down your throat as a child.

"Anyway." The man explains the rules. "Things are gonna run a little differently. Mainly, no collateral damage. The only ones you can have at are the targets. Check the dossier. If you hit anyone else your life becomes forfeit. Understood?"

"Really?" you ask.

He shrugs. "That's what they told me. I don't know. I've only been here a month."

You had waited a year for this. The same way, as a child, you had waited anxiously for playsets and puppies for Christmas and birthdays. Each new thing promising to fill a gape. Always abandoned from boredom in days. You had told yourself this would be different, everyone had said it would change you, but they lied through the same coward's teeth. A year of planning and saving, amounting to nothing. Just another present to toss to the gape.

◄

The copter drops you atop a hotel a few blocks from the destination. Take the elevator down to the lobby. Head outside and follow the sidewalk to the target apartment tower. Skim the dossier on the way.

The tower is thirty-seven stories, façade all black glass. Wait in an adjacent alley until nightfall, as instructed. Pacing, fingering the tranq gun (loaded with a single dart), practicing what you've been told to say to security.

Head in at 8:15. The lobby is dead. Approach the security desk.

"How're we doing tonight?" the guard says. A cigarette-scorched voice from a Shar Pei face.

You've already forgotten your lines so just whip out the tranq and fire, plug a dart in the center of his chest. Snarling, the guard tries to stand, to reach across the desk to your neck, but falls backward into his chair, immobilized.

Head toward the elevator. The chalky powder has integrated into your system, outputting signals to your fingernails, which will function as spoofed access cards. They will get you to the twentieth floor and even into most rooms, but the target is on the thirty-third, so additional maneuvers will be necessary.

Swipe your fingernails over the elevator card reader and smash the button for the twentieth. The car heaves upward, shuddering through the shaft, before gradually slowing. The speaker emits a bell tone and the doors slide open and you rush through, into an empty, door-lined hallway. Noise behind the doors—music, stomping feet, dancing, shouted off-key Christmas carols. Follow the hallway, placing your ear to each door until you find one with silence behind it. There—room twenty seventeen. Flick your nails over the card reader. Light flashes green and the lock clicks open. Turn the handle and slip on through.

The lights are out, and someone's sawing logs a room over. Keep quiet. Crouch and feel along the walls, down the hall, into the kitchen.

Here. There's a secret. The cabinets. Find the largest and empty it out—the cereal boxes and canned tomatoes and rice and bread. Gently and quietly, resting each item on the floor. Then crawl inside. Press the cabinet's rear panel. Press hard.

The panel falls away. The cabinet unfolds, unravels like origami. Creating spaces. Unfolding into ducts, tunnels, crawl spaces, shallow corridors that did not exist before, that only exist now because you are here to find them. Crawl in, climb through. The arteries of the building. They'll let you reach any room you choose.

Scale the crawlspaces, up to the floors the elevator wouldn't bring you. Feel the pulse in your neck as you near the target. A vibration in your blood. Crawl until you reach the dead end. Press the white panel in front of you, until it falls away, into a cabinet filled with flour, sugar and pancake mix.

Push though, letting the boxes and sacks thump to the floor, and crawl out into a kitchen. Bright white overhead light. Chattering a room over. Push yourself onto your knees, and from there, your feet, and remove the knife from your pocket. Unfold it.

Right there: a woman, middle-aged, steps around the corner into the kitchen. Her eyes click onto yours. The way her mouth pops open tells you she knows, that she understands why you're here—not the nuance, not the specifics, but the essentials. She's used to people wanting her and her family dead. Just like the dough bodies, but a completely separate context.

Before she can run or even exclaim, you grab her wrist, you drive the knife into her neck. She goes stiff, gurgling to the floor, the wound flapping open, a dozen garlic-smothered Cornish hens cascading out.

You don't shake. It doesn't mean anything to you.

Footfalls around the corner. A generic man appears. Aghast at you.

You move in.

It's amazing how many times you can stab a person in only a few seconds. As quickly as an arm can move. Your arm isn't even that fast but in no time the man is crumpled to the floor, coughing rubies from wet slits.

Head to the adjacent room—a lavish den. Two young children—probably only five or six—turn from the TV to you. They cry at their guardians' milk on your clothing and scamper to their shared bedroom (predictable). They're slippery but they succumb easily when caught, spilling small coins and buttons when opened. You wait till they stop breathing and head back to the kitchen to wash up.

A voice in your head—unfamiliar—tells you to get out, back through the cabinet. Climb the ducts to the rooftop and rendezvous with the copter. The voice asks whether you were detected.

Tell the truth.

"Any survivors?"

"No."

A sigh hisses inside your head. "Okay. That's fine. C-tier."

⌁

Back at the warehouse, Allie gives you the taser. A good weight. Maybe it was worth it.

"We also added another seven hours to your session," she says. "A token of our gratitude."

You consider tasing her right there. Stomping her head until her scalp cracks, until her jaw comes apart. But you think better and thank her and leave.

⌁

You return to the public housing complex, breaking into one of the units through the window and stabbing an eight-year-old girl in the face while she sleeps. Her mother runs in screaming and throws a chair at you but you hit her with the taser and she collapses, caving in, farting and pissing. You're about to kill her but you stab out her kneecaps instead so that she won't be able to chase after you, but she'll still live. This will be a story for her to tell now. This is the way legends begin, and a lasting legacy has always appealed to you. Capture video of the whole thing and post it to your feed. Nobody watches it, or if they do, it doesn't register—it's as mundane as a birthday cake or a sleepy puppy.

Your inner ear vibrates. Signaling that you're down to two minutes. The hummingbirds course against the sky. One stops, lowering toward you. A slight hiss. A dart fired, connecting with your neck. Nausea, vertigo. The world warps and you collapse to your knees, then forward into grass. *Blip*.

And you're back in your apartment, wincing out of slumber on your couch, stinking in days-old clothing, yeasty in your pits and crotch. Head filled with cotton and asphalt.

And for a moment you believe you had dreamed, not just the past few days but the entire world and life itself. That you dreamed of there being simply too much life, so much so that something had to be done about it. And that you of all people would be afforded the luxury of dealing with it. You believe it to be a dream the way you know dreams craft false memories, entire fabricated histories, so convincing, you may wake and believe what you dreamed was truth, until days later when it untangles and you realize those places never existed, those people never existed, you never did any of those things. But here the opposite happens. It's in the ache of your muscles, the material dried beneath your fingernails. It's the truest thing you've ever known.

He
Just
Takes
It

He gets shot in bed, first thing in the morning. The blast pushes his face, the inside of his face through the pillow and mattress, into the wall. Speckle and bits obscuring in ornate wallpaper. Bone and sinus.

They shoot him again on the porch, seven times during his first cigarette of the day, through his hand, his knees and thigh, his chest and neck and elbow. Smoke pours from the holes in his lungs. When he walks, bullets and shot grind together, offering new thresholds between organs in ways never conceived by G_d.

They'll shoot him at work, in the bathroom, and he'll fall forward into the urinal, wetting his chest and face. They'll toss him in the stall beside, lock the door from inside, and crawl back out beneath the gap below so no one else can get in. He'll wake up, shivering and weepy, vomiting lead shards, but he'll get up and get on with his day, and that's admirable, some believe.

He's shot on his way home. Seventeen bullets, caving his chest. The steering wheel falls from his hands, the tires hit curb and his Kia collides with vendors, middle-class families, and the unhoused. All of them will die except he, he will get up again, crawling out the back window and staggering down Ocean Avenue in the July inferno, gunpowder exploding between his joints.

They shoot him in bed, before he shuts off the bedside lamp. They shoot through every inch of his body—it takes fifty guns. Pushing him through the mattress, him becoming the mattress, making him the blood that soaks the mattress and fills the floor. The impossibility of vanishing. Still here, in vain refusal of each blast, crying *no no no no no*.

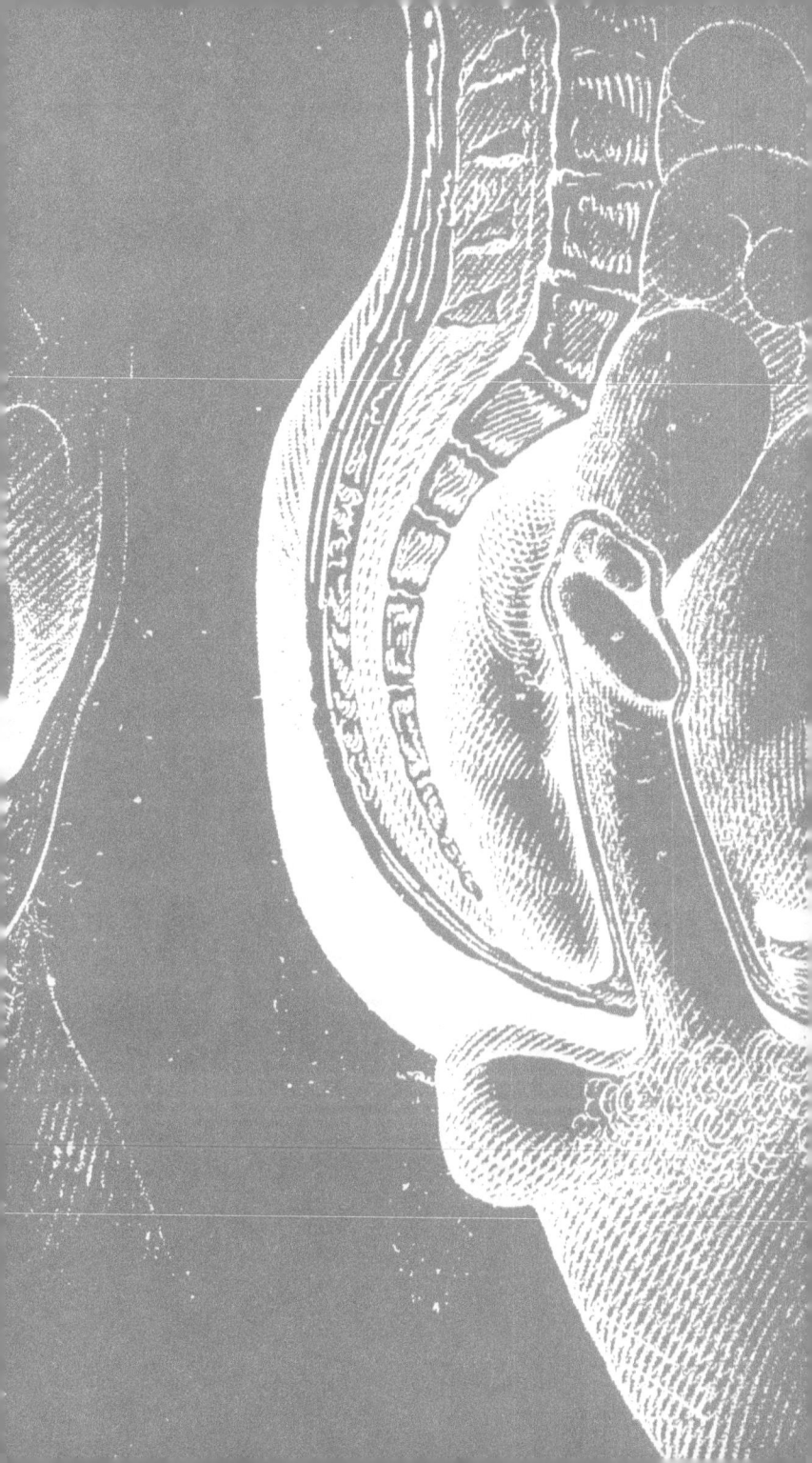

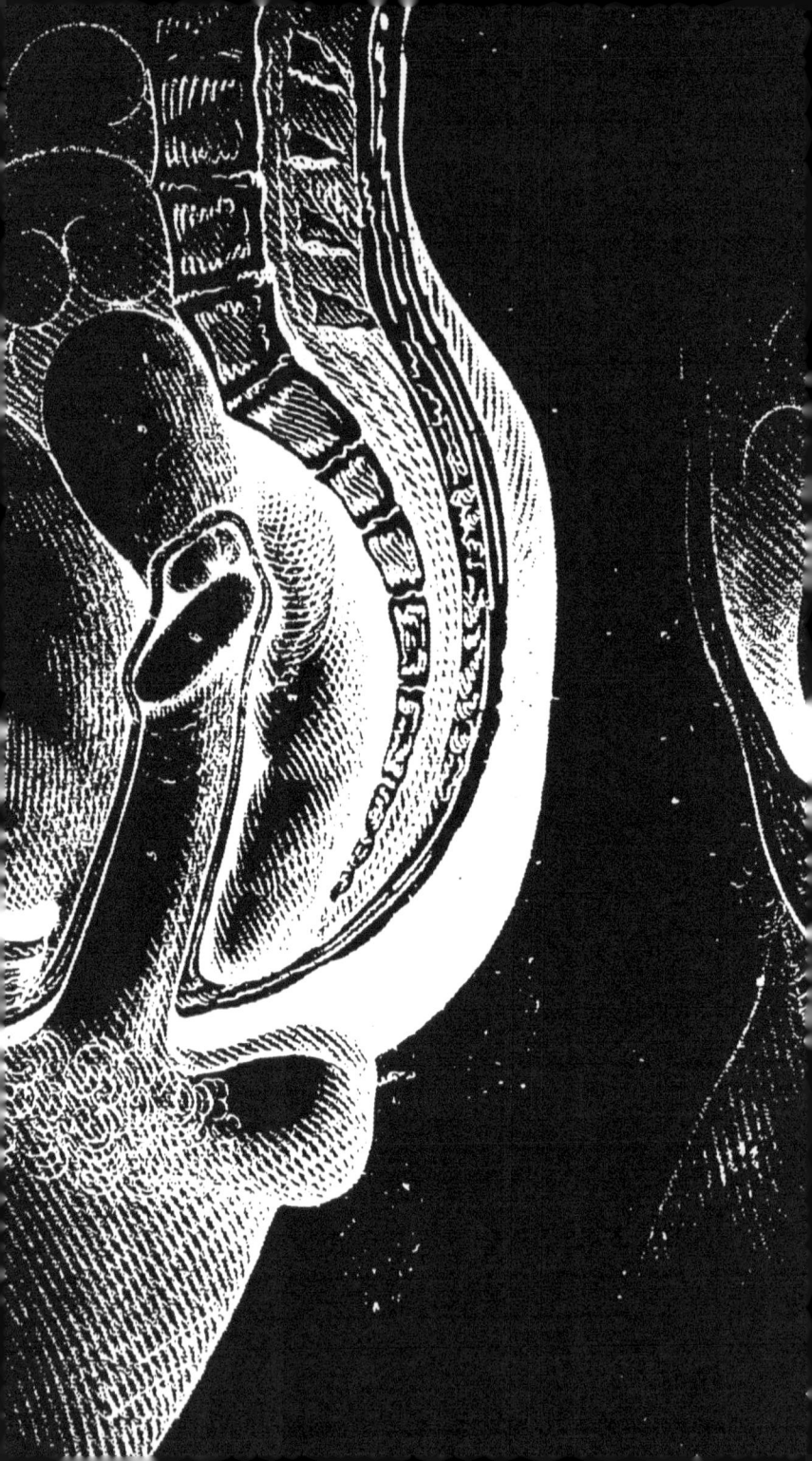

Poison Nurse

He dies beside me. I wake and he's dying, or he's already dead. The last of his warmth streaming out his penis onto my leg. An endless swamp shit reek choking the air, balmy but cooling rapidly. His eyes are open and googly. I shake him though I know. He dies beside me, he began dying inside me, if he'd never met me he'd still be alive probably but he did so now he's dead.

He said I tasted like a swimming pool. Like chlorine and a battery.

I liked him. I didn't love him but maybe I would have in a year or longer. Just because he didn't mean much now doesn't mean it isn't a real loss. So I cry, a little, when I roll him up in the bedding and call Arnold to come take care of it.

Knock knock knock-knock knock. I let him in, the first time in months. His hulking body, arms round, tight and stained tan beneath his uniform. Grey beard, grey hair in a ponytail, but whenever I think about him he's still a kid like when we first met. I hug him close. He returns it. "I owe you," I say. "I hate I only call you for this shit."

"It's fine." He lets go and nods past me. "In there?"

"Yeah. You want coffee first?"

"Nah, I'm good." He goes back outside and brings in

the stretcher, guiding it through the condo to the bedroom. I strip and slip into the shower. Hot rain. Getting the piss and stink off my skin. Washing my vagina's exterior and interior, his blood and remnants. Thinking about his mouth on my clit, I cry again.

Arnold gets the body out and loads it into the ambulance, then spends an hour making the room decent. The mattress is plastic sealed, preserving it. The sheets, the pillows, the lining, the blanket—all thoroughly wrecked, so he hauls it out and stuffs it in with the body. I replace the linens while he washes up. I offer coffee again and this time he accepts. I ask how he's been, and he shrugs. He doesn't ask me anything because he doesn't need to. He was raised right and knows not to twist a knife. He tells me he's sorry and wishes me all the best in life, and he leaves, and I do not sleep.

You're three years old. You wake with a bucket of water in your chest. Sharp coughs. Barking like a seal. Air shredding throat like rough soil. Mama wraps you in a blanket and brings you outside in the cool chirping night. She feeds you spoonfuls of honey and lemon juice. She sings and rocks you until you can breathe normal again. This is the first thing you remember about her.

I pull into the clinic seven minutes past my shift's start, crushing an Adderall between two quarters and dumping it in my coffee, then crossing the parking lot through licking sinister heat, through sliding glass doors down a long hall on carpet blooming with tacky palm fronds and mangrove. Roxanne's at the front desk, thank God. Glancing up from a book, she smiles at first, but then takes in my face, my sunken eyes, my paleness. "Oh sweetie, you look like shit."

I grab my tablet from the cubbies. "I feel like shit. Shit doesn't cover it."

"Shit's the only thing that covers it. Shit covers everything."

"Yeah. Fuck. Whatever. How're you?"

She plays with her pen, swiveling herself side to side in her chair. "Oh, you know. Awful. Just awful."

You're eight. Running off your lawn into the brush and mangrove. Tracking Key Deer, gathering up shells, wading in streams. Half a mile down, there's a tall wooden bridge no one uses anymore. A terminated bridge, no beginning or end, just a middle standing over ankle-deep water, three times your height. Pretend the bridge is a ship—the top deck of a long sunken vessel.

Years from now you'll bring a boy here.

There's a rope ladder, leading to the top. Give it a tug—it feels secure. Put one hand on a rung, then the other, your feet following. Climb to the top deck to set the sail. Sun glancing off the water, throwing confetti over the bridge and your body. Reaching the top lip of wood, you begin pulling yourself up. A sensation. Something touching, touching your hand. A brush—minuscule tiptoes over your knuckles. You tense but maintain your grip. You feel it again, and it shakes something dissonant within your belly. And then the thing peeks over the side of the wood—a leg, then three legs, then eight, attached to a juicy brown lump.

Letting go, you fall backward, to the water, to the sand beneath. Throwing your hands backward to break the fall, they hit water first, then the sand all dressed in dead coral, skidding through it. Something sharp slips between your right thumb and forefinger.

You yank back your hand, bringing it to your face. Ragged white flesh, erupting red plumes twirling diluted in the already wet. Then the real sharp comes, infinite sting and the hand turns to fire, the fucking agony running up your arm to elbow, like a thorn bush beneath your skin, twisting around.

You are certain this cannot be reversed. You are certain your hand will be like this forever.

Run home in a scream and weep.

Mama meets you at the door. "My God, what did you do?" Taking you by your good hand, she pulls you inside to the bathroom, pushes you onto the toilet seat, grabs a towel and wraps your wound in it. "What did you do?"

You just cry and yowl.

"Alright, alright." She opens the towel. It's nothing but red. "Jesus." She twists on the tap water and guides your hand beneath. You scream, pulling away, but Mama's grip is strong. "Stop it. Let me do this, or your hand's gonna rot off." Give in and let her wash it. A million needles in tender flesh. You whimper while she says "Shhhh, you're alright."

She finishes and washes her own hands, and you withdraw yours and look at it. A clean tear in the crotch of your hand. The wound smiles, with pink gums and pearly teeth at the back of its throat. Gape back.

Mama pats the wound dry with a paper towel, then leads you to the medicine room. She lifts you onto the examination table and retrieves a canister of gel, a sterile spatula, gauze and a non-stick pad from various drawers and shelves. "This," she says, "keeps the outside from getting in." She scoops a wad of pearlescent gel with the spatula and smears it over the grinning wound, then places the sterile pad and wraps it. "That's the most important part."

You never see any other nurses or doctors besides Mama. A nurse is as good as any doctor, she says, and she's the best there is. "Only difference between a doctor and a nurse is the paycheck." In two decades you'll learn this to be true. "Plus, I'm your Mama. No one knows you better than I."

Mama undresses, washes, and redresses the wound twice every day. While it's undressed, take a peek. Watch the wound change—growing foamy with white blood cells, stitching together from the corners of its mouth and the back of its throat. In two weeks, it'll seal up. In a few months, you won't even be able to see the scar.

It's so many bodies. Grinding against their biomes, wearing down, coming apart at the micro and macro. And when that happens, the bodies come to me, to a white room where we play it white and sterile, trying to keep the outside out and the inside in.

All of my bodies. Old bodies, mostly. It's Florida, wealthy Florida. So it's a 57-year-old lawyer with a ruptured testicle. A septuagenarian's taupe swollen calf. The puncture wound in a retiree's foot. Bodies wilted or calcified, opened to reveal to me. Feeling along creped flesh, I observe and I identify. That's my medicine.

It's my sixth appointment this morning. I knock twice and open the door and the breath gets knocked out of me. This body. Muscle under baby fat. Soft taught unwrinkled skin. Newly-defined cheekbones. A boy, blonde and tan in a white Monster long sleeve, blue shorts, slides. Thick arms and calves, a little chubby.

I glance at the tablet. Sixteen years old. Remembering him, from his physical maybe four years back. I had him turn and cough and his body went stiff and eyes were glassy—maybe the first time someone had touched him like that (or the second time—a cruel secret). He was puny, then. Barely anything at all. Now he's something new.

"Hi. I'm Yvonne. Not sure if you remember me."

He looks surprised, scared even, but bobs his head. "Yeah." His voice buckles and scrapes—the grit of puberty.

Skimming his chart. "I hear you're not feeling well."

"I'm sick," he wheezes, rolling the words into a coughing fit.

"Sorry to hear that. What feels sick?"

"It's hard —" A big, deliberate inhale. "It's hard to breathe."

"Are you a smoker?"

He shakes his head.

"Even pot?"

He shakes his head again, but his scent gives him away.

"Alright. Let's take a look." His blood pressure, his temperature—both normal. I watch the way he breathes. Pulling slow through his mouth. Like low wind. He holds it a few moments. Exhales raspy.

There's a performance here.

"Hop up on the table." I pat the vinyl. "And take off your shirt."

He does so. A slight, pursed out belly, firm and smooth save a trail of hairs beneath his belly button, descending toward his groin. I place the stethoscope between two handsome peach nipples. "Breathe in."

His chest rises.

"Breathe out."

And falls.

Nothing. No tightness, no rattle in his chest. Nothing but air passing unhindered through bronchioles and alveoli. Could probably get more cardio but he seems healthy enough. I pick up the tablet, swipe back through his chart, and tap it on the desk. "I don't know what to tell you. I'm not finding anything."

"No —" he moans, forcing a cough. Ramping up the act. "It hurts."

"I can prescribe antibiotics." I take a pen from the desk and click it. "You want that?"

"This—this happened to me before." He says it too fast. He loses the rasp, but catches himself, bringing his voice back to a deep mumble. "I mean—I was—I was sick like this. Before. And I came here. And they—they gave me cough syrup."

There it is. "With codeine."

His eyes shift to the floor. "Maybe. I think so."

I click the pen in and out. "You're getting antibiotics. Come see me if you still have symptoms next week."

He looks me in the eyes, and now he really does look sickly. Who knows what the stakes are. Maybe he promised his friends he'd score. Or there's some freshman girl, all fully developed since sixth grade (estrogen in the water, estrogen in the meat, estrogen in soap, plastic and every-thing), and he wants her fucked up so he can pull off her clothes beneath his parents' stilt-house. Or maybe it's just for himself—after school, sipping at the bottle till he can't stand or jerk off anymore.

Stupid things seem so important when you're young.

Whatever. Fuck it. Life is disappointment. Get used to it.

I hand him the script. His face purses into this gor-geous pout. Perfect like a conch shell. He takes the paper and fumes out.

I close my eyes. Inhale his scent. Like clean salt. And inside me, it feels like a glass filling with water.

The needle stirs.

I bounce on my soles, from one foot to the other, then grab a fist full of sterile pads and stuff them in my pocket. I head out to the front desk and tell Roxanne I'm taking lunch.

You're eleven. You and Mama are walking through the flea market (painted signs made of driftwood, a table of air plants, a table of knives and swastikas, a table of sunglass-es) and it tears you. You don't know what it is but it tears you. Like a dog hooked its tooth just below your belly and gave a tug. You're having fun today so you try to not act like it's bothering you, but with each step there's the tear, forcing a grimace.

"What's the matter?" Mama says.

"Nothing."

"Doesn't look like nothing. What's hurting?"

Pat the spot just below your stomach.

She touches your forehead. "Is it pain or nausea?"

"Pain."

"Are you bloated?"

You nod.

"Can you jump up and down for me, baby?"

You make a small hop and the tear—oh God—it shoots through your body. You double over and cry out. People turn and look.

"Okay, let's get you home."

"Why?" You don't want to go, even with the pain. You want to be out with people and bric-a-brac. At the house, you're always alone.

"If it's what I think it is you're gonna need all your strength."

You stop by the hospital and Mama runs in, keeping the A/C on for you. She comes back with a piece of paper. Then you stop by the CVS and she comes back with a bottle of pills.

"What's going on?"

"I think it's your appendix, baby."

You get home, throwing up on the way to the front door. Inside, she cleans you and sets you on the couch. You have no idea what's coming.

It's five days and nights of dogs tearing you up, of screaming and throwing your guts, of crying sweat, soaking shirts and cushions. Days and nights of heat, a sun's worth, nuclear, of melting down, swelling, expanding balloons, water particles moving faster and faster, drenching, burning off into the air. Boiling brains. You ramble, talking sugary race tracks and dough bodies, convinced you've learned a way to end the world just by thinking and obliterate all the past you thought you knew. Five days and nights in Mama's lap, sucking pills from her fingertips, ice chips, of cloth wiping lips, forever wet, her palm cupping your head like a puppy's.

On that fifth night, the fever breaks. The tear rolls back into a numb ache, barely there, almost like a friend. You finally sleep, something that could be described as sleep and not Hell, not the ruined nerve you've been tied to. You sleep, but Mama doesn't. She still sits and watches you, and when you wake her eye sockets are deep and shadowed, her skin a greyed pale. She hugs you close and you sleep again, together.

Affliction is an education. There's no better way to understand your body and what it's capable of. Whether it's your body in revolt or being invaded from without, affliction bends you. It reshapes. It exerts control.

But with the correct tools and practices, you can exercise your own control. That's all medicine is. You can reshape the body just as an ailment will. You can return a body to how it existed before it was stricken. You can strengthen it. You can shape it to what you desire.

The boy's alongside Overseas Highway, walking, swatting brush with his hand, mammoth palm fronds tearing in the wind above him. I hit my blinker, pull over to the side and roll down the window. "Hi." Flashing teeth and peeking over my sunglasses.

He stops, flinches like he's been caught in something. He looks over and recognizes me, and I watch the panic deepen. "Oh. Hey."

"You need a ride?"

"I don't know." He looks left to right, like he's in a

trap. "Nah, I don't think so."

"Ah, come on." I lean over and push open the passenger door. "Get in."

He checks his flanks again, then comes forward and gets in. "Thanks." He forces a string of weak coughs.

"Oh quit with that shit. Nothing's uglier than a shitty bullshitter." I hit my blinker and merge back onto the highway. "And you're real shitty."

He says nothing.

"So where're we heading?"

"I live on Bailey's. Off Watson."

"Nice."

"I guess."

I get down to it. "So why do you want codeine anyway?" He puts his fist to his mouth, like he's going to cough again. "I said stop. Talk to me. I'm not a cop." Holding the smile.

"I don't know," he says. "No reason."

"Yeah right," I laugh. "It's not a weird thing. It's natural. Most boys want to experiment."

He doesn't say anything.

"That stuff can be bad news though. Especially at your age."

"God, you sound like my mom."

I bite my lip, looking at his throat—the newly acquired tangle of Adam's apple. "Well, I'm not."

"Whatever." Pouting again, looking out at the sea, beautiful and perfect.

The needle stirs.

"Everyone likes to get high. I get it." Silence. "I can help, you know."

"I don't know what you're talking about."

"I said cut the shit. I'm not a cop. And I'm not your mom."

He stuffs his fingers in his pockets. "You didn't help before."

"This is different."

"Yeah?"

I pull into a Cumbies, coasting behind the store into a dark parking spot, a swamp swaying just ahead.

"This isn't my house," the boy says.

"No shit. Are you on Signal?" I take out my phone.

"Yeah. Of course."

"What's your number?" He gives it to me. I tap it into my phone and slip it back into my purse. "You'll get an address from me in a couple days. What's your worst subject?"

He gives a dopey little look. It's cute.

"In school. What class do you have your worst grade?"

"I dunno. Science."

I roll my eyes and back out of the parking spot, back around the shop and onto the road. "Tell your parents you got assigned a biology tutor. You can come see me after school. I'm on the bus route."

"For what?"

We hit a red light. I lean back into the headrest, looking him up and down, biting my lip gently. I want him to notice. Or maybe just the needle does. "So I can help you."

‸

You're twelve and Mama is giving you your annual physical. She listens to your heart, to your lungs. She feels the lymph nodes in your neck. She puts her fingers on your spine. She tells you to flip back over on the table and take your underwear off. She tells you to spread your legs. She says there's going to be something different this time, but not to be scared. "I'm going to just put one finger in. It might be a little uncomfortable, but be brave for me."

You say okay.

Feel her fingers press just below your stomach. And below that, a pressure. A breach. Feel her reach inside, across the smallest possible distances.

"Ah!" Mama shouts. And the pressure releases, she's yanking her hand back. You look up and she's staring at her gloved finger, a bead of red sprouting from the tip. She sees you watching and pulls her hand down by her side, hiding it. She smiles, nervous. "That's enough for today. How about some ice cream?"

⌣

I drop the boy off, back a few houses before his so his parents won't see my car, and head home. I get inside, go to my lab and check on my newest psilocybin crop. Another week and they'll be ready for harvest. I grab a chocolate cap from the mini-fridge and pop it in my mouth, chew and swallow, then head to the bathroom and pee. I pull off my scrubs, bra and underwear and run the shower.

Washing myself, thinking about the boy. His eyes, his lips, his arms, his belly and his thighs. Space throbs. Light smears. The needle trembles. I barely towel off and head to the bedroom.

It still smells like the boy who died here. His name was Terry—a gorgeous spring breaker from New Jersey who showed up at the clinic needing his stomach pumped. Once he was in the clear he told me he needed a ride back to his Airbnb, so I offered. On the way, he grabbed my phone and punched his number into my contacts. He said he wasn't supposed to be in town for much longer, but he could change his mind if persuaded.

He was fun.

I brush my wrist up my belly, across my breast. Glow building in my sternum. He would circle my nipple with his thumb, letting friction catch on the areola bumps. He'd breathe gently in my ear and I'd squeeze my thighs to-gether. Warm light in my belly. He would move his mouth from my ear to my neck, to my shoulder, to collarbone. My nipple, firm and sensitive, would disappear between his lips. Sucking air as his teeth grazed it.

Breathe in, then out.

I slide my middle finger down past my belly, through the tuft of hair, parting my lips, pressing down on my clit. Rubbing a slow moon, remembering his mouth on my thigh, beautiful plump lips on my pelvic bone. The way he tasted me, even as I pushed him away, like he couldn't help himself. Like he was addicted to what's inside me. And that last time, sliding in, clutching my hips to pull me further onto him. The way he grinned looking down at me.

Light swirls and ripples. I buck, arching against the mattress, and discharge. Gasping. Sheets soaked in sweat.

My head stops spinning and I get up, wobbling from foot to foot toward the lab. I tear the wrapper off one of the sterile spatulas I stole from the clinic and scoop it up inside my pussy, pressing against my walls to capture my lubricant, and withdraw. With another spatula, I scrape the fluids into a glass vial, then place it in the mini-fridge. I toss the spatulas in the trash, go to the bathroom, pee, wash up and head back to bed, collapsing on the mattress, flipping on the TV.

Terry's on the news, or at least his name and a picture from when he was still alive. I always know it's coming, but it doesn't make it hurt less. Discovered by kayakers, tangled in mangrove. The authorities call it a drug overdose, leading the anchors into a segment on the opioid epidemic.

⌒

You're fourteen and meeting your new boyfriend for the first time. Dennis. You meet Dennis on the internet. He messages you, saying you have "beautiful cheeks." He's your type—big Jewish nose, a little chubby, beautiful brown eyes. Ask how old he is. Twenty-four, he replies. Tell him how old you are. He doesn't respond. Go to bed sad.

But the next day there's a new message from him. Soon, you're talking on the phone. Ask him to come over.

"What about your mom?" he says.

Tell him she's at work, that her shift lasts all night.

All you hear is breathing on the other end. "Okay," he says finally.

He comes over. He's stiff and shaky but you lead him to the bed and you lie on your sides and make out for an hour. He barely speaks, and when he does it's about how beautiful you are. He touches your waist and belly. You crawl on top of him, pressing all your weight down, both your clothes still between you. He takes his hands off and lies there stiff.

Roll off. "We can do other stuff," you say.

He tenses beside you. "Yeah?"

"Totally," you say, nestling into him.

He's quiet. Listen to him breathe. Then: "Can you strip for me?"

You smile and kiss him deep. You get up and put on Mike Jones, dancing a sequence you'd long practiced in the mirror. Pull off your jeans and grind little circles in the air with your ass, looking over your shoulder, giving a smile and wink, hoping he can't see you tremble. It feels like a movie. Tell yourself it's perfect. Pull off your top and watch him stare, thirsting at your waist and breasts. He undoes his pants and pulls them off. You unclasp your bra, shaking it free, letting your breasts flop, and shimmy your panties down. He stays clothed in his shirt and underwear, stroking his cock through the fabric. "You're so hot," he says.

Slink over, climbing his lap, your knees on either side of him, straddling his clothed cock. Put your mouth next to his ear and breathe. "Should I get a condom?"

"I don't need one," he says, and takes you by the shoulders and pushes you to the bed. He lays down beside you and works his penis out of his boxers, stroking, staring at you.

A cold snap through your spine. You tense, feeling your nakedness, the moment rotting. Ask: "Do you want me to do anything?"

"You can touch yourself too. Just lay right—" he moans "— like that. And make sounds."

Lay there. Moan. He groans quiet. His skin turns slick and moist. He works harder and harder, and goes *uh uh uh*. *Uhhhh*. Strands of wet white burst over your skin.

Put your hand on his belly and kiss his neck.

He bolts up, stands fast, yanking his pants back over his knees. "I'm sorry," he says. "I got to get home."

The world shrinks, collapsing inward, just a little. "Okay," you say.

He heads towards the door. "I got to get groceries."

There was a guy in college (another who died) who said that the only thing anybody wants is control. Power over another. He said that all relationships are just exercises in power, dressed in delusion and tradition. Especially romantic relationships. *Especially* purely sexual relationships.

He said that everyone gets it wrong. Everyone thinks that men only care about the physical, and women only care about the mental. But actually it's the opposite. He said that in every survey of long-term heterosexual couples, men's greatest complaint about their partners was a lack of companionship and emotional bonding; women's greatest complaint was a dwindling sex life. The fact is, he said, more than anything, men want to be adored. They want to be worshipped. They want a slave to dote and ego stroke. And this makes them profoundly vulnerable.

Women, however, desire sensation above all things. They seek to own men's bodies, in order to be filled by them, as the female life is vacant otherwise. So, by biologically intuiting the vulnerabilities of men, women seduce through coy looks, childish whimpers and other maneuvers of deception. Melting men down, fucking them hollow, until their souls are destroyed. He said that since time immemorial women have ruled the world through men's bodies.

I laughed in a manner that didn't reveal its mockery, and said I'd never heard it put that way before, "that's such a unique take on things," etc. But in truth, what he said scared me. The possibility that what he said was generally bullshit, but true specifically for me.

I dress in scrubs the first time the boy comes over.

Sometimes it puts them at ease to view me as a professional. I'm nervous so I swig a third microdose and pace in front of the door, waiting.

He's almost fifteen minutes late. Dressed more or less the same as when I last saw him. Unwashed—B.O., oily hair, that faint dead bleach stink of semen. That'll need to change. It will, in time.

"What'd you tell your parents?"

"I dunno."

"Did you tell them I was your tutor?"

"I said I was going out. They don't give a shit what I do."

"You sure?" I peer through the blinds into the parking lot. Wind pushing the palms, Key Deer lumbering toward the trash bins, but no unfamiliar vehicles. "I don't want a mini-van rolling up on me."

"They don't care." He glances around the room, at the mini-lab, at the chaise lounge sealed in plastic. "So you said you're gonna help me?"

"Yeah. I am. But you're gonna have to help me, too."

He rolls his eyes.

"I actually think you'll enjoy this."

"Yeah? You've got some good shit?"

"Yes. If you behave." I point toward the chaise. "Sit." He does so. In the mini-lab, I collect a thermometer, a sterile sheath, an alcohol swab, a 2x2" square of gauze, a roll of tape and a syringe, placing them all on a stainless steel tray. From the fridge, the vial filled with my discharge, diluted with saline. I uncap the syringe, jab the vial, draw the contents, and return the syringe to the tray. Then I head to the kitchen and fill a glass with ice chips. I return to the chaise, placing the tray on the end table, and ask him which arm I should do.

"What?"

Tapping the syringe. "You got a problem with needles?"

He shakes his head. "But what's in it?"

"It's a blind study. If I told you, it'd skew the results."

"Is it safe?"

"Do you think I'd give you something if it wasn't safe?"

He considers the syringe, the rest of the tray, and me. "Okay. Do my left."

I sterilize the middle of his left shoulder and jab, inject, and withdraw. He doesn't flinch. "There we go. Good job." A tiny bead of red. I cover it with gauze and tape it over. "Why don't you lie down."

"I'm fine like this."

"You won't be. Lie down."

He lies down.

I sit in the chair beside him and pull a small lined trashcan next to the chaise. "If you have to vomit. Don't try and stand. That'll make it worse."

He says nothing, but nods. The minutes pass. His face twists into a grimace. His hands move atop his stomach. I touch his forehead. Warm, moist. Venom interacting with his blood.

"I'm gonna take your temp." I take the thermometer from the end table and place a sterile sheath over it. "Open."

He opens but immediately retches. He tilts his head over the chaise and pukes a viscous orange stream into the trash can.

"There there." Stroking his hair, letting the curls wrap my fingers. "It's alright."

He retches and vomits again, watery yellow. He gags

and gasps. "What's happening?"

"Shhhh. It's alright." Dabbing his lips clean with wet cloth.

"What're you doing to me?" He rolls onto his side, curled, drooling onto the plastic. The needle trembles, and I smile at this—what my body is capable of—but stop myself.

"I'm making you strong." I move from my chair to the chaise, sitting inside his curl. An erection presses through his shorts into the side of my ass. I pinch up an ice chip from the cup and place it against his lips. "It'll take time." He sucks at the chip. "But you'll get there." As it melts down, my fingertips meet his lips and he gently sucks them too. When it's melted all the way, I remove another chip and place it in his mouth. He accepts and crunches gently.

He groans. "You wouldn't hurt me, would you?"

I try not to laugh but I do, a little. I explain that the truth is, most nurses are idiots. Everyone trusts them because they have a degree and wear scrubs, but that doesn't mean anything. It's even worse with doctors. The truth is that you don't got to be anything special to be a nurse or a doctor or a surgeon or a senator or anyone with station. The truth is, they're all just people, so most of them are average or a lot worse than that.

Forgetting my point, I pick up the tablet, jotting notes while he tremors on the chaise.

You're fourteen and Dennis is jerking off on your chest, watching you rub circles between your legs. Together and apart. It's been a month and that's the extent of your relationship now. He comes over, you make out, he jerks off on you and he leaves. He's always finished before you are, so you stay in bed and rub your clit while his cum is still on you.

But not on your birthday. On your birthday you dress up in purple fishnets and a mini-skirt and black strapless top, no bra. You paint your fingers and toes metallic purple, your lips a matching hue. You put on the music he likes.

Watch for his headlights to come up the driveway. When they do, step out so he can see you, swaying in the night, warm and electric like skin. When he gets out, run up and wrap your arms around his neck. Wrap your thighs around his knee and squeeze. Whisper in his ear.

He pulls back, looking you up and down. "Wow," he says. He looks side to side at the neighbor's houses. "Maybe we should get inside."

Lead him to your room and push him down on the mattress and straddle him, kissing, sucking, lapping at his lips, working around to his ear. Whisper: "I want my present."

Feel him tense beneath your weight. "I-I'm sorry … I … uh didn't —"

"I want you." Kiss his earlobe. "I want you inside me."

He pauses, then gently pats you on the back. "Okay."

You hop off him, grinning big and horny dumb, grabbing a condom from the dresser and stripping to nothing. He takes his pants off but keeps his shirt and underwear on. You grab his cock, warm and firm, and pull it through the opening. You tear open the condom's wrapper, unroll it onto him, and hop onto his lap, guiding him inside you.

Pressure. So tight at first. Like it won't even fit. But then the breach, it slides in and it's like light and heat shooting straight through you.

Place your feet on either side of his thighs and pump up and down on him. Looking down, watching it slide in and out. He looks down too. He says that you're so beautiful. He grabs your hips and swings you over onto your back, thrusting hard and deep. A nice long ache, in and out, hard and slow, your calves wrapping his hips, clenching him deeper inside. Pounding heat and light. A balloon filling with water. Pulling his face down, pressing it against yours, sighing in his ear.

"*Ah*," he gasps. Like pain.

"You okay?" Grinding against his pelvis.

"I'm fine." He pumps, sweat dribbling off his forehead into your mouth. Speeding up, like a machine pushing inside you. He gasps and groans again. Louder. Louder. The water pours inside.

He holds his breath. His body stiffens. Releases. He pulls out and falls beside you onto his back, heaving. The condom, half-hanging off his penis, smeared with blood.

You've gotten your period since you were ten, but didn't think it was time. Must have lost track. The blood has to be your own.

You swing your arm and leg over onto his torso, pulling close, laying kisses on his cheek and ear. "Whoa," he says.

"That was greeeeaaattt," you say, not knowing whether it was or not.

"Yeah," he exhales.

"You okay?"

"A little dizzy," he says.

"Want some water?"

"Maybe." He closes his eyes. "Yeah."

Gently crawl over his body, kissing his forehead. Then

head to the kitchen, humming to yourself. Head swollen with vision and potential future. Dates in Key West, fancy dinners, drinks and nightclubbing. Him tugging you by the wrist to an ancient cemetery where you lie him down and mount. Lying together on the beach, watching egrets overhead, surf lapping your thighs. A home for the two of you that you'd carve out from the mangrove.

You fill a glass with tap water and return to him. He's sweating through his shirt, clutching his stomach. "Here you go." Hand him the glass and lay back down beside him.

"Thanks." He takes a sip, trembling. Ask again if he's okay. "Yeah. I will be."

✌

Removing my clothes, stepping into hot night. Sweat joining with the wet in the heat. Insects and animals clicking, chirping. Wind flushing through fronds, over my body in waves. Closing my eyes, I imagine going back, not to my earlier life but further, beyond my mother and father or any of my family. Even this country. Back to old dead continents. Worlds of worship. If the world and the people in it could know my body and its capability, it would be worshipped. They'd throw boys to me, and my body would never be in want.

Either that or they'd toss me to fire. Maybe even today they would. Never too late. Maybe even better that way.

The boy returns the following week. I greet him in a tank top and tight black bicycle shorts. The needle shivers when he looks at my legs. He's unwashed again, so I make him shower. "Most boys your age already learned to manage their hygiene. Guess you'll be a late bloomer." I give him Tazorac and instruct him to apply it daily. I give him money and tell him to buy body wash, shampoo and deodorant or he can't see me again.

The session is more or less identical to the first. Once shot up, he curls around me, and between bouts of vomiting, I feed him ice cubes and let him suck on my fingertips. Once it's all done and he's good to go home, I give him two grams of psilocybin chocolates and drop him at the end of his street.

But the third week he doesn't show. I message him. *Where are you? It's important that we keep our schedule.* And it's true. Cultivating tolerance requires a strict, deliberate routine.

But no response. Anxiety climbs into my shoulders. It whispers, telling me I was wrong to pick him. A lapse in judgement, a stupid side effect of my grief for Terry. And it hits that maybe the reason he's not responding is that he's gone. The anxiety twists. And if he *is* gone—his parents. They could be going through his phone. They could be seeing these messages. They could be putting it all together.

Pacing the condo, one room to the other, waiting for sirens, for flashing blue lights in the parking lot, I get a reply. *Sorry. I don't think I'm gonna come anymore.*

Relief washes, then another, separate panic. *Why?* I type. *I miss you.*

I feel like shit. This was always a possibility. Maybe I was wrong. Maybe he wasn't made for this.

The needle stirs. *Can I see you?*

Nothing for a minute. Then: *Okay. Get me at Matthew & Ortega.*

I pull on my tight purple cocktail dress and drive out, sky ebbing pink and peach, like my skin and his pressed together. Turning onto Matthew, I find him at the corner, hunched. He looks weak, decayed. That's just how it is at this point, before he's conditioned.

I pull over, lean over and push open the door. "You had me worried."

He steps toward the door. "Why?"

"I thought I wouldn't see you again." Repressed people believe the reason guys go to strippers and pros is just for tits and pussy, but that's not it at all. All they want is to feel desired. Missed. Because chances are they aren't getting that anywhere else. Once you understand this, it's the easiest role to play.

He hesitates, then gets in the car.

"Why didn't you come back." I bite my lip, frowning small and pretty.

"I told you. I feel like shit. That shit you shot me up with. What is it?"

"I already said, it's a blind study. If I told you, it'd —"

"Is it heroin? Is this because I tried to get codeine? Is this, like, your dad catches you smoking and makes you smoke the whole pack?"

Fucking disappointing. "It's not heroin. I'd never."

"Then what the fuck is it?"

"I already said." I pull over to the side of the road. "Look at me." Pushing my sunglasses down the bridge of my nose, so he can see my eyes. "Do you really think I would do anything to hurt you?" I lay my hand atop his thigh. He's shaking.

He stares at me. Weak. Almost like he might cry.

The needle stirs.

He looks down in his lap. "No."

I smile, lean in and plant a kiss on his cheek. I merge back into traffic and bring us to my place.

He huddles, wrapping his waist with his arms on the chaise. I return with the syringe, the gauze, the tape, but also two hits of acid I'd been saving for a rainy day. I lick my fingertip and place it to one of the tabs. "Let's do something different tonight. Open up."

He shakes his head.

I pout and pop the tab in my own mouth. "Come on. I'll still give you your take-home chocolates." I pick up the other tab. "Open."

He opens. I place the hit on his tongue and leave it there. He closes his mouth around my finger and sucks as I withdraw. I smile and give him a light playful slap.

He points at the syringe on the table. "Aren't you going to do that?"

"In a little bit." I sit across from him. "I think that hit will help you with the nausea, so I want it in your system first."

"Okay." Some tension falls out. His posture loosens. "Cool."

"So how much longer do you have of school?"

"Two years."

"Nice. Do you know what you're doing after?"

He smiles sheepish, shakes his head.

"That's fine. I did all sorts of bullshit before I started doing this. I mean, my job." I catch him looking at my cleavage. "For a while, I wanted to be a chemist." I arch my back and lift my neck. "You could be a model, you know. Or an actor."

He laughs. Blushes. "Nah."

"No, really, I could see you in a GQ spread or, like, on the CW."

He shakes his head again. "Thanks. I'm actually really into music."

I smile big. There it is. "Oooh, that's very cool. What do you play?"

"Some guitar. And I make some beats." He looks away, smiling but still embarrassed. "And I rap."

Flashing big teeth, reaching out a hand, touching his knee. "Oh my God, that's so hot. That's like atomic. Can I hear?"

"Nah," he laughs.

"Come on! Spit something. Give me some bars."

He grins and leans forward, resting his elbows on his thighs. He opens his mouth, starts, stops, then—

Got a real long knife and it gets real hot
Smokin' too much weed and downin' too many shots
Got too many girls I can't tell'em apart
So I keep to the shadows and try not to get caught

He laughs a little. Shakes his head, cheeks rosy. But I keep looking at him, scraping my front teeth over my bottom lip. I start snapping in rhythm. He jumps back in.

Now I got a warrant and the smoke got me worried
Signal blowing up, bitches want me to hurry
But I don't give a fuck 'cause you know I stay lucky
Rollin down the block and they all look at me funny
Got a wide hat, got a perm
Gonna slide back, gonna learn
Bitches don't mean nothing but a really nice time

Just hanging in the summer and we feelin' real fine
Tempest got me rocked off margaritas and marinade
Blood clots got me runnin' like we got no intensive aid
Biiiiiiitch, I hear these kids afraid

He shrugs and laughs again. "Those last bits were off the top."

"Oh my God." Cooing, clapping my hands together. Making a show of it. Inside, I'm laughing. At him, yes, but there's more to it. It's dumb and ridiculous, but I feel fifteen again, laying in fields smoking cigarettes with a boy (someone real, another boy, a different boy who dies) trying to impress me. The acid beats inside me, beating me like a drum, and it beats inside him too—the sway, the ripple, the slight loll of his head. It's like a rope pulled through me and tied around him. He sways, and I sway too.

He lies back on the chaise, rubbing his chest and face. "Hey, sorry for being weird. Thanks for picking me up. You're really cool."

I stand and retrieve the syringe and pad from the platter. "Thank you, sweetie. You're real cool too." I sit beside him, take his arm and find a vein, jab and inject. He rolls to his side, curling around me. The usual hard-on pressing through his jeans into my thigh. I pull the waste basket beneath his face and feed him ice chips with my fingers. Half an hour passes and he doesn't vomit. I ask if he's nauseous.

"Yeah. But not as bad as it's been."

"Good." I feed him two ice chips and slide off the chaise to the floor.

"Hmmm?"

"Shhh." Folding my legs to the side, resting my elbows on the chaise. Grabbing his belt, unbuckling. Working his jeans' button through the eye. Unzip and open.

"Wha—" He tenses.

"Shhh. Relax." I wrap my fist around the front of his boxers and squeeze. It flexes back. "Thank you for being here," I whisper.

I reach inside his boxers and pull his penis through the hole. Uncut—thick, glistening tip. It smells like gauged ears and old pennies. Ringing it lightly with my fingers, I give a long, soft stroke.

He shivers.

"I've never seen one this big," I lie, placing my mouth over it, dragging my tongue around the glans. Bobbing, bringing it further into my mouth, sucking my cheeks in, creating vacuum. He tenses. His cock pulses. I graze the tip with a tooth.

"There's a knife inside me," I say, breathing it in.

He spasms and heaves. He coughs. He leans forward and pukes into the waste bin.

I ignore it. I stay on his cock, taking it in palm and twisting, tracing the glans with my thumb. He heaves yellow bile. The reek permeates. I'm miles away from turned on, but that's not the point. This is just training. Classical conditioning. He'll learn to associate the nausea, the fever, with my lips around him, the wet warmth of my cheeks and tongue. He'll never run off again.

⌃

It's 5:14 AM and Mama's walking in the door from her shift, finding you in the living room. Not crying, because you've cried everything you've got. Completely cried out. Tell her you're sorry, you're so so sorry. You truly believe that this will be the last time you ever see her again.

Bring her to your room, early sunlight carving through the blinds, falling on Dennis's rigid body in the dark roiling swamp of vomit and piss. She gently covers her mouth and nose. She pulls you close with her other arm. "It's okay."

She tells you to go back to the den. She goes to her own room, and you can hear her through the walls, talking on the phone. "Bless you. Good Lord, I owe you I owe you I owe you." Then she hangs up and comes back and sits beside you, wrapping you in her arms. She asks you to tell her everything.

Tell her. All of it. Tell her you're sorry again.

Deep inside, you believe she is going to take your life away.

A knock at the door. *Knock knock knock-knock knock.* Mama opens it. A young broad man, dressed in scrubs, stands in the frame. "Ms. Williams," he says. And then looks at you. He introduces himself as Arnold. Mama leads him into your room.

That's how it goes, every time until Mama dies, and then it's just Arnold. Establish a pattern early and you'll never disappoint anyone. You make a mess. Someone else cleans it up.

✦

Two sessions later and he's ceased vomiting. His spasms diminish, his fever hums low at ninety-nine point seven. He still lets me feed him ice chips, sucking and licking them out of my fingers.

"Any nausea?"

He shakes his head.

"Good." Tussling his hair. "That means you're getting stronger."

"Cool."

"I sure think it's cool." I place an ice chip between his lips. He sucks it into his mouth, crunches and swallows. I let my thumb rest there on his bottom lip. He waits, breathing gently on it. Then he tips his face forward, taking the digit into his mouth, sucking gently, swirling his tongue around.

The needle shivers.

I withdraw my thumb and wipe it on my blouse. "You can sit up. I'd like to try something new." Uncrossing my legs—spreading them slightly, so maybe he can see up my skirt—I pat the top of my right thigh. "Come here."

He looks confused, but stands anyway, a little woozy on his legs but steady enough. He comes over.

"Sit." I pet my thigh again. He sits. His ass is soft but strong. I lay my wrist and forearm across the top of his thigh, just an inch away from his groin, and rest my chin on his shoulder. "Remember what happened a few weeks ago?" I whisper.

He takes a deep breath.

"What I did?"

"Yeah," he exhales.

"Did you like that?"

"Yeah."

"Good," I coo. "Do you do things like that with other girls?"

He nods.

Breathing him in. Scrubbed clean. Like plastic pomegranate and salt water. "What do you do with them?"

"What do you mean?"

"You fuck them, right?"

He nods.

"You finger them?"

He nods.

"You eat their pussies?"

He nods.

Cervical tissues swell with fluid and press upon the needle.

"Are you good?"

His body tightens, compressing. "What do you mean?"

"Do you satisfy the girls you're with?"

His face goes red. He turns from me. "I dunno."

"It's okay." A light kiss on his earlobe. "Stand up. I'm going to show you something."

He gets off my lap, turns his back to me, fumbling with the front of his pants, hiding himself.

"Don't," I say. "Don't hide. Turn. Face me." He does so, full erection pressing through his jeans. He looks down and to the side. "Look at me," I say. He does. Hooking my thumbs beneath my skirt, I pull off my underwear, already glazed wet. The boy trembles. "Kneel," I say, opening my legs, pointing to the floor just in front of me. He does. "Now this is important," I say. "Disobey, and you can never see me again. Understood?"

He nods.

"Good. You are to do exactly as I say. No more, no less. Disobey, and I will *never* let you see me again. Understood?"

He nods.

"*Understood?*"

"Understood."

"Good." I smile big. "Touch me."

He reaches out a tremoring hand toward my lap, my

pussy already slick and puffed. I reach down and spread myself.

"You're going to put your fingers in me. Only two. Your middle and your index on your right hand. Only those." My own two fingers press against my clit and rub a slow circle.

His fingers enter with ease. The ridges of his knuckles rub against my walls as he pushes in and pulls out, slowly, gently, in rhythm with my own rubbing. I tense my seat, the back of my cervix, keeping the needle in place.

"Reach further," I say. "You won't hurt me."

He does, and his fingers press against the bulb of my cervix. I spasm. He begins to withdraw his fingers, but I grab his wrist, holding him inside me. "Stay there. Stay right there."

"Okay," he whimpers.

"Now," leaning in, smiling, "I'm gonna show you some real magic." I tell him to curl his fingers, like *come hither*. And his fingers curl, pressing his tips into the sponge of my ceiling. And I fill with oceans and storm. Shake and inhale. Becoming nothing but wet. A flood, a torrent. Primordial throb. A phantom heel on my spine, making me arch, threatening to snap me in half. His fingers pulling me apart. I want all of him inside me. His entire body. To pull him up through my opening, from his cock to his hips, his torso and limbs, his head. All inside me. His hands stroking circles around the base of my cervix, his neck bending backward, pressing his lips, his teeth, his tongue into spongey wet.

The needle buzzes. It shakes in insistence.

The needle slips out.

"*Ah*." The boy shouts, a sharp exclamation, and reels back from me, onto his ass, cradling his slicked hand. A small bead of blood on the tip of his index.

"Oh sweetie," I say, leaning forward, out of the chair toward him. I take his hand and pull him to his feet. "I'm sorry 'bout that."

"What?"

"Nothing to worry about," I lie.

"What the fuck is that?"

"It's an IUD," I lie and smile. "A girl's gotta be safe. You wouldn't want a little surprise, right? Not at your age."

"Oh." His breathing slows. "Alright." His world pulls back together into something rational and knowable. "Yeah, alright, I get that."

I kiss his earlobe and rub my nose against his cheek. "Let's get you cleaned up." I bring him to the bathroom and run the sink. Standing behind him, my breasts pressed into his back, holding his hand beneath the water, coating it in soap, scrubbing it, then rinsing, coating, and scrubbing again. I slide down to the floor beside him, open his pants and breathe on his cock, letting it fall between my lips, twirling my tongue around the tip. Reaching down and rubbing my wetness, I tell myself this could go on forever, and I'd be happy. This could be my life now, me and him, eating mushrooms and colliding forever in four walls, A/C and artificial light. Sucking his cock, rubbing moons into my clit. This could be all that we have, forever, and that could be alright. Coming together as vibration, as a smoky orange light. This could be enough this time.

ᴧ

The needle shakes, furious. It threatens. It tells me it will tear me apart from inside if I disobey. It tells me it knows best. That I worry too much. The needle tells me the boy is my soulmate. The needle caresses me from inside, knowing if it were to press any further it would puncture, it would burrow, until it was no longer inside me, until there was no longer a me to be inside.

⌒

I tell him to come over Saturday. Not for a session. Something different. I tell him to tell his parents he's staying at a friend's house. He says he won't have to say anything, his parents won't care.

I come to the door in a purple strapless sundress, no bra, barefoot. Lights dimmed low, music already playing— low wormy grooves, like massive bodies rubbing against one another. I open the door and he's dressed up, in long khakis, a pink and blue Polynesian shirt. His eyes go wide at me, smiling and swaying in halftime to the music, pushing my hips side to side. Watching him watch me. "Hi," he says. He tries to hide his smile but it breaks through every time. "You look beautiful."

"Aww." Reaching out, squeezing his wrist, I gently tug him inside. "Thanks, sweetie."

"I brought this." He reaches into his breast pocket and pulls out a poorly twisted joint. It makes me laugh a little, making me young again. I grab him by the back of the neck and kiss him. "I love it. That's beautiful."

We sit on the chaise, him behind me, me between his legs. He lights the joint and pulls deep. Before he can exhale, I twist my head and open my mouth to his, breathing in his smoke. We lap tongues, and I pull back, snickering, taking the joint from his hand. I take the hit, hold it, and tilt my head back into his chest, parting my lips. His lips meet mine, catching my exhalation. He runs his hand down the center of my chest before cupping my breast. Pinching my nipple between his thumb and forefinger, pulling in a circle. I arch and suck his bottom lip.

The needle stirs.

Turning and climbing onto his lap, my breasts fall from the dress and he catches them in his mouth, circling each nipple with his tongue, gently grazing his teeth against the tips. I push him backward and press my mouth to his, sucking his lips, brushing my tongue over his. Licking his teeth. He presses his groin into mine, rubbing against me dry to the synthetic beat. "Take off your pants," I whisper. He keeps humping, sucking my neck. I pull away, rising up off of him. "Now." He jolts beneath me, wrestling his belt open, his fly, squirming the jeans down to his ankles, kicking them off. His penis slips through his boxers' opening, plump and glossy with pre-cum. My fingers encircle it, running up and down the shaft. Just two long pumps. He sighs deep, and I climb atop his lap.

I hover my pussy above his cock, bringing it down lightly until it just barely touches. Connecting our wetness. He runs his hands down the small of my back to my buttocks. I gyrate my hips, dragging myself across his glans, letting it spread my lips gently. His body goes rigid, and he pushes himself up off the couch, his hand on my ass pulling me down toward him, and he enters me, slightly. I put a foot on the ground and lift myself off, letting the shaft rest against my clit. "No," I say.

He moans and tries to push himself up inside me again.

"No," I repeat, and wrap a hand around his throat, thumbing his Adam's apple. Sliding off his lap to the floor, between his thighs, I envelope his cock, licking my lubrication off his shaft and tip. He moans, tremors and giggles.

But then he stops. "No," he says. He grabs me, pushes my head off his penis. "Your turn." He grabs me by the shoulders, so hard it may bruise, and throws me onto the chaise, onto my back.

He parts my knees with the backs of his hands and kneels between. Reaching a finger inside, then another. Pressing against my cervix. I suck in, I tense, I hold back, and the needle holds too. He pulls the tips of his fingers back, into the spongey ceiling inside me. He strokes and I arch. He leans forward and puts his lips to my clit. And I let him. For a few moments.

Shake out of it. "Stop," I say, placing my foot against his shoulder and pushing him away. But he's strong. He swats my calf and my foot slips past his shoulder. He pulls my hands from his head and holds them down by my sides. He puts his lips and tongue to my pussy and drinks me.

The stomach is actually remarkably good at breaking down the toxin. He may have some nausea, some light hallucination, but it shouldn't be so bad.

Then he stands, holding my waist, and he slips inside me. He fills me, a slow piston grind, felt on every one of my surfaces.

I don't tell him no.

He feels the ridges of my walls caressing his shaft. He feels his glans press against the plump bulb of my cervix. What he doesn't feel is the needle slipping out from behind it. It's so fast. He doesn't feel it slip inside his urethra. He doesn't feel the needle widen it. And in the throes of fuck, he doesn't feel the tear in his urethral lining, the exposure of his blood to my venom—all that he's been training for.

The wound widens, and then he does feel it. He tenses and yells, but stays inside me.

"You alright?" I ask.

He shakes it off. "Yeah." And he thrusts deeper into me and I feel the needle lodged, pulling when he pulls, and it hits me like a gust, like a torrent, like an egg through a serpent's throat. It makes me gasp and shake and we gasp and shake together, and maybe we will always be here in this shape, and maybe this lasts forever.

Dennis. My uncle. A boy named Sanjay. A boy named Austin. A man named Trevor. A boy named Yuze. A boy named Omar. A man named Liam. A boy named August. A boy named Angel. A man named Sal. A boy named Benjamin. A boy named Ji-Hoon. A boy named Oliver. A boy named Terry. A boy.

I message him and ask how he's feeling. He says he's alright and asks when I can see him again. I tell him Wednesday.

He's twenty minutes late. Eyes sunken. Complexion a wilted bronze. Strained inhalation, deep sighs.

I touch his elbow, guiding him inside. "How are you?"

He sucks dry mucus through his sinus. He exhales and his chest rattles wet, like God blowing on a lake. "I'm fine. I missed you."

He leans into me and I tuck my chin around his neck. "I missed you too." I let him kiss me and press himself into my waist. "Can I take a look at you first?"

"Okay."

He lays down on the chaise and unbuttons his pants. I take his temperature (101 degrees), check the lymph nodes in his neck (very swollen), give him a sip of water, unzip him and pull his pants and underwear off all the way. His penis red and erect. Looking close, it's two reds. A red like a bug bite and red like wine. Infection and dried blood.

I kiss him on the forehead. "You sure you're alright?"

He nods, lifts his head and catches my lips in his.

Pulling away. "Why don't I do something for you this time?" I fill a bowl with warm water and grab soap and a wash cloth from the bathroom. Alcohol swabs and antibiotic cream. Sitting beside him, I swaddle the wash cloth around his penis. Moving it gently around the flesh. He tenses and coos. Like a time when I was a child with Mama, except I'm her now, as well as myself, all at once. I dunk the cloth back in the soapy water and return it to his penis, wiping the crusts of red off the tip. Infected swelling on the glans. Wrapping it around the shaft, I give three long strokes. A snake around a branch. He gasps and grabs my arm. "I want you," he says.

"You don't want me to take care of you this way?" Circling the base of his glans with my thumb.

He shakes his head.

What he said when he got here.

The needle trembles.

He said he was fine.

He said he was fine.

It'll be okay.

Shaking it away, I stretch toward him, letting him kiss me deep (a cold taste). I remove the cloth, bowing my head back to his penis, briefly slipping it between my lips. Bobbing slowly, twirling my tongue, up and down, letting its tip touch the back of my throat. He bursts in my mouth. A salty white universe. I swallow, letting it die inside me, resting my head on the chaise, next to the softening, shrinking cock. He traces my ear with his fingers, stroking my hair. "God, thanks," he says. "That was the best."

I don't say anything.

"You alright? Sure I can't do anything for you?"

"Nah. I'm fine." I lift his shirt and kiss his belly. "Maybe next time." And maybe that's how it goes. He, unlike the others, returns to me. Strengthened and renewed. It continues, it proceeds infinitely. Maybe next time, and maybe next time, and maybe next time, and maybe next time.

No palace more fit to rot. Born in the corner tower, a beam of mansion carved across an entire state. When the sun was high and everyone could see, your family owned modeling agencies, credit unions and pet stores. Then dusk crept over and guided them to a separate trade.

Three thousand and seventy-three rooms comprise Penis House. Home to at least a thousand souls and their personal effects and actions.

These are the ones you know of.

COUSIN CLIFF

Dresses as the Rwandan genocide every Halloween. He wants to tell you something.

"I've got a picture of you. When I hold it, it feels like your hand."

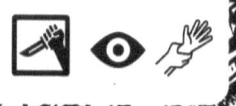

DEN

The stench. Mouse bodies in couch cushions, crushed beneath her weight.

It's intentional. This is a place to be woozy. The things you can't stomach become opportunities. New comforts, acquired tastes.

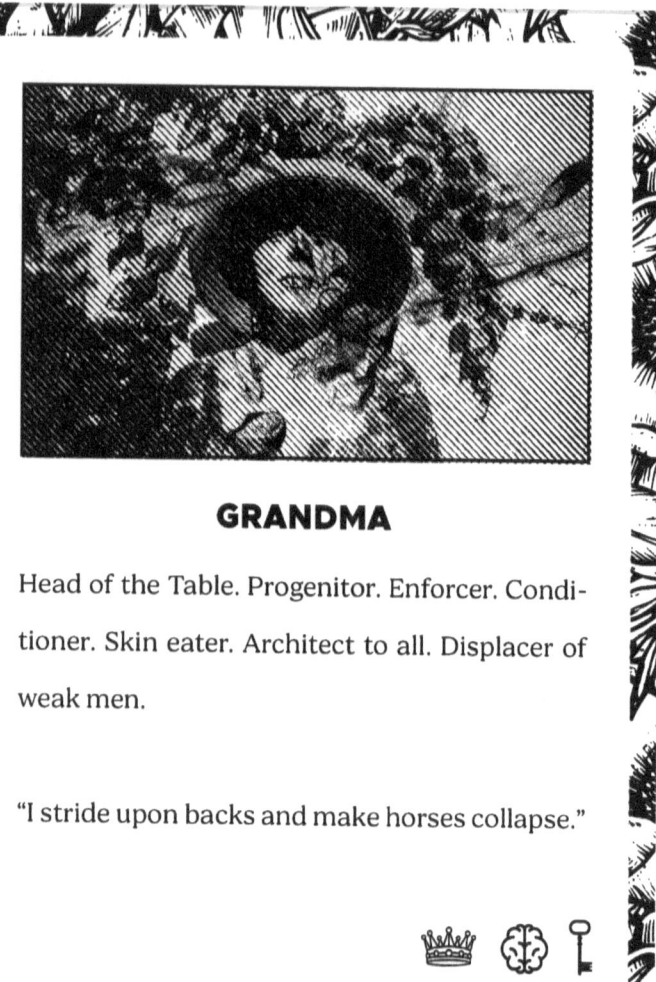

GRANDMA

Head of the Table. Progenitor. Enforcer. Conditioner. Skin eater. Architect to all. Displacer of weak men.

"I stride upon backs and make horses collapse."

THE ORCHARD

When you were little you'd run between the trees, tearing off apples and crunching them between your teeth. So thankful that every child could live in such luxury. That the world had charmed not only you but everyone in it. Dumb to the other children of Penis House dwelling beneath your shoes.

NIECE NANCY

Born half outside the family. Her father a peasant but the mother so lovely.

Grandma asks that you keep an ear out for her (snitch blood).

"I want to go home."

Wake in Bottle Nest. Hundreds of bottles—Snapple, Mountain Dew, Glaceau Vitamin Water, et cetera—emptied or half, filling your bed, spilling to the floor, eclipsing end tables and all other surfaces. A bottle for each day you've resided here.

Before you were alive, this space was majestic. That could not do. Time recognizes only ruins, and you went to work immediately, in fear of being forgotten.

You were still children, but close enough to grown that you could kill if need be. A tick clamped to your inner thigh. Plumped and beigey. (Ticks sprung from void when G_d left the Earth). You pulled it off, leaving that warm rosy bumper behind, and taped it to the tip of a pencil. You took it into the walk-in closet and mounted it on the wall with more tape. With an aerosol deodorant (your father's) and a Bic, you sprayed flames over the tick's plump little bod until it blackened and curled and disappeared.

You can piss in anything. Failure is only what's visible.

The aerosol could've inhaled up the flame, suckering up into the canister and bursting, bursting up your palms and hand bones. The wall could have catched fire, reducing the house to cinder. You didn't care. You wanted to bring that thing to the end.

A space's quality is proportional to the secrets kept within.

BALLROOM

The dance. The ritual. Host to state fingers (your father) and those responsible for all you know and love (your other fathers).

The pit opens, hands are taken, and the worthy are guided to the rest of their lives.

AUNT SHERRY & BABY PUCE

"A diamond in her eye,

A piglet dipped in lye"

Even he knows better. There will never be a time

when he isn't a burden upon her. Everyone will

know it, believing him oblivious.

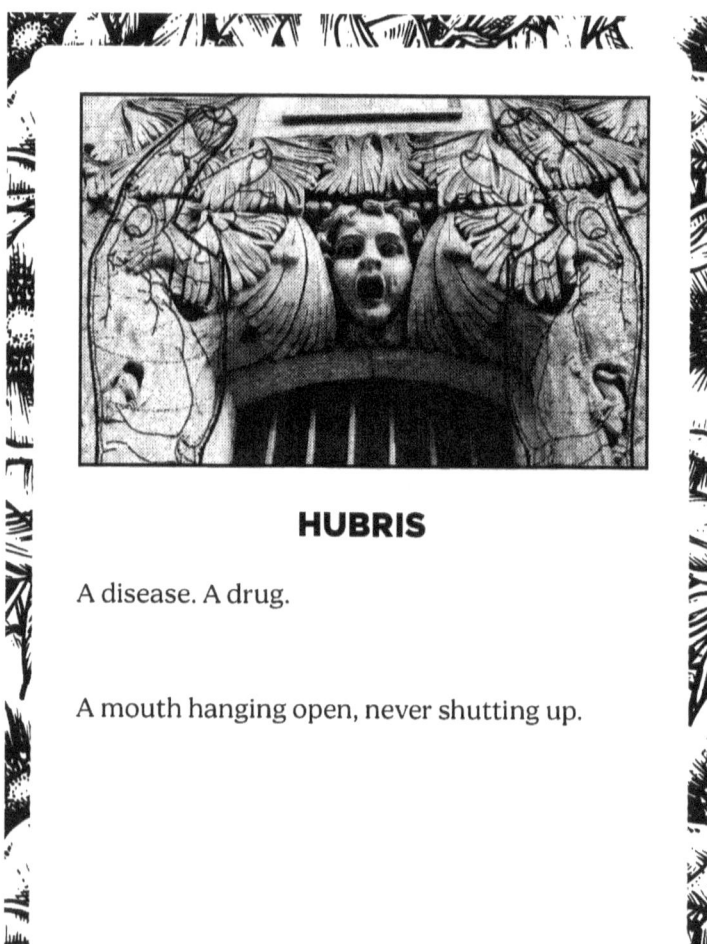

HUBRIS

A disease. A drug.

A mouth hanging open, never shutting up.

NEPHEW TODD

Too quiet. Weakling. Clings to the knees. The fault of the mother. Distaste for kissing and nakedness. Inoperable. Wrongly spared.

"Please stop."

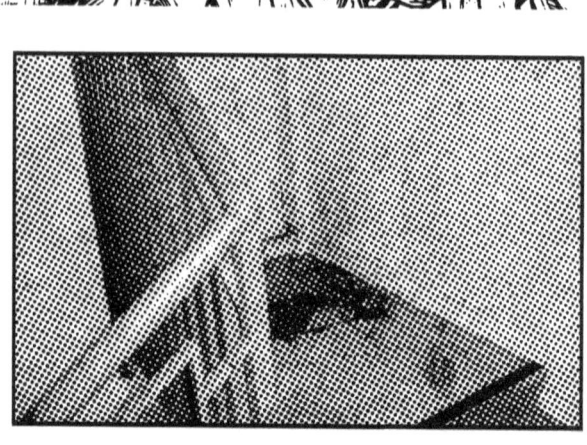

EXTERIOR STAIRWELL: A

Not a safe place. Dogs or dog-hearted men, men with dog tongues and red-bulbed hot lipstick dicks running from the crotch up to their stomachs, breathing hard and starved of meat.

Break some teeth if you're gonna swing.

The bed sucks at your body like a
crib. You lift yourself forward
and up, letting the mattress'
tacky lips peel from your back.
Powdery creped skin dripping from
your frame like a sheet. Is it
yours? It' s not like any you can
remember.

The outer chambers. Where you
were born. Where you'd sit at
the window, gazing down on the
great expanse of Penis House. The
lanterns and ramparts, the homes of
people you own. A secret you prefer
kept.

The Moth Closet. Filled with moths. A
thousand palm-sized moths. Devouring
fabrics and cottons and now devouring
each other. Generation after generation,
hatching and dying and eating their
own. Devouring children, their olds.
They love it here. The only thing they
ever knowed, the only thing they evered
loved.

So would you have wanted to eat
her clothes? Another way you've
failed her?

That time, as children, when you laid
across the tile, and let go of your bladder,
and the hot yellow sputtered over your
thighs and knees. You kept still, inhaling
the reek, divining your future. Fate exists
so long as you stay true to it.

COUSIN HENRY

Killer of children. Grandma's boyfriend. The False Tyrant. Hand to the Table.

"Often I wake up falling."

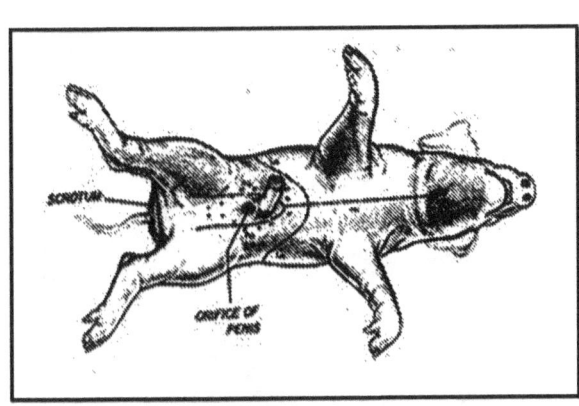

PIGLET DICK

She'd leave the dick on the pig when she cooked it. She'd giggle and point, saying it was your favorite part, before carving off the glans and dropping it on your plate. You'd gnaw it, rubbery slick and foul, tears trickling down your cheeks while everyone else laughed.

CREEPY SECRET

There actually is a cure for the summertime blues.

Don't let Grandma find out.

UNCLE LAWRENCE

Veteran of Bottle Nest. Close talker. Toadie by blood. Asks questions as whispers. Begs at Grandma's feet for entrance to the labyrinth.

"Even through the wall I'm aware of your taste."

SECRET PLACE

Why are worms in the house? On the cutting board, in the bathroom sinks. They work in reverse. Falling upward into your face, burrowing through pores into the fat of you.

The floorboards whine and warp,
shellacked by generations of
blood, feces, amniotic spill.
The room—its trinkets, set upon
dusty dressers and shelves—send
twinkles up your spine. Tiny
porcelain mother dolls. Mud-
dy nostalgia. Walls pocked with
cubby nests, where as a child you
would burrow between the plaster
and sing to the mites. A space
between joy and dread.

Your family conducts a ritual in the form of industrialized agriculture, genocides in seven countries, lavish galas, and globe-spanning human traffic. An attempt to change the name of G_d, and therefore the nature of the world.

Trace the walls, beams of uterine
oak, scanning over the photos of
men and women whose lives were
beyond the house's walls. Dust
your fingers over the porcelain
statuettes, slip a bleach white
pig into your pajama pocket. You
can almost hear it squeak, but
keep your fingers wrapped tight,
smothering it in skin and dirty
cloth.

You weren't an only child. You forget this, you pretend to forget this, you pretend to forget this for so long you no longer need to pretend. There were other children. What did you do with them?

Far beneath broken earth, the Penis shudders.

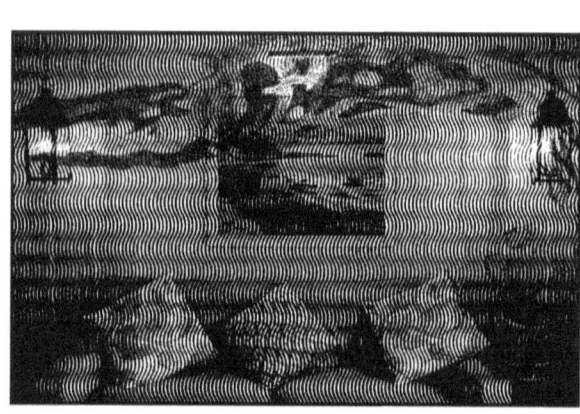

CUDDLE CORNER

Yes, you were of a protected class. No matter. Still you were scathed. There's fogetting and there's refusing to remember.

Make amends, or be wronged once again.

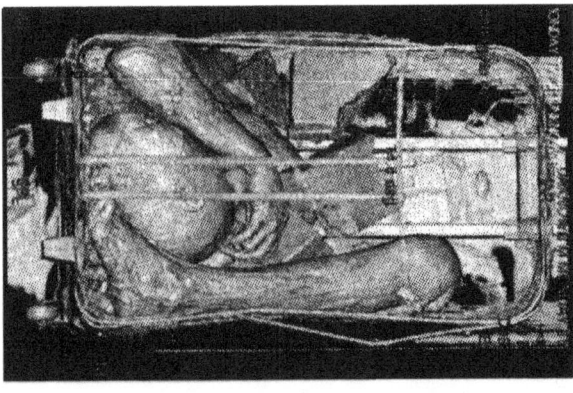

You can only be a head, almost. You can't be a leg or a cock. You can't be a vein or a tendon. That isn't what a person is.

Toss to ruin everything. Or maybe it's the best decision you've ever made.

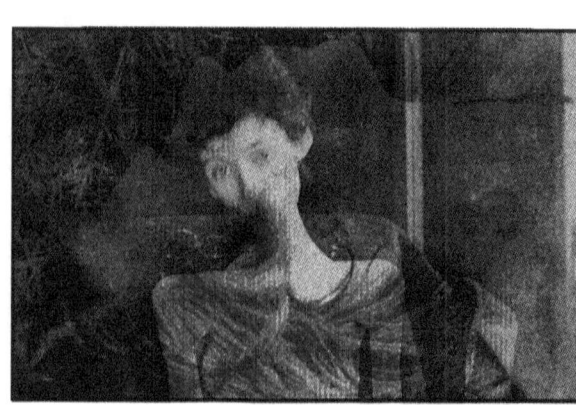

ELIZABETH WILLOW

Blows over in a gust. Falls behind the washer and drier. Slips beneath couches and bed frames. Hardly noticed, barely anything at all.

"Hold my breath."

✝ 💀 🌷

SHABBY STUDY

Where Dennis resides. Never realizing he's here. His dreams filling volumes, spinning him out across time, across the continent. We may all be curtains should he decide to wake.

PILE OF HOOVES

It's a pile of goddamn hooves!

Some say Penis House exists upon an island in a whale. Others claim it lies in the center of the city, on a forty-acre grassed plot surrounded by fifteen-foot razor wire fences. I've heard (and you have too) that Penis House rests far underground, that it was constructed just after WWII with atomic fears. Some say Penis House has always been here, existing many places across time.

You can't remember if this house ever belonged to you. Only in other's hands, just as you were in their hands. For how long? Decades, a hundred years, a thousand? It's difficult. The house is a diorama standing in a single circle of light, a star cut from a cloudless black sky. It doesn't even feel like a wound. The inky lake sits beyond the window. A curled rope lying beneath its surface—a noose for drowning cattle. You were once condemned, but those same hands pulled you from the depths and pounded water from your lungs. It was a lie when you thanked them.

You can't remember ever eating here. You can barely recall passing through. You can't picture the walls or floors even when you're here. Just blank where a room should be, where a room should be, where a room should be. Blank where a room should be. It's blank where a room should be.

Do you know of the tunnels? Of the second house? Identical to this one, but inverse. A second family too, but all with different names and faces. They have a Father and Grandma too, but the children are different. No need to even think about them.

A finger trap. Lamprey in the walls.

201

UH OH

You tried to do something good for once. Your sister called you a traitor. They locked you in the Moth Closet. Not yet the Moth Closet then. Just a place for locking you in.

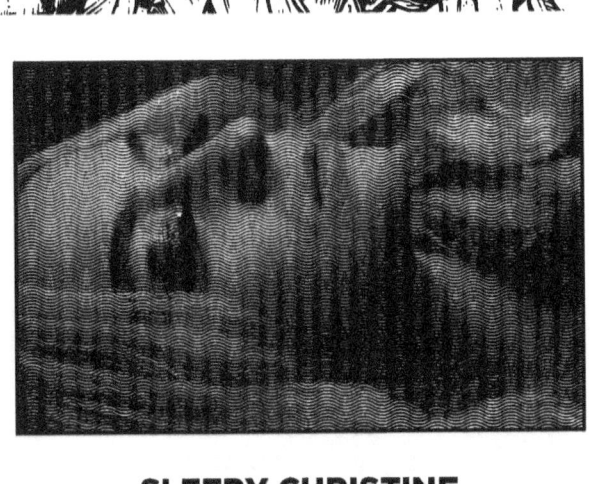

SLEEPY CHRISTINE

Covered in pee.

You can shake her, you can leave, but you can't make her speak.

THAT BEDROOM

Familiar scent.

Linens and coiled serpents.

A rose stem run through you.

THE CHAFF

Children born, inspected and determined. Those unfit for the house tossed to the labyrinth. Knotted heart of tunnels, dispersing outward, stretching through soil and sea. The children feed upon the fallen and come of age crawled to fresh brothel and prison. They learn to welcome it.

A thump from below, somewhere beneath the floorboards. Like blood-wrung eardrums. A wandering body or wet machinery. And you remember. Not just her hands. Her outline. Her face. The woman with yellow cake sticky on her lips and cheeks, her oily kisses. The way her knuckles danced like panicked bucks. The way she changed your landscape, the texture of your skin, with her rot and stain. A secret. A tumor to always be within.

You hated food. You'd stay in the bathroom (before it flooded to ruin), staying for hours, stuffing toilet paper down your throat, until all your insides were paper, your skin was paper, your hair and fingernails and eyes and teeth were paper.

There's a room with walls covered in cardboard, cardboard made to look like buildings, cardboard on the floor with lines down the middle like a street. Cardboard phone booths, cardboard cars, cardboard lampposts, cardboard fountains in a cardboard park. And if you spend longer than the least amount of time, it all sort of shimmers and blurs, and it's like you can feel the breeze and smell exhaust and hear the speech of those not trapped here. You look at the ceiling and the ceiling's a sky and the sky is blue, extending forever, wind blowing all around you.

Covered in bloods. Dry bloods, burnt bloods. The knifes rusted and dulled. Stove hissing a mild perpetual leak, sucked out the space through a broke up window, saving your life and the house's too. The refrigerator broke a year ago, or ten years ago, or maybe it has always been, but still you fill it, with hairs and hornet's nests and pieces of animals you've snatched. You pretend it's cold in there, and sometimes it is.

She is the thump. Clutching half a dozen candles, stalking the halls. When she thinks of you, she giggles and it makes you quake.

The closet held your parents' long coat, parka, winter coat. For long they still smelt of them, because they were inside them, some-where. Now here you burn meats. Walls blasted to black and ash. You need to burn the meats or the meats'll make you puke.

Every window a one-way mirror, reflecting inward.

WOEFUL BATHROOM

Now you've really done it. Hands, eyes, teeth and genitals all infected. Never washing off, no matter how hard you scrub.

Live with what you do.

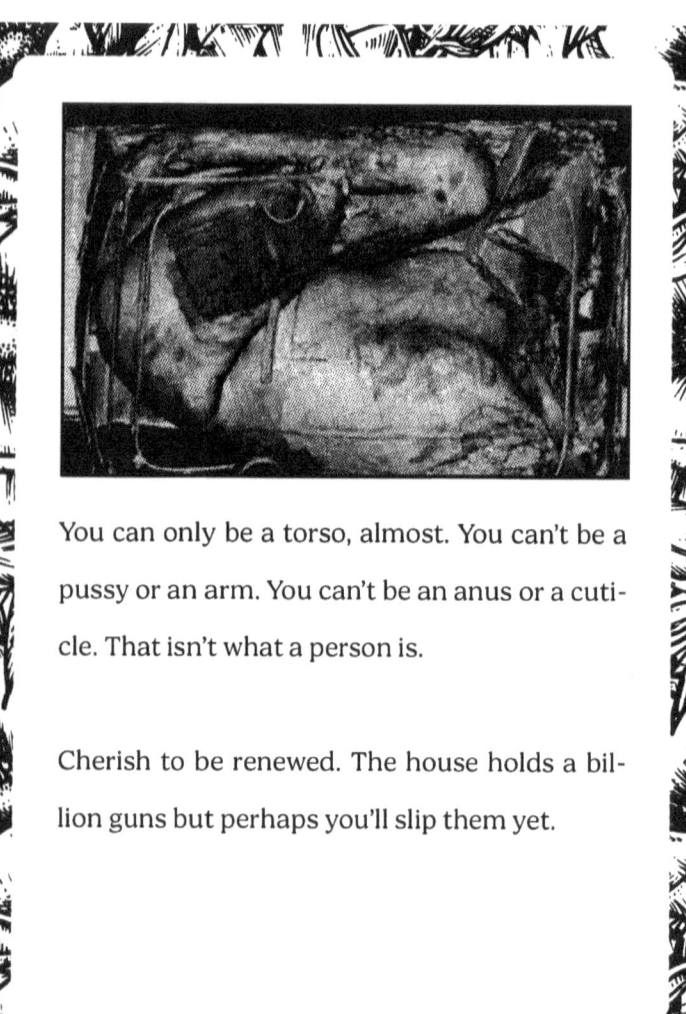

You can only be a torso, almost. You can't be a pussy or an arm. You can't be an anus or a cuticle. That isn't what a person is.

Cherish to be renewed. The house holds a billion guns but perhaps you'll slip them yet.

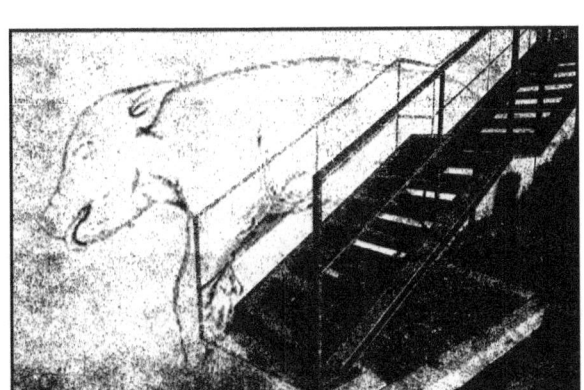

EXTERIOR STAIRWELL: B

Tell yourself you were born into it. It will not define you, it will not determine your path. You could be free of its influence if you wanted to be. It isn't your fault. Say it - in a miniature voice, held tight behind your lips. Say it to stay upright, to keep the tears off your face.

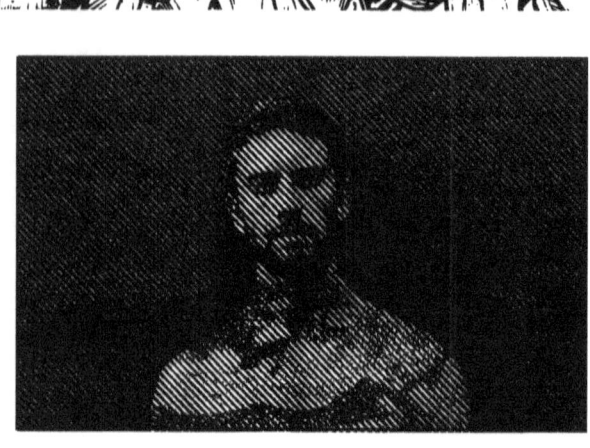

THIRD UNCLE WADE

True heir. Proved strength above blood. True Tyrant. Slayer of fathers. Skin soft as a waterfall and smells of your bed.

"My love is a box. My love is a shackle."

They die in cribs. You nail up the coffee table, a pair of shutters, a chair across the door. You tape over the seams. They're in there still, grew, grown, growing. Their bodies swole, the real swole (the real real swole), filling the room with gas. The gas liquiding, turning flesh, coats of skins, blooming fractal petals of skins, coating the walls and furnitures, before bloating and poppering again, filling the room with more gas, liquiding again into skins, another and another coats of skins. Over and overs. By now it's swallowed everything.

The pics are still there, tucked in wetted bursting boxes. You know what they are. You'd sooner burned the entire house before seeing those pics again.

They still think about you.

Your skin always belonged to them. Even when they tried to send you away, they wished for your skin to remain.

THE GAPE, A MAW

It's all over the walls. There is always another staircase; another void-drenched catwalk. The monsters with your friends' and fathers' faces. Every window a mirror. Every other person a twin. A gorgeous tomb to run through. No need to see sky again. No need for suns or kisses.

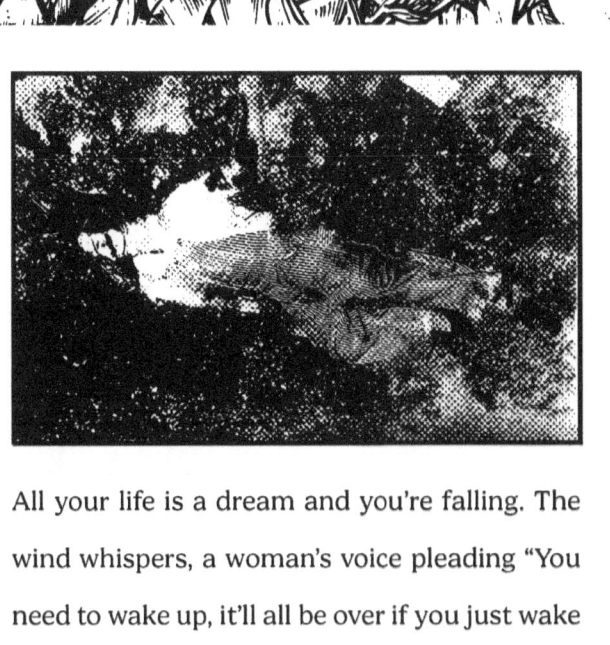

All your life is a dream and you're falling. The wind whispers, a woman's voice pleading "You need to wake up, it'll all be over if you just wake up." You scream back "You're wrong, I need this, this is the only thing I have." It isn't even that great a lie but you keep repeating it, over and over, while the planet below refuses to grow closer.

You will return to your bed, letting it suck you to sleep. You will dream of a child with a face you once recognized as your own. A child who pulls a thin silver knife from the swamps (those just half a mile from where you really live). The child will carve a new world with that blade, at once sensical and just. One inhabited by soft nuzzling animals and hands that don't clench and carve. A world you can think about without shaking, without bawling into your pillow. A world you won't need to push far away, down into your soured gorged intestines.

Or maybe you will not dream at all. A hole pulls open where your mind was. You will wake to a new day in a life you can't recall, wearing skin you no longer recognize. The thumping down below, the bed sucking skin. You'll fumble the tiny white pig in your pocket, squealing frantic through the cloth, crying to get out.

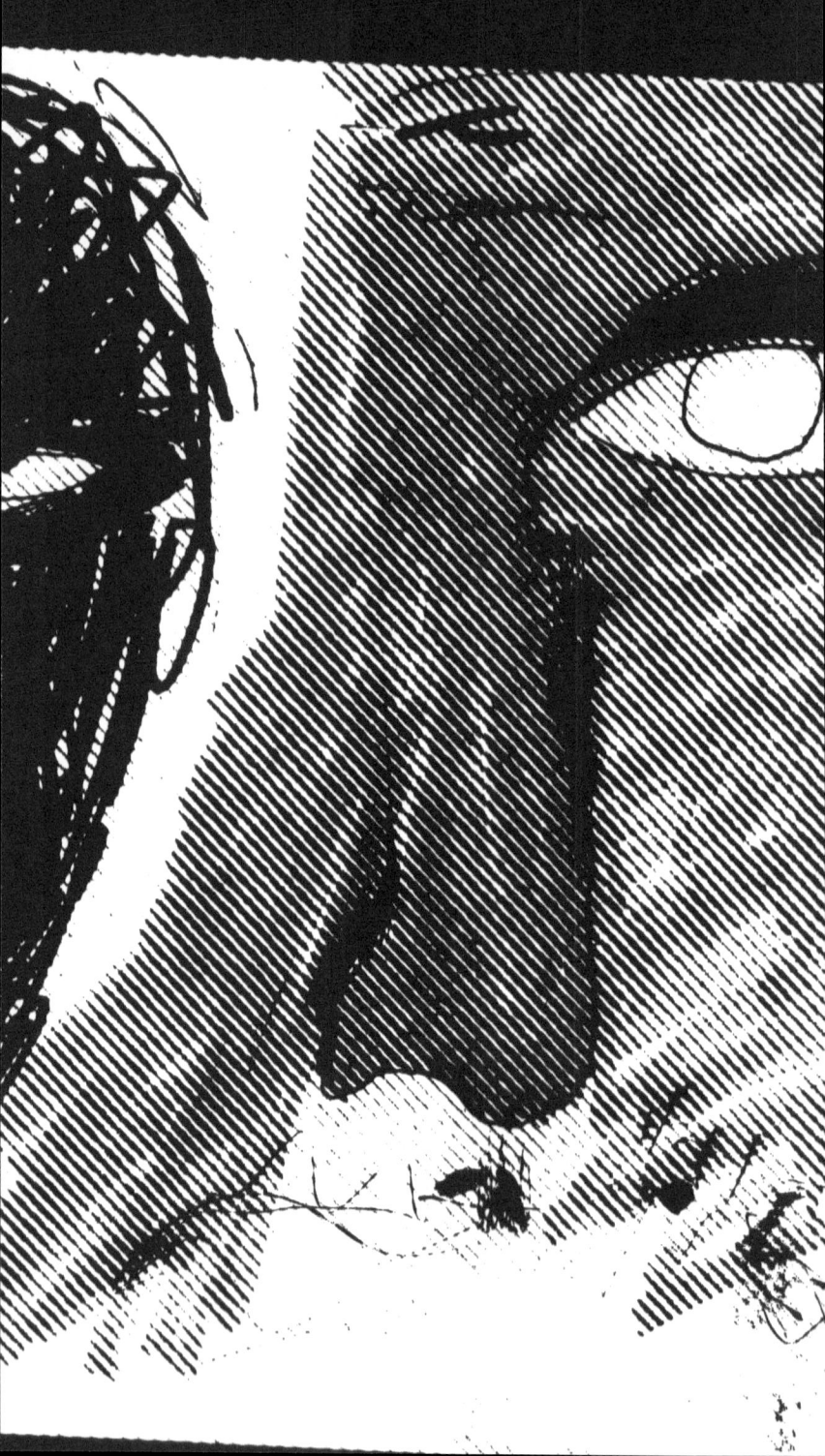

Mantra

Board up

    Bury

        Burn low inside

            and never let it go.

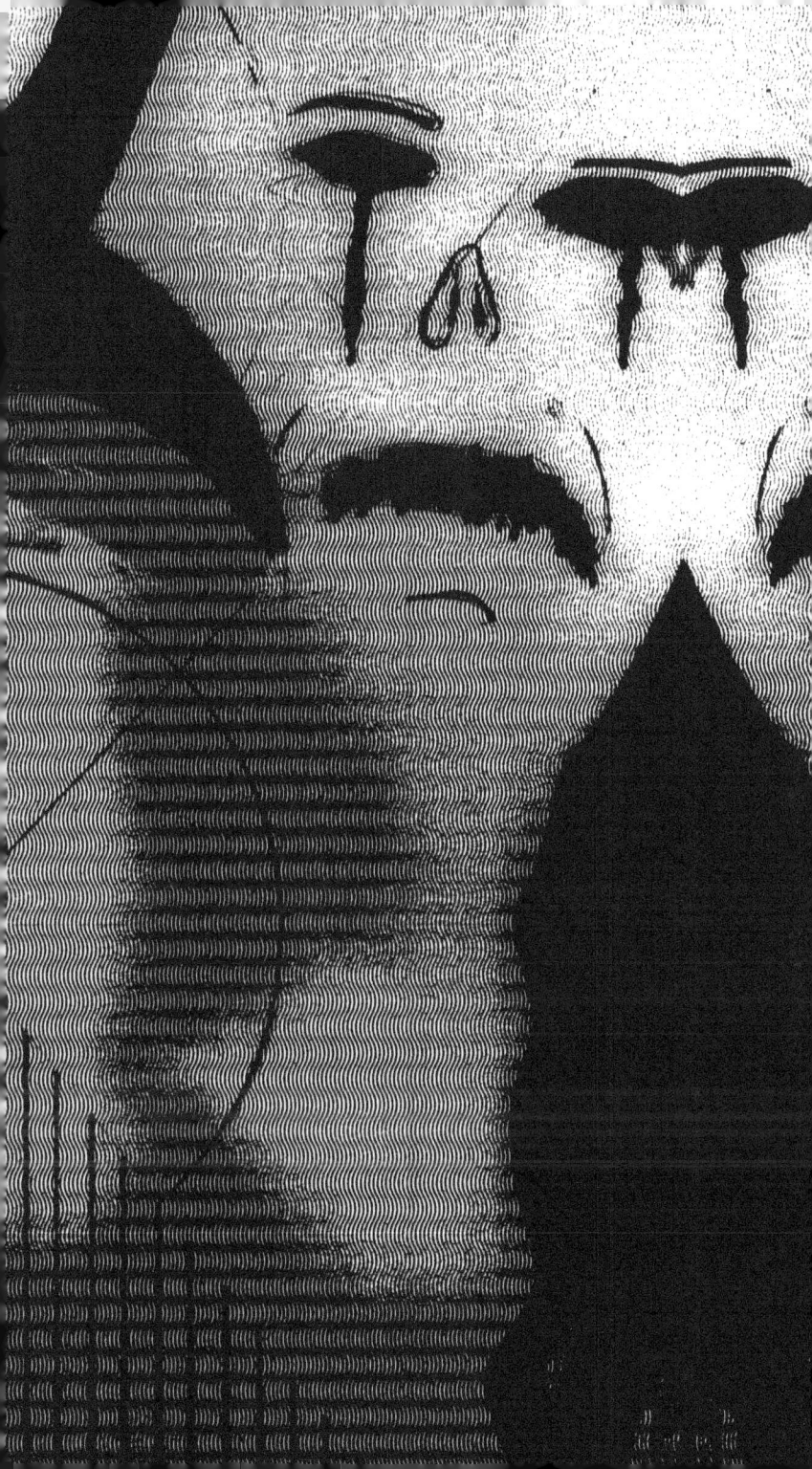

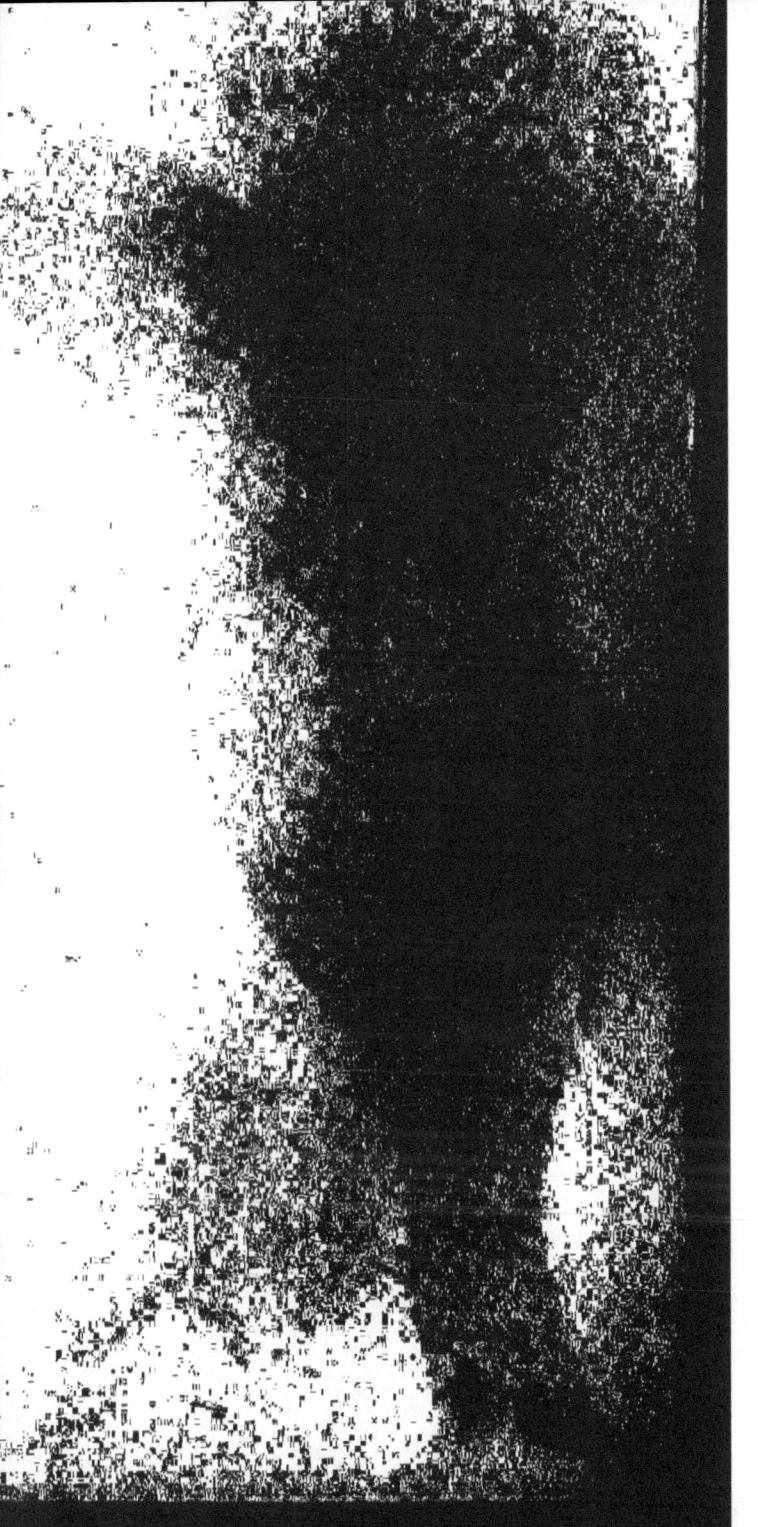

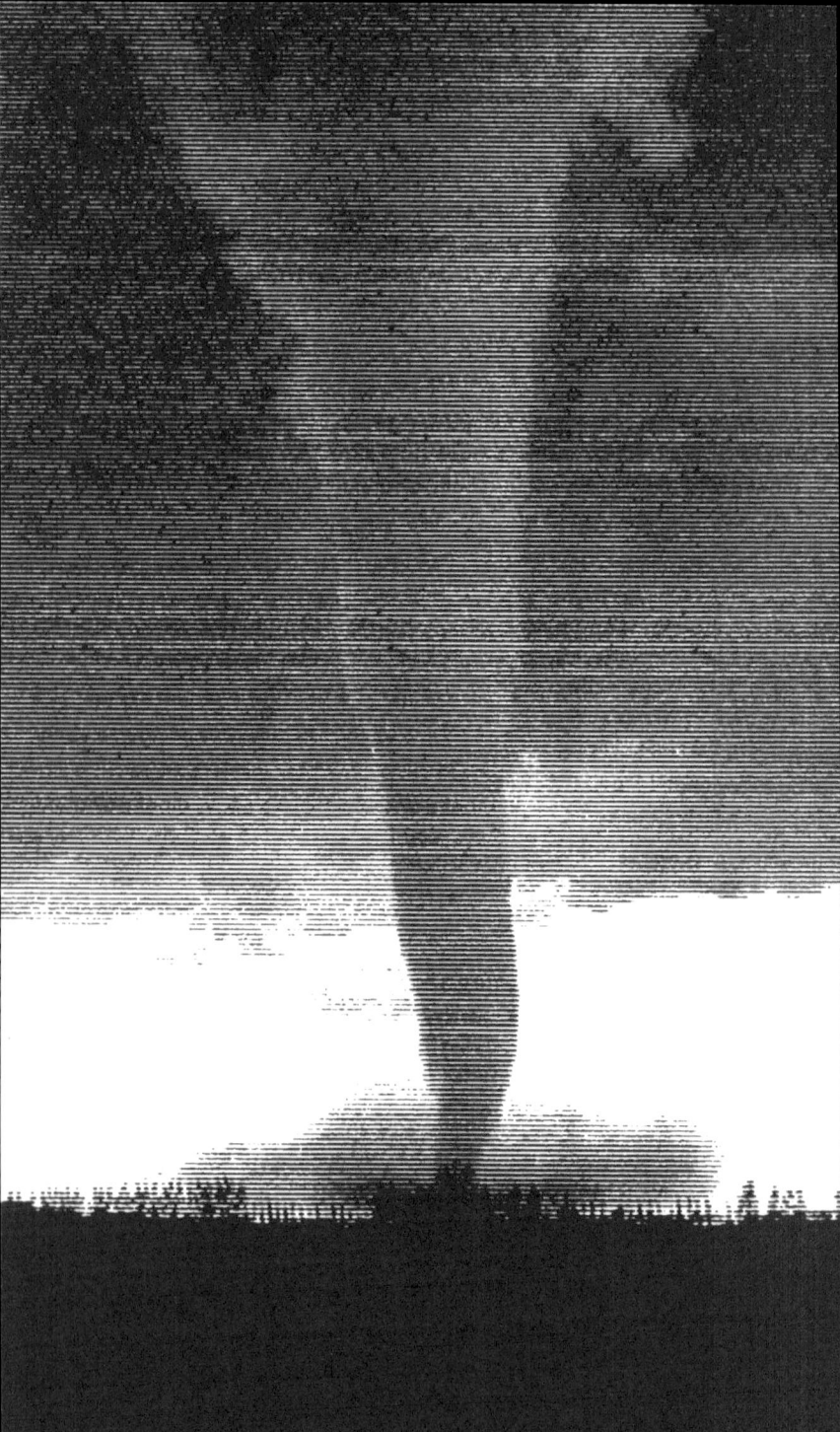

Puppy Milk

for Matthew M. Bartlett

It's like a toothache. It takes over everything. A patch of rot grasps a nerve and the world falls away. Your body disappears, your pasts and futures dissolve into a single intolerable present and all you are is a throbbing sweaty toothache. Like it's the only thing you've ever known.

They aren't the words I'd prepared. They come in the moment, like a wave crashing through me. I don't even look at the paper crumpling in my hand. I close my eyes and it all comes out between gasps.

You said you didn't believe in free will. That's what war is. My body isn't my body. A pale tooth. The world's a pale tooth. A twirling spear drilling through the spaces. All the spaces. It's a twirling tooth. A pale tooth. A twirling bone. The world's a twirling beak. A pale tooth. A pale bone. The world twirling like a drill. A twirling tooth. A pale bone. A pale drill. Twirling like a tooth. A bone. A drill. A bone. A tooth. A drill. You don't even know. It's the music that used to be you. In your ear. In the air. You don't even know. A twirling tooth. A pale bone. A pale drill. Twirling like a tooth. A bone. A drill. A bone. A tooth. A drill. A tooth. A bone.

A drill. Drilled milk and cum. A bloody fucked tooth.
Fucked bloody. Drilling. A tooth. A bone. Spins and
spins and spinning milk and cum. Milk and cum. So
much and all you can do is stop breathing.

I breathe in. My head tips forward, my lips press into the
microphone (Warm and sticky. Why is it sticky?). I exhale and my breath hisses through the room. I jolt upright.
Back in my body. Back in the room. In the café. All Sedo-
na-red walls, curving bulbous plaster giving a shoddy illusion of something organic, like the walls of a cavern, like
we're all trapped in this tiny wet pocket. All of us—me and
Derrian and Chelsea and the other Leeds High burnouts,
encroaching on the shitty old bohemians. All of us packed
in and robbing each other's breath.

Hesitant clapping. The open mic emcee taps my
shoulder. "Um, cool. Thanks Nicole." I look away and
wobble off the stage. "Okay, next up we have Mya W. Let's
give it up for Mya!"

I drift between the chairs, gently bumping into shoulders, toward Derrian and Chelsea in the back. Derrian
looks away, at her shoes or over her shoulders. Like she's
trying to hide. Embarrassed, for me or of me. But Chelsea
stares me right in the face, and that throws me off. She'd
been in her own little world all day, big puffy headphones
wrapping her ears, fist clutching a Walkman, thumbing
the radio tuner, barely saying a word.

"That was different," Derrian says, forcing a laugh. A
solitary *ha*.

"Where'd you hear that?" Chelsea asks, still staring, almost like she's staring through me—not all the
way, but past the skin, the muscle, the bone. The ques-

tion crawls inside my mouth. It pries at my gums. "What?" I say (What's she on? Am I on it too?).

"What you said up there." She's almost shaking. My jaw throbs in sync with her tremors. "Where'd you hear that?"

White. Sticky white. "Nowhere," I say. I believe it but it doesn't quite feel true.

Derrian finally looks me in the face. "You don't look so hot."

I wipe my forehead with my sweatshirt, smearing a charcoal birthmark on the sleeve. A wet achy fever beneath my skin. But I don't tell her that. I just say I need some water and push through the clusters of people to the pitcher between the stage and bathroom. Empty, except a few dying ice cubes and a limp lemon sliver. I head to the counter and wait while three customers crawl through their orders. It's the busiest I've ever seen the open mic. All strange smelly bodies pressing into each other, chatting over the awful up-talk poetry honking through the PA. I hate it, but it's the last place in Leeds that'll let kids hang out.

The barista—I've seen her almost every Friday this past year but still don't know her name—waves me in. "What can I get you?"

"Water."

"Water's over there." She points toward the pitcher. "*Next.*"

"It's empty." Sweat pours down my forehead, into my eyes, distorting her features. Making her blurred, bloated, monstrous.

"What?"

"Pitcher's empty."

"And?" She clenches and unclenches her jaw.

"And?"

"And what, you didn't bring it with you?" She slaps the bar. "I can't leave the register. Bring it up so I can fill it. *Next*."

Pushing back through the crusts and failed Rainer Marias, I grab the pitcher and head into the bathroom. The mirror stretches across the entire wall. I almost don't recognize myself in it. Like I'd been dipped in water and aged two decades. I look like my mom.

That fucking toothache. Stuck in the back of my jaw. Like I'd been gnawing gunpowder. Tiny explosions. Buzzing. Like the enamel's vibrating. Stirring up my pulp.

White. Swirling, smelly white. A swirling white tower. Twisting milk and cum.

Last fall, Derrian and I copped a quarter of mushrooms off this townie spanger, Dennis. He chewed our ears off, all this stuff about fungal intelligence, these massive networks of membrane that mushrooms use to communicate. He said that tripping is just mushrooms' attempt at communion with us. "It's translation," he said. "They're making your brain think the way a mushroom thinks. That's all that tripping is."

Hours later, Derrian and me were rolling in the leaves, giggling, listening to them crackle—an almost horny sound. I closed my eyes. A mass of scaley meat, a world's worth of heaving wet snake flesh wrapping my body, wrapping the Earth's entire skin. "Yooo," I said. "I'm feeling a little snaky right here." Derrian laughed and threw a fistful of leaves at me.

That's almost what this feels like. Almost. Not like snakes. A world of milk and cum, spilling over the world until there's no air left.

I shake it away. Squeeze my eyelids tight and open them again. Back in the ladies' room. In my body. Mom's

236

face in the mirror, staring back at me.

I fill the pitcher in the sink and glug it down—the whole gallon in one go. Yanking fistfuls of paper towels from the dispenser, wiping my face. Then I drop the pitcher in the toilet bowl and leave.

Onstage, a middle-aged man in a Panama straw hat hovers over the microphone. "Come *on*, America. Listen to your *brother*. You used to call him *Jesus*. Listen to your *mother*. You used to call her the *trees*." I pop up on my toes, scanning the room for Amber. Her narrow pale face and spiraling red hair. She'd told me at school she was coming tonight. Forgot? Lying? Whatever. I head back to Derrian and Chelsea.

"You good?" Derrian asks.

I lean close to her face. "Can I ask a weird question?"

"I'm used to it."

"Did you dose me?"

Chelsea scrunches her forehead, eyeing me.

Derrian laughs. "Dose you? Like, did I roofie you? Bitch, I'm not that desperate."

"Like with acid or something?" There was a guy at school who got dosed at a party. Some prick rubbed liquid LSD on the back of his neck. Had no idea what was happening when he got home. Tried to slit his wrists but his folks caught him just in time. "Anything like that?"

"Come the fuck on. Are you really asking me that?"

"I know. I know. I'm sorry."

"You sure you're okay?" She presses the back of her hand to my forehead, like my mom when I'm coming down with something.

I step back. "I'm good. Sorry. I just need to smoke or something."

She drops her hand to my shoulder, squeezing it like a

giant leech. "Then let's book. You done here?"

I make one last scan for Amber. I almost think I see her onstage, but it's another red-haired woman, older, probably in her 20s, reading from a Moleskine: "My heart is a robin's egg, and my fingers are feathers, lifting me from another broken shell."

"Yeah," I say. "Sure, I'm done."

⌁

Outside's a warm, damp thaw. Patches of white dissolving on soggy dead grass. Storefronts blacked out, gaping voids under glass. Not even the spangers are out. The streets wet and dead. An inversion of the café. Dead, maybe, but at least enough space to breathe.

Derrian pulls a cigarette from her pack and sticks it between her lips. She's about to light it but stops. "You hear that?"

I do. This warbling—barely audible beneath the wind and lamp noise, but it's there. A single sustained note. Singing, maybe. A stagnant, violent sound. My teeth wiggle and ache. A heat inside. In my gums, in my jaw.

Chelsea pulls off one of her headphones. "Over at the park."

"A concert," I say. It's like the singing is inside my mouth, prying at my teeth. "Spring concert or something."

"Let's check it out," Derrian says.

"It's just a choir or whatever. Boring shit." I don't want to go. My teeth don't want me to go.

"We've got to cut through there anyway. Let's check it out. Just for a minute."

Our sneakers clap against the sidewalk, echoing off

hollow buildings. Empty storefront after empty storefront. Only the occasional headlight cutting out from the hill ahead as proof we're not alone. The singing grows louder. The note bends gently, like a warped record. It rubs against my teeth. I run my tongue over the enamel, wetting the gums, but it doesn't stop the ache.

A voice calls out across the street. "Woop woop!" A man kneeling on a stoop. Long ratty hair stuffed beneath a stocking cap. A torn-up bomber jacket, camo shorts over long johns.

Derrian claps and smiles. "Yo Den!" We dash across the street. Good old Dennis. "What's good?" She gives him a hug.

"You know." He pulls back and shrugs. "Same old same." He points at Derrian's cigarette. "Think I can buy one of those off you?" He digs into his pocket, fistfuls of change rattling.

"You can have one dude." She takes one out and hands it to him.

"Danke." He lights up, inhaling deep, holding it, then exhaling long and slow. "What're you ladies up to?"

"You know. Just came from the open mic. We're checking out whatever's going on at the park."

"Pulaski Park?" He turns and spits on the sidewalk. "Nah, you don't want to be there."

Derrian smirks. "Why's that?"

"Bad scene. Just real bad news."

"It's just a concert or something. You don't like music?"

"They're giving their children away." Dennis rolls the cigarette between his fingers. "Real ugly business."

Chelsea goes stiff beside me, but Derrian keeps smiling, forcing her laugh. "Who is?"

"Coward parents. You know, scared people are the most dangerous people in the world."

Derrian chucks him on the arm. "We're tough. You know that."

Dennis grimaces. "I know. I still wouldn't go there if I were you."

"How 'bout if I promise we'll be careful?" Derrian gives him another cigarette and leans in for a hug. "It's good seeing you, buddy. Be good, okay?"

"Yeah, I'll try."

I nudge Derrian once Dennis is out of earshot. "What was that about?"

Derrian wipes something out of her eye. "He's fine. He's just sick. He's trying, but you know. It sucks."

I drop it. The drone rises with every step forward, pushing against my skin, through my lips. My teeth buzz like a bee colony.

⌄

Pulaski Park glows between city hall and the Academy of Music. A glow that spills into the street. Lanterns strung from tree and post; torches pounded into the ground. A bonfire. At least a hundred people, dressed in jeans and button-downs, or skirts and blouses. They hide their faces in masks. Papier-mâché animals—pigs and horses and roosters and goats. They circle the park's central pine tree. Hundreds of small paper circles tied to its branches, like a skirt of fungus. As a child, I'd look up at the pine in terrible awe, unable to fathom how a tree could grow that tall and wide.

A band—a fiddler, an accordionist, a tom player— walks the crowd. It's barely music—a shrill keening, an approximation of a cicada's hum. The voices—this looping, warped falsetto, the timbre of cats drowning—comes from everywhere, from every person, from behind every crude animal mask.

Chelsea pulls off her headphones, staring at a couple dressed as matching otters. She stares like they're on fire. "We should go. Can we go?"

"Yeah," Derrian says. "Let's book."

We maneuver through the bipedal rams, rabbits, serpents. All staring at us now. The keening scrapes at my teeth, slipping beneath the gumline, prodding my jawbone. Through the bodies, between the pine and bonfire, I glimpse a stained wicker cradle, rocking gently back and forth. Something bursts beneath my gums and I grab my face and look away. Derrian pushes me along and we break from the crowd, onto a path toward the concrete steps where I knocked my front tooth out when I was seven. We descend and cross Pulaski Parking Lot to the South Street underpass and the dirty trail beyond.

⌄

Tall metal lamps light the path all rosé beige, the season's first moths tapping at the bulbs. Clots of fresh mushrooms encroach the path, around my feet. I kick a patch. Spore motes explode and lift through the lamplight. Another kick, another milky cloud rising, drifting in waves, into my face, up my nose, down my throat, into my lungs.

We hop off the main path onto a thinner vein, scaling the hill between the woods and society. We push through brush and thorns until we reach it: The Pod. A mass of thick vines curled into a round hut. We discovered it last summer, figured someone homeless had built it to sleep in, but we never saw anyone use it except other kids getting high. We dragged a fallen tree trunk inside to use as a bench and made it our own.

Ducking inside, Derrian and I call "Not bitch." We take our seats on the rotting log, Chelsea stuck in the middle (but she's still lost in her headphones, staring quietly at the rusted coffee can blooming with cigarette filters). Digging into her backpack, Derrian removes her glass bowl and weed, then packs it and lights up. I ask her if Amber said anything about coming out tonight. She lifts her head back, blowing smoke through the vine ceiling. "You've got to stop chasing that." And hands the bowl to Chelsea.

"I'm just asking if she said anything."

"You're in for a whole world of hurt if you keep after her."

"You only know, like, the persona she puts on. I know —"

"You know I love Amber," Derrian says. "I love Amber. But Amber's fucked up. It's not her fault, but she's fucked up in so many ways and hasn't even begun working toward rectifying that shit. You're gonna get wrecked if you go down that path, that's all I'm saying." Shrug. "Anyway, there's like literally millions of girls out there."

Chelsea flinches in her seat. Coughing through the bowl, blowing the weed out. "Oh shit." Clutching the right headphone to her ear. "Oh shit."

Derrian roars. "Those were my fucking headies." Reaching across me, she yanks the bowl from Chelsea's hand.

"Holy shit." Chelsea presses the headphones tighter, pressing so hard it's like she's trying to cave her own skull in. "I found it." She pulls them off and pushes them at

Derrian. "You've got to hear this."

"Nah. I'm mad at you now." She pulls her baggie from her backpack and loads a nug into her grinder.

Chelsea turns to me, forcing the headphones into my hands. "Please. Listen."

I slip the headphones over my ears. A voice like pebbles dragged by a river. A hornet's buzz pitched down to a low rasp:

A bone. A drill. A bone. A tooth. A drill. A tooth.
A bone. A drill.

I pull the phones half off. "What is this?"

Chelsea's eyes crack wide open. "I've heard it. You've heard it too."

My teeth go alight. Like they're bursting, frothing with pulp. Melting down to tendrous nerves. Entangled in radiation.

White. The world. Everything white. All a dense, silky light. No, not waves or particles. The texture. Milk. Milk. Soft sour milk. A flood of it. A tower. A white twirling tower, as wide as a mountain, as wide as the Pioneer Valley. A churning tower of sweet old milk, pungent like semen, flushing up into the sky. Twirling like a drill. A tooth. A bone.

The bodies inside. Hundreds of thousands. All our bodies. We can't move, we can't speak. Just flushing upward into the sky, a torrent of rank milk and cum.

"Yo. *Yo.*" Derrian's voice. The world drifts back. No white. Just sooty night and thin blades of moon spilling through the gaps in the Pod's ceiling. Derrian hands me the bowl. I wave it away. "You sure?" She takes another hit and cashes it. "Bus should be coming soon. Let's get back."

Stuffing the bowl in her backpack, she rises from the log, ambles onto the trail and down the hill.

Chelsea gapes at me like I have a gun for a face. "You've seen it," she says.

"What?" But I know.

"You've seen it. The tower."

The white simmers in my spine.

I stand. "I haven't seen shit."

Chelsea grabs my elbow. Skinny fingers like bones. "Can I stay at your place?"

"Tonight?"

"I don't want to go home."

I pull away. "Okay. Sure."

The voices are gone. The accordion, violin and tom. Everyone vanished. The bonfire doused, though the torches and lanterns remain, flames dwindling. A gust tears through the ancient pine, and the paper circles flip and sputter on its branches. Chelsea grasps at them, putting her face close to see what's written. Derrian jogs ahead toward the bus stop. I'm staring at the stained wicker cradle. My teeth buzz.

"Come on," Derrian shouts. "It's gonna be here any minute."

"Just a sec." I step toward the cradle. A black lace veil lays over it. A sound inside—a whimper. A slurp.

"Yo!" Derrian yells. "I see it, it's up the block."

"Just a second!" My gums ache and throb. I pinch up the veil and let it fall over the side.

A puppy. White and brown. A beagle, maybe, coiled inside the cradle. Shivering, its mouth pressed to its loins.

Whimpering, suckling. Suckling gently on its penis. Not licking or gnawing. Suckling.

It stops. Removing its mouth from its penis, its maw sticky wet white. It looks up, straight into my eyes, and smiles like a person smiles. In a hushed sweet voice, a toddler's voice, it asks: "Want to know a secret?"

⌒

I was four and my mother fed me an apple. It had gone mealy—the first mealy apple I'd ever had. I had loved apples but this felt wrong. I didn't understand the texture. In my young dumb mind, it could only mean one thing. "It's poison," I yelled.

"How could you say that?" my mother cried back at me.

"It's poison," I wept. Believing mother to be a witch in disguise, serving tainted apples as I had seen in a film or cartoon.

"How could you say that about your mother?" My father scolding me for daring to slander her name. Neither of them willing or able to grasp my perspective—the naïve terror of my age and vulnerability. Both I and them enthralled by a sense of supreme betrayal. It was weeks before they'd look at me the same.

⌒

The bus drops me and Chelsea off a quarter mile from my house. We barely speak the rest of the way. I don't tell her about vibrating teeth or towers of semen or puppy secrets and she doesn't tell me about any of the things she's seen.

My parents are already asleep when we get in. We

head straight for my room. I flop on my bed. She sits at my desk. "I don't know how much left I got in me," I say.

"It's okay." She looks down at her Walkman. "You can go to sleep if you want."

"Okay." Twisting onto my belly, closing my eyes.

Pale marble towers. Taller than trees, than the mountains. The scent of animal lactation. Driven between the river, white water rising up the banks. Soaking the soil to sludge.

He's standing there. I can tell it's him, though his back is turned to me. A scalp and shoulders I've known my entire life. He turns, and his face is a flower. A fruiting. A bloom of flesh. Like Amber's orange pussy rotting beneath my tongue. He steps forward and the slit pours white.

I wake up drenched. Face stuffed in a pillow, a rotten ache pounding in the back of my mouth. Slipping my fingers past my lips, I feel along my gums. Dry and swollen. I twist upright and tap along the night table until my hand finds the water glass. I glug it down in one go—washing the ache, but not diminishing it. I feel for the lamp and switch it on. A crack of beige light. The room throbs. An empty room. Alone. Chelsea's gone.

I go out to the hallway. The bathroom door is open, a black void inside. I creep downstairs, slipping through the den, the dining room, the kitchen. She's nowhere.

I head back to my room. My foot kicks a chunk of something, something plastic on the floor, sending it skittering across the hardwood into a patch of dirty clothes. A plastic charcoal brick. Chelsea's Walkman.

Picking it up, running my thumb over its surfaces.

Rough on the back. I flip it over. Stalks and dots and infinity signs carved into the plastic, just above the battery cover. I turn it sideways. Two dots, a dash and six numbers: *88.1-89.3.*

I place it on my desk and climb into bed, but I don't get to sleep.

⌃

The weekend passes. I call Chelsea but each time it's six rings before cutting to the answering machine. Monday comes and she isn't in school. I ask Derrian if she's seen her, if she's talked to her. "No." At lunch, I hit the cafeteria payphone and call her again. Six rings, then answering machine. My gums flex and throb.

⌃

Mom and Dad look at me different now. Like they're reading my thoughts. They hardly even speak to me anymore. They'll smile, but there's a great strain in their eyes, like jets of water pounding on their optic nerves.

Mom makes cream of mushroom soup for dinner. Whole creminis that burst on my teeth like dead mice. I get through two bites and ask to be excused.

I hear them talking downstairs, when they think I'm asleep. My father's voice: "It's got nothing to do with what you or I want." Inaudible. "You make me sound terrible."

Silence. Then a single rising note. Mom wailing. Fried rasp. Weeping.

My teeth shake. An awful pressure. Like worms, botfly larvae crawling beneath the enamel.

White. Sticky sloshing white. A sea of white. Stinky milk and cum. Submerged in it. My head floating just above the surface. Hands at my throat. I reach up and pull at them. Familiar textures—hairy knuckles, ill-trimmed hangnails, the pads of rough callus. My father's hands. They push me under, into the thick smelly white. I thrash my arms and legs but the hands are too strong, too steady. They push me far below, further even than his reach. My world is slick greasy white and when I scream it floods my mouth, my throat, my lungs. Sticky rotten and hot.

I snap awake. Sheets soaked through. A knifing headache. My mouth filled with warm copper.

The moon's gone tonight.

I switch on the lamp and the room comes alive with light and opaque brown dots and dust motes. Little dancing spores. I spit in my palm—red swirling in clear and white—and wipe it on the comforter.

Crawling to the end of the bed, I reach out to my desk, grabbing Chelsea's Walkman. I put in my earbuds and flip on the radio. A wave of static. A wall of hissing flies. Thumbing the tuner. Crackly blasts of country music, then top forty, and more static. Watching the dial, rolling the tuner, back and forth between 88.1 and 89.3.

The voice. I hear the voice. Gravelly and hollow, almost like water. It crackles against my eardrums. Like a wave crashing through me.

> *...and won't even blink. Blood is so thin. You don't even know. When it comes down to it, there isn't anyone who'll let blood stand in the way of dry land. Ever more cats in bags and ever more bags in rivers.*

My teeth vibrate in time with his cadence. An almost comforting throb, like an old friend's caress. An agony I'd miss if it were gone.

I listen until sunlight cleaves through the window. I switch off the radio and twist onto my belly. I blink, and when my eyelids flip back open my mom's yelling it's time to go to school.

⌁

Chelsea still isn't anywhere and Derrian still can't reach her (I've stopped calling, I know it's useless). I tell my teachers I have cramps and spend half of each class in the bathroom, thumbing the radio tuner on the Walkman. The voice is never on the same station—it drifts. Never really a station at all—somewhere between them.

> *Seed will go to seed will go to seed will go to seed. Goats make promises with fathers, but goats are always goats. Goats never care about our words, let alone promises.*

⌁

I pinpoint the tooth. At first, I thought it was my entire jaw but it's only a single tooth. My right bottom molar. I open wide and pinch it between my thumb and forefinger and feel it quiver, buzzing like a fly. I wiggle it side to side—loose in the gum, but when I yank it won't pop out. Throbbing burning copper. I spit red and white into the sink and twist on the faucet, flushing it away, spiraling around the ceramic into a deep black hole.

Pliers. Pliers pliers pliers.

Downstairs, through the kitchen, out to the garage. Even though I've never seen Dad fix anything, I know he has a toolkit. Every dad has a toolkit.

I trace the walls, pulling tarps off bikes, coolers, snow tires. A shock through my gums. Impossible agony, like my tooth twisting, like it's trying to spin around, or burrow deeper into gum. I buckle in half, sinking to my knees, hissing and spitting on my nightshirt, trying to keep quiet. Closing my eyes, it's pure white, dripping out and smearing across my cornea. Open again, shake it away, clenching my jaw, trying to push the pain out of my mouth.

Then I see it, tucked between the trash bins and the volleyball set: a broad grey box.

Leaning against Dad's SUV, I step toward the box. And there, I glimpse them resting atop the trash bin. Two ovals, each the size of a face. Two papier-mâché ovals, lumps running down their centers, like snouts. Twin gaping black eyes punched through each of them, staring up at me. Dull grey stubs rising from their foreheads. A pair of goat masks.

White. Dripping white. Dripping from my eyes, my ears, my lips. All my insides clogged with white.

I beat my forehead with my fist until it goes away. I spit copper onto the concrete floor, then unsnap the toolbox latch and flip open the lid. Nails and screwdrivers stab at my hands. There. Round rubber grips. A pair of needle nose pliers, greasy and old. Tucking it into my sweatpants, I head back to the bathroom.

I no longer see white. I don't need to anymore. There are

other ways to prepare.

The cops find Chelsea's parents but they don't find her. Her mom's body is half-hanging out the front door to their house, burned to grey. Almost just bones. Chelsea's dad's body is burned to black, a skeleton curled into a fetus beside the toilet. She left the dog alive, locked in the pantry. They can't find her brother.

It was stupid of her to do that. Only brings attention. A stupid mistake, but I get it. I hope she'll be alright, though I know that's probably impossible now.

You have to wait it out. Wait for the tide, the tower, the torrent. By then, there won't be any cops, or hierarchy. You'll only have your parents to worry about, and their hands, and even then, they'll be too preoccupied with reaching dry land. A tooth. A bone. A drill. Twirling in space. A torrent of rank, mucousy milk. I can wait. Lying awake, sitting up when my door creaks, finding my father in my room, clutching an object I can't quite see. I can outwait them. When the tower comes and blocks the rivers and drowns the valley in cum. The torrent. A tooth. A bone. A drill. Then I can run free.

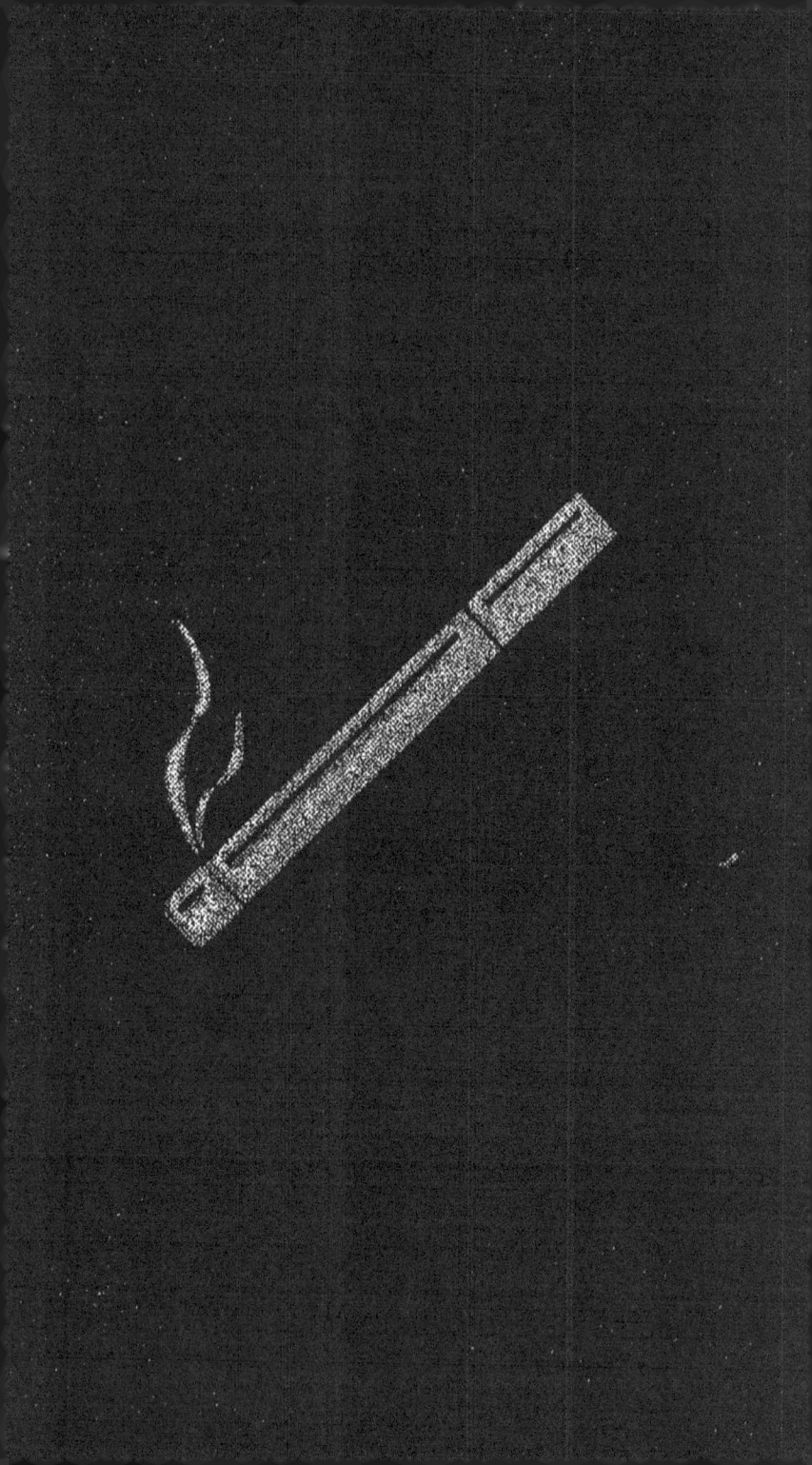

A Favor

She asks for a light. You reach in your pocket and dig out your Bic, strike the flint, and touch the flame to her cigarette. She inhales. The tip roils cinder. A line of flame draws down the paper, crossing the band, down the filter. It touches her lips and her entire face is a blaze. Engulfing, disappearing her hair, climbing down her throat, down her shoulders and arms and chest and belly, down her pants to her shoes. Washed in pumpkin light. She waves her arms, spinning in circles and howling.

You run.

The Frightened

The letter arrives a month in advance. It's been eleven years. You didn't think you'd ever hear from him again.

You are graciously invited to celebrate Frank and Diane's union.
The Elwood Hotel
53 Parrish Blvd
Providence, RI 02903
May 31, 2019 - 7:00 PM: Pre-Game Bash
June 1, 2019 - 3:00 PM: Ceremony Followed by Reception

Providence. Cities breed nothing but uncertainty. Uncertainty and goblins. You can't stomach it, ever since fleeing to the country. Where you live now (population six thousand, two hundred and eighty-four), you generally know who you'll see, what situations you'll encounter. But anything can happen in the city.

You place your revolver and some cartridges in your suitcase, between the linens.

It's an hour drive, two hours on the train, and a fifteen min-ute taxi to the hotel. The Elwood's façade is bronze and marble, the rot of jazz, a broad golden portico above revolv-ing doors. You smoke a cigarette before entering, watching the park across the street. Tents scattered across the green and dirt. Homeless milling—tens of them—independent from one another, reading books, petting dogs, drifting out from their designated areas to haunt regulars, requesting change and smokes. Like spit particles, like germs.

Halfway down your cigarette, you glimpse one preying to-ward you. Long ratty hair stuffed beneath a stocking cap. Camo shorts, a torn up bomber jacket. A smile like rusty razors, like falling icicles. You toss the butt and head inside.

The lobby is all ornate gold-painted trim, purple and emerald wallpapers; black with curling pinks and greens in the carpet. The space is broad but clogged, about a hundred people arrived. Milling faces—faces unknown, strange faces, and faces from high school. Faces like bags filled with water. Aged and reduced, their potential obliterated. You hold your breath—as though doing so would turn you invisible—and weave through the crowd, peripherally scanning for people who might recognize you, so that you may better dodge them.

Particularly the groom. What does he even look like now? What could eleven years have done to him?

Having successfully avoided any and all familiar faces, you enter the registration queue. Bulbed men and women chattering about home ownership and children. Shrill hateful voices, amplified by the acoustics. Drilling your ears like bad frequencies. Like hornets buzzing.

A massive hand claps your shoulder. Like a hand wrapped in steaks. You flinch toward it to a face you almost recognize, like a face you'd known that'd been blown up like a balloon and deflated again. Wrinkles and jowls. An elder, battle-scarred ape. But his eyes, the smile carved in his face. You know him. The groom. Your friend.

You made it.

You nod and tell him of course. You wouldn't miss it for the world.

His lips scrunch. Eyes moist and trembling. He pulls you in for a hug. If he applied only a bit more pressure his arms would crush you into his chest.

The queue moves forward, and it's just about your turn.

Don't let me keep you. We'll catch up later.

Stepping away, he pauses a beat, turning back to you.

Thank you. Truly. Thank you.

The front desk clerk gives you your key card, your room number, and some disquieting news.

CLERK: *Have you been informed about the security compromise?*

You have not.

CLERK: *It's the transients. I'm sure you saw them outside.*

Yes. You did.

CLERK: *They've infiltrated. Wandering the halls. Nights usually. It's the weather, you see. They don't have rooms, of course. They can't afford them.*

Of course.

CLERK: *We've done our best to respond. But there's only so much you can do.*

And what does this mean?

CLERK: *Just be wary. You'll be safe in your room. I can assure you of that.*

The elevator is full of mirrors. Walls of mirror, reflecting infinitely. Sipping your image and spitting it back at you. Your face. Your face is terrified. Your face is furious. Your face is untrustworthy.

A bell dings and the elevator shudders at floor seven. A woman steps in.

You look her over. She won't return the gaze. She's smaller than you, maybe muscular beneath the baggy sweatshirt and pants. You look for filth on her clothes and skin. Sniff the air, trying to determine whether she belongs outside. Reading her body language, deducing whether she'll try to rob you.

The bell dings at floor fourteen. Your floor. You get out, the doors close between you and the woman, and she continues her ascent, leaving you alone in the empty hallway, with only the buzz of old wiring.

Ornate carpeting beneath your feet. Pink flowers curling around metal spoons. Like heroin spoons. Such an odd design choice. Maybe a mutation, a passive effect of the transient invasion. The outside taking over, tainting and altering the world, without even their knowledge of doing so.

You head down the corridor, lined with more mirrors, floor to ceiling, spitting out your visage. Each looks like an attacker, rounding the corner, about to grab hold of your shoulder and pull you into a corner.

You lock the deadbolt and slip the guard chain into place. You remove your shoes and pants. Removing the revolver from your luggage, you load it with cartridges—how soothing as each presses snugly into the cylinder—and place it on the bedside table.

The plan is to seclude here until the ceremony. The only place you're guaranteed safety. An embassy in hostile lands.

Glancing over the room service menu, you settle on a light soup and salad, and call down to the restaurant. An automated message informs you that due to the event, the restaurant will not be able to provide room service until June 2nd. But you were prepared for this, gathering fistfuls of take-out brochures from the lobby.

You settle on Chinese. Vegetable lo-mein and an order of steamed vegetable dumplings. You call it in and the woman on the other end says they will deliver to the lobby.

The hallways. The elevator. All crawling with homeless. Men and women with knives, dirty knives and needles. Shoving you to the ground and taking all that belongs to you.

You ask if they can bring it to your room.

No. Pick it up in the lobby.

You cancel the order. Pick another restaurant. Italian. A big plate of spaghetti and extra garlic bread. Call.

Alright, you can pick it up in the lobby in about forty minutes.

Can't you bring it to my room?

No, we only deliver to the lobby.

You cancel and pick another brochure.

Lying in bed, failing at sleep, your stomach twisted, trying to devour itself. The phone rings.

You pick up. For a brief idiotic moment, you think it's one of the restaurants. They changed their minds. They *will* bring your food to you.

THE GROOM: *Buddy!*

He shouts over music and crowd chatter.

THE GROOM: *Why aren't you down here?*

You lie. You say you don't know what he's talking about.

THE GROOM: *It's a party. Y'know. Pre-game. Come on down.*

You tell him you're tired. That you're the sleepiest you've ever been. That you need your rest for the big day.

Something changes in his voice.

THE GROOM: *Get down here right now.*

You tell him that you have to get some sleep, and hang up, sprawled in bed, wide awake.

Footsteps pound down the hallway. Drunken cackling. Side parties stomping above you. An orgy in the room adjacent. Apes unleashed. You hear every movement. Hours of it.

And something else. Like dry fronds scraping the brick outside. Skittering. Appendages tapping at the façade. You see it in your mind—a man with thin spider legs, leering in windows, seeking children and invalids to suck dry. Keep your eyes squeezed tight, for if you were to see something it would suddenly become reality.

Another set of footfalls clunk down the hall. A lumbering gorilla. The sound halts at your door.

Years from now you'll laugh about it together. Old stabs, old wounds. Your terror. His refusal to accept the things he cannot control, and the consequences that accompany those refusals. But that will be years from now. Right at this moment:

His meaty fists slamming on the door.

The wood buckling from the weight of his shoulder.

Finally, the wood cracking around the strike plate, the bolt tumbling to the carpet. The guard chain stretching and snapping. The door giving way, the groom, your friend, falling through splintered wood but still on his feet, shirt unbuttoned, sleeves rolled up, face bright pink and eyes ringed dark.

THE GROOM: *The hell you doing?*

I need to sleep.

THE GROOM: *You should've come down.*

His enormous calloused frame lurches forward.

THE GROOM: *Disrespectful.*

Grabbing the revolver from the bedside table, you barely take a moment to aim before pulling back the hammer and squeezing the trigger (you never keep the safety on). *Pop.* Pull and squeeze, pull and squeeze, pull and squeeze. *Pop pop pop.*

Only one shot connects but it shoves him backward into the hall. You run to the door and push it closed. The wood is shattered down the middle but it still closes, as closed as it can be now. Watching through the crack, the groom, your friend, rises to his feet, clutching his shoulder. You push a dresser, the end table, a plush chair in front of it, listening to him stagger down the hall, bellowing and striking walls.

You return to bed. Pull the blankets over your head. The phone rings but you don't answer.

The next morning, there's a knock at your door. Pushing the furniture away, you gaze through the crack, ignoring the red speckling the doorframe. It's a bellhop, uniformed in black and purple. He tells you the ceremony is about to begin.

You take the elevator to the ballroom. A purple and emerald hall with tented ceiling. Ornate frescos beneath the trim—mean-faced cherubs encircling a boy, holding him down, pushing his face into dirt.

You take a seat on the groom's side, in back and far from anyone else. The ceremony's already begun. The bride—someone else from high school, but who you never knew, really—has already been given away, and now stands, facing the groom, his arm in a white sling, the officiant standing between them.

Faces turn to grimace at the sight of you. Faces you recognize, and you're certain they recognize you.

The groom, your friend, holds the fingers of the bride with one hand, his good hand. They smile into each other's wet eyes. You almost begin to cry. You reach toward your hip and caress your holster.

You dodge the reception, the dagger eyes from everyone who knows who you are and what you've done. You consider seeking out the groom, just to say hi, maybe apologize for last night, but he's nowhere to be found.

Ride the elevator to the fourteenth floor. Down the hall, past the mirrors, to your door, which had been replaced with fresh, unbroken wood during the ceremony. You swipe your card and step inside.

Another breach.

A window thrown open, sucking A/C into hot wet night. The stink of ape sweat. A wooden chair smashed to pieces beside the desk.

The bed.

Your bed is occupied. A man in a black suit atop the mattress, facing away toward the open window. You know who it is immediately, even before the white cast drawn over his shoulder gives it away.

The groom stands, turning to you, a leg of the splintered chair in his fist. His face flattened, neither a frown nor smile. Nothing. Pulling his damaged arm away from his chest, he tears off the cast, grunting like an elk. Circling around the bed, he slowly advances, saying something. You hear the words but your brain refuses to decipher them.

You say please don't. You say you don't want to get hurt. You yank the revolver from its holster, pull the hammer, point, and squeeze. *Pop.*

The bullet twists the air and connects as intended. Spinning through his right eye, spitting out the back of his head, releasing pale mist like sliced grapefruit. He staggers, smashing into the dresser. Pushing off the drawers onto his feet again, he continues his approach, snarling. Wolfen. A red wet bulb for an eye.

You tell him to stop.

He halts. Studying your face with his one good eye. He says something again. You hear the words but refuse to accept them. Dropping the chair leg, he turns, rushing the gusting window. Bracing his hands on the frame, he steps through onto the ledge, one foot, then the other, fast and fluid. Just before vanishing, he turns and gives a quiet, solemn smile.

You rush to the window. Lights of the city bloom through soup fog. And the groom, clutching the façade, scuttles down the bricks like a mantis. You watch until the fog consumes him and you're alone again.

You wake early and pack, hoping to avoid as many people as possible at check out. Descending in the elevator, you're thankful it doesn't stop at any other floors. The car's light shines *L*, the doors slide open, and you step out.

The lobby is filled. Wet swollen faces, both familiar and foreign. They turn to you, meeting your eyes. Glowering.

Speeding along, keycard in hand, you navigate the bodies toward the front desk. Eyes scanning for the one who can harm you, who has every reason to harm you. You slip into line. Only five heads until the front desk. Holding your breath again—still that stupid hope you can shrink into invisibility.

A finger taps your shoulder.

You turn. There's no surprise here but it still sucks the air out of you. It's the groom. Your friend. A wad of gauze taped over his eye, another padding the back of his head.

You shake. You say oh my God. You say I'm so sorry. You say I didn't know what was happening. You say you didn't know what was going to happen. You say you're so sorry. You say. You say.

He gives a tired smile.

THE GROOM: *Come meet the family.*

But you have to check out. You say you have to check out before ten.

He looks up toward the brass clock overlooking the lobby. The face reads 5:48.

THE GROOM: *Come.*

You follow him to a hall shooting off from the lobby, connecting the hotel to its restaurant. He gently takes your elbow and guides you to the bride, still in her wedding gown. You ask her how it's going.

THE BRIDE: *Oh, you know. Terrible. I got canceled last year.*

You clarify that you were asking about the wedding.

THE BRIDE: *Even worse.*

The groom, your friend, wags a finger at her, then leads you down the bench to two small children.

THE GROOM: *This is Evan. This is Angelica.*

He picks up Angelica and gives her a kiss on the cheek. Evan hides behind the groom's broad calf. Their faces look almost exactly like your friend's, when he was young, and you were too.

It was decades ago, both of you in your late teens but already old friends, friends since freshman year, failing out of life together. He had taken you to a party—no, just seven people on the couch splitting joints and growlers. Someone had made a blow dart shooter. A simple plastic tube. Everyone took turns shooting thin silver darts into beer empties lined on the mantel. *Thwip*. But when it passed to your friend, he tilted the tube downward and shot the needle straight into the host's shin.

He said it was an accident but that always felt like a lie. What would it matter, the outcome's the same. But even then you still kept beside him. That isn't the reason you closed off.

His silver hair. The crags in his face. Years distend. Such terror. You know it, it's true, but only partly. Epidermal shedding, sowing fresh allergies, discarding the old. You mimic. Discarding the old. The friction of other people, even those you've loved. Discarding when their faces rub you raw.

He, his wife, his children.

The world, and your life within it, shrinks as you travel back home. The train's compartment more cramped, the highway's lanes narrowed. Earth's curvature almost visible. Sun and moon pass overhead three separate instances by the time you reach your apartment.

And the apartment has shifted as well. Now only a single room, and hardly that. A walk-in closet. The ceiling lowered to your chest. Just enough space to lie down in, so you lie down, and the walls pull in further, the ceiling descending till it nearly touches your nose.

Tell yourself it's fine. That it's actually what you wanted. That you hadn't planned on ever standing again. Relinquish. Find empowerment in doing so. Find sleep in the one place where no one can find you.

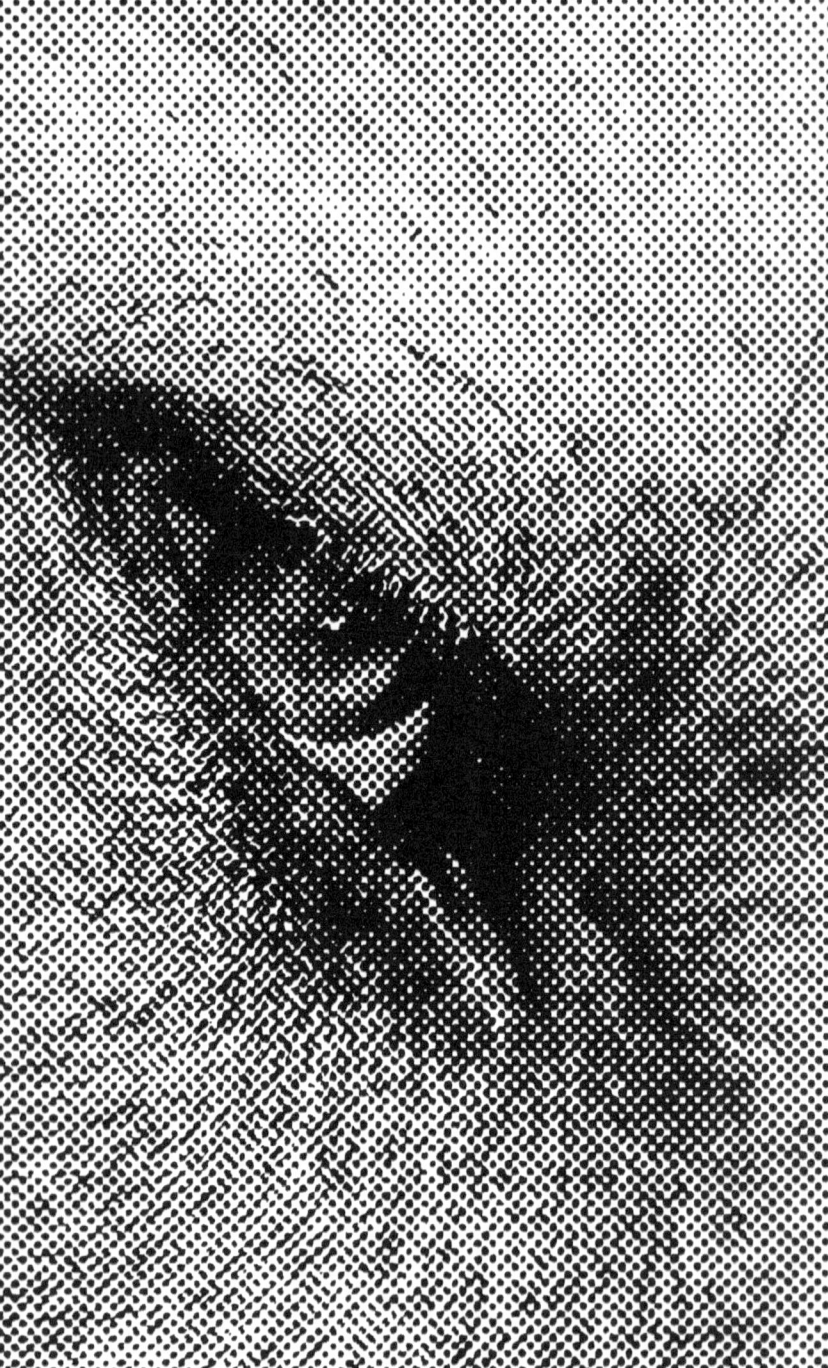

The golden retriever smiles, encircled. Her name is Lavender and she believes she is loved. Encircled by the mother, the father, the son, his wife and their child.

Lavender watches hummingbirds through the window. Following as they flit from stalk to stalk on a feeder, a gift from the son to the mother and father for their anniversary. The mother and father complain that the hummingbirds possess such nasty temperaments—dashing after one another, battling for exclusive rights despite there being plenty of space and sugar water for all.

The child pets Lavender's ear.

Three days ago, the son, his wife and their child arrived at the mother and father's house. Together, they walked through the neighboring woods, following a restful brook. The child, in her rubbers, hopped through shallow water, pulling stones with sparkling minerals from the stream, holding them up to the sunlight, smiling at the glittering, before shoving them into her pocket. The adults discussed the emerging war, until mother finally exclaimed, "*Enough*. It's the first time I've seen you in six months, I don't want to talk about it."

A tick—a perfect evil bead—perched from a thicket,

raised its appendages and grasped Lavender's fur. Scaling leg to chest to neck to head to ear, the tick—undiscovered—crawled to bare skin. A canal. A tunnel. The tick entered.

Now, this morning, a pressure swells inside Lavender. A pounding, deep in her ear canal, just beside the drum. The pulse of her blood being drunk by the tick. She doesn't understand. She walks in circles. Whining. Pawing her ear.

"Oh who's a silly girl?" mother laughs, rubbing Lavender's neck in a brief pause from her circling. It soothes. Distracts. For a moment, Lavender believes this affection will cure her of the pressure and ache as she becomes lost in the sensation.

But mother's hand withdraws, returning Lavender to the wrongness inside her. The tick swelling. The size of a briolette.

"Is she okay?" the son says, scratching Lavender's rear. Lavender barks.

"She's fine," mother says. "Just a silly girl."

Lavender barks again.

"Did she eat?"

"Of course," father says. "I fed her before you got up."

"Maybe she needs to go out?"

"*No*," mother barks, fed up with the questioning. Desperate for a pleasant visit from the people she remembers loving. "She was just out. She's just being silly."

Lavender whimpers. Failing to comprehend. She barks. Failing to communicate.

"Hush." Mother gently bops the dog's nose.

"Grammy," the child says, running to her grandmother's leg. "Doggy hurt."

"Oh no no no sweetie." The mother scoops her granddaughter up. "She's just being a big goofball."

"No no. She hurt."

"She just wants attention."

Beneath them, Lavender spins, pawing her ears, keening. Trying to mold her whines and grunts into vowels and accents. A noise her keepers can understand. Stamping her feet, tapping a message in an undiscovered language. The tick swells, the pressure grows. Her body invaded, turned alien. Home turned unrecognizable. Her family turns their heads away, distracted by a new discussion, another hummingbird lit upon the feeder. She flails at empty air, at the carpet, at a wall, as though sunk through thick old water, fathoms down, where no one can see.

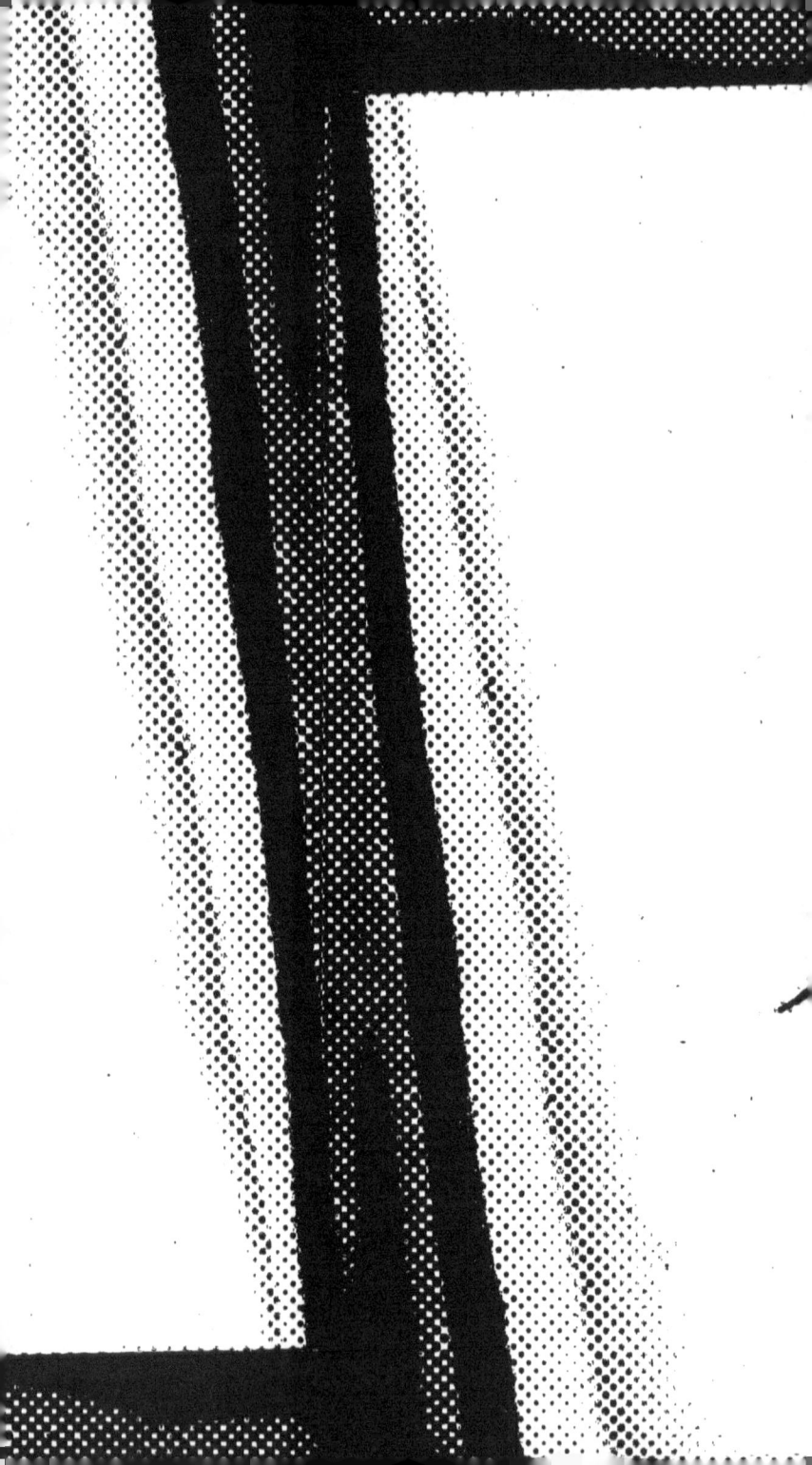

Highway Wars

**based on a concept by
Justin Davis Jacobs**

It's almost every night: I'll be driving home when some cocksucker rolls up behind me, running their brights, blowing out my rearview, flooding my vision with blinding white. Maybe it's by mistake, maybe it's intentional—a jackass trying to fuck with me, but it doesn't matter. The outcome's the same.

So here's what I do: I grab the rearview mirror and tilt it just so until their headlights shine right back in their fucking eyes. Rub their faces in it. See how they like that. And I'd like to say that what happens next is that the car behind me wobbles side to side, overcorrecting before careening off the road. Headlights gone, nobody's problem now.

But that never happens. Not once. At best they switch off their brights or they accelerate and pass. The definition of anticlimax.

Lynn hates that I do this, and I've been doing it longer than we've been married. She says I could get someone killed. I tell her that if you run your brights right behind someone, you deserve to crash.

"You'll just piss 'em off," she says. "What if they follow you home?"

"No one's gonna follow me home." And no one has.

Not yet. Chickenshits, all of them. But ever since she mentioned it, I've been praying for one to try.

❧

I hate driving during the day. The sheer congestion of it. We've convinced ourselves that every space needs to be filled, so we fill them with cars, every single day. So I mostly work evenings into nights. But not today. Today, I signed up for a morning-to-afternoon, because it's a longer shift and I need the hours. So I'm out of the house at 9:00 AM, which is just more salt in the wound. I try to never be out of bed before noon.

At least it's summer. There are three fucking colleges in this town, so during semester the commute is even more of a nightmare. Clogged with living garbage in tank tops and pajama bottoms. Tan muscled trash babies in sports cars racing up and down narrow avenues, tossing empties from windows and running over strays. But for now, the students are gone—oh so thankfully gone—and the streets are wide open, the whole world feels open, the sky open, the sun is gold, and even though it's horrible to be awake this early, the ache is ignorable from moment to moment. A twinge of sensation that could be interpreted as warmth and life inside me.

I slow my '99 Camry—rattling with age, trembling grey like a frail horse—to the North Pleasant Street/Kellog Ave intersection in the center of three lanes, heeding the red light. Flanked by two others—a blue Honda Civic to my right, a white Kia Sedona idling in Left Turn Only. The light clicks to green and I ease off the brake but this fucking, this *fucking* Honda Civic just guns it, swinging out in front of me from the right lane, nearly clipping the Sedona turning left, blowing past us onto Kellog. I smash the horn and the Sedona does the same and I catch a glimpse of the kid driving: tank top, wavy ball of surfer hair. Face like a male model's.

A fucking college kid. I always forget—some students stay on campus through the summer. You can never get rid of all of them. Like fucking ants.

If he's heading where I think he's heading, there's a spot I can cut him off. So I stomp the gas. The Camry shakes and heaves but complies, engine moaning, under-inflated tires pulling at the blacktop to push me forward. I keep it ten miles over the speed limit, and the street is mostly empty so there isn't much to worry about. Up ahead at the Main Street intersection, I'm blessed with a fresh yellow and zero oncoming traffic, so I press the gas harder and whip the wheel left and gun it down the way, passing the bookstore and Indian restaurant and Black Sheep Bakery. Past the pizzeria and Women's Club and *boom*—right there, the Kellog Ave outlet. I swing left and there it is—the blue Civic heading straight toward me.

I wrench the wheel till the hood points toward the sidewalk, then pull the Camry in reverse, evening it out so its side is blocking both lanes completely. Blue Civic would need to go up on the sidewalk to get past me, and even the most reckless shitty kid is unlikely to pull a move like that. I shove the car into park.

The Civic arrives, slowing to a halt. The kid starts honking. I roll down my window. "You can't just do whatever the fuck you want, man."

The kid scrunches his face. Baffled. Stupid.

"I saw what you did back there. You cut us all off."

The kid rolls his eyes and leans out the window. "Are you fucking kidding me?"

"You can't just do whatever you want, dude." I shrug at him. "Other people live here."

"Get out of the fucking way!" He screams, pounding on the horn. "Jesus Christ, *go*."

I think about getting out. I think about getting my bag. But there's too much daylight and this is already too blatant, too provocative. I pull the car out of park. "You think about what you did," I yell. "This isn't your god-damn mom's house." I swing left, pulling forward, opening the roadway. He guns around me through the empty on-coming lane, screaming while he passes, the words indecipherable, just noise.

The joke is that literally everyone around here has worked MSC Data Capture at least once or twice in their life. It's the easiest job in the world to get, and even easier to keep. Dialing the public, reading survey scripts off a computer screen, inputting the data. That's it. All you have to prove is that you can speak and hear and they'll hire you, even if you otherwise can't perform the position's other basic functions. There are guys working here who can't pronounce half the script—dudes who can't *read* half the script—but they still thrive here, because none of it actually matters. (There's this kid—Bruno fucking Bailey, this real wild Southie—who rolls joints at his desk every other shift. Never been caught). It's a numbers game where the numbers don't matter. All you got to do is show up and put in the minimum. Not the kind of place you'd want to get stuck at if you had any ambitions. The only way you'd consider it a long-term prospect is if you were fucked for life.

I've been here thirteen years.

I'm late, as usual, rushing in through the sliding doors, exhaling a quick "hey" to Shane the security guard, then into the dialing room to sign in at the supervisors' desk. Paul, one of the supes, looks up at me, then at the clock, then at me again. "You're seventeen minutes late."

"Traffic."

He arches a brow, cocking his head toward the rest of the room. "Everyone else made it on time."

"I very much doubt that. Sincerely."

"It's a figure of speech."

"Look, please —" and it's a surprise even to me that I'm already almost crying "—please please please I don't need this today."

Paul snorts his wide pig nostrils and tosses his pen on the desk. "Honestly, I'm just making conversation here."

"Great. Fun. Thanks." I drop the pen on the sign-in sheet, grab my headset from the filing cabinet and head to my station.

The dialing room is big and beige—ten long desks each split into twenty-five stations on either side. Each station equipped with a touchtone landline phone, an autodialer, and a desktop computer that was already old in the early aughts. A quiet, ambient hostility—a factory floor but white collar, without even the superficial benefits of American myth.

The higher-ups randomize the seating chart every day to keep us off balance, so you never know which station you'll be at or who you're gonna be stuck between. If you're lucky, you get Cynthia Falla and Jerome Powers (at least those are the names they use while dialing. MSC Data Capture allows for pseudonyms), because they're total fucking pros with insane completion rates, so you never have to worry about small talk. But today I'm between Hilda Swan and Ricardo Boston. Ricardo Boston is always organizing and re-organizing his pills at his desk, and grunts and curses whenever he gets hung up on (which is almost always). Hilda Swan just stinks of gasoline and pee. On the plus side, she has a surprisingly great completion rate, so she barely stops to chat. But today she's nightmarishly ripe, canceling it all out.

I plug in my headset, sit down, and stuff tissues between my eyes and glasses so no one will see me weep.

⌁

"Now my third sister went to live in Louisiana to be closer to her father-in-law, and we weren't real close to begin with so I was fine but Mama was real put out. And this wasn't my sister with the drug problem. She lives real close and I still see her, sometimes."

The respondent has been talking for five minutes. I had asked whether she had had a physical in the past twelve months and this is her response. MSC Data Capture requires that I state the question a full three times before marking it as a refusal and moving on, but I can't get a word in. I can't bring myself to. She said she lives alone and it's apparent she hasn't spoken to another person in days.

The survey is supposed to take twenty minutes, if your demographics qualify. We've been on for thirty-five and haven't even passed the screener questions yet.

"My mother lives in Carl Junction and she has her

entire life, except when we lived in Clarksdale but that was long enough ago it doesn't really count."

A hand reaches out in front of me and clicks mute on my headset receiver. The hand is attached to Malinda, another supervisor. Only twenty-three. Way too young to be in that role, but I guess she possessed a severe enough face and personality to qualify. We all resented her when she got promoted, though most of us would rather self-immolate than supervise this place. But no one here would waste an opportunity to be resentful.

"You have to end the call," she says, arms folded, eyes fixed in resting glare.

"I can get through this," I say. I haven't had a complete in weeks. It doesn't actually matter because this place will never actually fire you because of performance alone. A written warning at most. But there are people here who'll show up without pants because they forgot to put on pants before leaving home and *they* get more completes than I do. Jesus Christ. At my last performance review, the supervisor just shrugged and told me that maybe my rates are so low because I'm just unlikable. Fuck. "I can do this," I say.

"No, you can't. End it. I can't fucking take it." She stomps back to the supervisor desks, puts on her headset and glowers at me. I click myself off mute and try asking the question a third time.

⌄

People see me and they see an ape. They see an ape pulled over my skin. A stupid disgusting orangutan blowing snot, batting at objects he doesn't understand—trying to make them work in ways they were never intended. Stupid fucking shirt and sweatpants filled with garbage stupid disgusting ass ape. They look at me like I'm not worthy of life.

The sun's still high when I get out. Again, this almost never happens, and I hate being out during daylight—more people and that means more cars, more wolves feuding for the head of some fraud hierarchy. But I know it makes Lynn happy because it means we can actually have dinner together. I can't remember the last time. So I swallow it down and grip the wheel tight, telling myself it's worth it.

I take backroads to dodge traffic, but even then, there's no escaping people. Spilling out of houses, out of the sky, bubbling up from the earth. Building new structures, new complexes, casting dust and shadow over the old world. Future ruins, and of course new roads to reach them.

So many people, too many people, and on a strip of blacktop between vacant rolling fields I get stuck behind one. A woman in a merlot Chevy hatchback, swerving back and forth across the lane. Through her rear windshield, I see her hand lifted in front of her face, clutching a phone. So predictable. Split between worlds, she glides over the painted lines, before overcorrecting and kissing the shoulder.

Up ahead, maybe a few dozen yards, I see the bicyclist.

Bicyclists and pedestrians are always paying the price for driver negligence. Everyone knows that. But there's something more to it. A real animosity. The fact is: drivers despise bicyclists—they view them as an impediment to their vehicle's sovereignty. Bicyclists and peds are just reminders of social obligation, a responsibility to others, and there's nothing drivers hate more. Sealed away from all others and their disgusting oxygen atop thrones of plastic and metal, glass and pleather—drivers loathe their responsibility to fellow travelers more than anything. Because driving is like any drug. You never want to care about anyone else when you're strung out.

My muscles tighten as the Chevy rides up on the cyclist, driver still clutching her phone, weaving back and forth. The hatchback veers left over the centerlines, and for a moment there's this hope that she sees the bicyclist, that she's giving the rider enough space, that she understands precisely what her vehicle is cable of inflicting on a human body. That she's simply doing the right thing. But then the car yanks back toward the shoulder, and its tires cross over into the bicyclist's space.

I lay on the horn.

The cyclist sees it coming and maneuvers, dodging the Chevy's bumper, swerving off the road, wobbling, then falling sideways to the grass. The hatchback proceeds down the road, oblivious to what it'd done.

I don't pull over to see if the cyclist is alright. I press the gas, keeping the Chevy in sight. The Chevy cruises past the turn I usually take to get home. I take my foot off the gas and touch the stem for my turn signal. *Fuck it.* I stomp hard, blowing past my turn in quiet pursuit.

⌄

She pulls into an empty driveway to an Easter-yellow bungalow and barren lawn. I roll on past and keep driving until I'm two blocks away, before slowing to the curb and shoving the Camry in park. I pull my bag into the front seat and open it.

All I need is my hoodie and hunting knife, so I remove each and just sit. Pulling on the hoodie, running the AC, waiting for the sun to sink, sky shifting from pink to charcoal. The block fills with hazy blue moonlight and I get out, knife folded, held tight in the hoodie's pocket. The night breathes hot and waxy. The sweatshirt is like a trash bag, wringing out moisture, but the hood feels like a mask, and that feels like safety. I bob down the avenue, behind the bushes, between the street lamps.

Pretend to disappear. Become objective, just a perspective from a vantage point. What do you see? Single-story houses, passably manicured lawns, stone walkways, trellises, wind chimes, political signs. Crows. Squirrels. But no people. Not a single person outside.

Too perfect.

I reach her house. The lights are on inside, and that's scary, but it only *feels* scary. You can't really see through a window when there's light on your side and darkness on the other. I'm as good as invisible. So I step onto the driveway and unfold the knife.

Crouched at the rear of the Chevy, I peer over the trunk at the house. No movement through the yellow-lit windows. I look down at the tire, grip the knife, and cover my face with the inside of my elbow. Stab. The rubber's tough but it gives, it opens, it lets me in, and the air pushes back, pissing back the blade. I look up at the windows. Still no one there.

I crawl along the bumper to the other rear tire. Stab. Release. The rubber sinks, flattening into the asphalt. I scuttle along the passenger doors to the front of the car. Stab into rubber. Air hisses out the wound.

A hinge squeals, a door slams. A bellow. "*What the fuck are you doing?*" The driver, the woman, standing there, a silhouette in the doorframe.

I run. I don't even think, I just turn and run. I run even though generally no one gives chase, no one gets farther than the end of their lawn. Most people aren't that stupid. They know I have a knife.

But you never know.

So I run. I run for blocks, I run until my lungs give out and I toss myself into some public bushes, shaking, heaving, trying not to puke. Righting myself, I peek back, squinting through street lamps' pale light. Glancing at the other houses, the lawns.

No one. Not the woman, no neighbors, not even pets wandering. Just croaks and buzzing; crickets sawing and frogs screwing.

Crawling from the bushes, I keep left and circle the neighborhood, back to where my car is. I get in, stuff the knife and hoodie into my bag, and drive home.

⌒

I don't delude myself. I know this is only getting her off the road for a week, tops. But last year, at least four hundred people died on Massachusetts roadways. An average of at least one person per day. And because of me, there will be at least three days where that woman isn't on the road, and maybe somebody will live because of it. I don't know. I just don't know. I know it's a Band-Aid on an amputation but what else is there?

⌒

Lynn cries and screams when I get home. "Why didn't you *call*?"

"I had my phone off," I say. "I mean, the battery died." I toss my bag in the spare room where I've been sleeping.

"Well, what were you doing?"

"Just driving around. I lost track of time. I'm sorry."

"I thought you were fucking *dead*."

Massaging my temples. Needles in my lobes. "I said I'm sorry."

She sniffs the air. Trying to pin a scent on me. "Were you out with someone?"

"What're you talking about?"

She looks down into the table and doesn't look back up. "Were you with someone that I don't know about?"

"Jesus Christ." Voice cracking. "Like anyone else would have me. What the fuck."

Her face twists like a rag and she bawls. "Then what were you doing?"

"I was fucking driving around. I like to drive around." And this is true. Sometimes I'll take Route 116 up to Conway on a winding gray serpent, pushing through conifers as tall as office buildings. Even during the day, the road is empty and free, like the beginning of the end of humanity, like the world is beginning to come back, and only I am around to witness it. "You never think about this shit when I'm out late."

"That's different."

"Not really."

She sinks into her chair and looks away. "I wanted to have dinner with you."

⌃

I always need to know I can exit any place and any situation at any moment. Never get stuck in a corner. Never get boxed in. So I keep my bag close.

Inside my bag:

- One pair of clean pants
- Two clean shirts—one short sleeve, one long
- One sweater
- One hoodie
- Three pairs of clean socks
- Three pairs of clean underwear
- Two bottles of water, unopened
- Five cans of Chef Boyardee ravioli
- Flashlight
- Phone charger
- Burner phone and charger
- My birth certificate
- A crowbar
- The hunting knife

Thank God we never had children.

I can't believe she hasn't left yet. Or kicked me out. But in fact, I know precisely why. She's terrified of the disruption it would cause; of becoming spinning, alone. The horror of re-entering coupling, the bars, the matchmaking websites, faceless strangers messaging, desperate to own and plug your body. I know her too well. She wasn't built for that shit. Me being the way I am is already a blow to her sense of stability, but if I left it'd be even worse—or at least that's what she's convinced herself. Our dissolution would signify a failure—a failure of her faith in herself and me and us; of so much irreplaceable time misspent. It's a genuine fear, therefore an exploitable one, and as much as I tell my-self I'm not exploiting it, deep down I know the truth.

∾

Summer allergies. The worst thing in the world, the worst fucking thing. You can never understand unless it happens to you. All day and all night blowing ropes into stupid lit-tle hankies. Little disgusting crumpled tufts filling up my car, filling up my station at work.

"You got a cold, man?" Dante Paris says, covering his mouth with his hand, peeking over at me and my station. Usually, he's one of the better dialers to be stuck beside, because usually he minds his own fucking business. But usually is only fucking usually, apparently.

"It's these fucking allergies," I tell him, muting my headset, huffing the tissue, blowing dry sticky slugs. "And you know what? It's worse than a fucking cold, because a cold will end. But not this shit. This is just my fucking life now." I open the tissue and peer at the slug—tinted rust—then crumple it, tossing it into the station's corner. "It's not fucking fair. No one—no person, animal or oth-erwise—deserves to deal with this shit. I mean, *look at this*." Gesturing at the pyramid of crumpled tissues. "Do you know how much tissues cost? I don't want to have to pay for this shit. It's so fucked."

"Okay, man," Dante says, angling away from me in his chair.

I hit the autodialer. Three rings. Voicemail. Enough time for my sinuses to fill with more warm thick slugs. I stuff my hand into the tissue box. My fingers scrape noth-ing. Look inside: nothing. I pat the pile of used kleenex—

all soaking wet, unusable. Jesus fucking Christ.

Maybe just wait it out. I look up at the clock. Two hours left.

I get up, heading past the supervisor desk toward the bathroom.

"Hey!" Dennis calls out from the desk. Fucking Dennis. No supervisor takes his job more seriously than fucking Dennis, and that makes him the worst person in the world. Worse than anybody. Worse than Jean-Bédel Bokassa. He taps the sign out sheet with his pen.

"Look —" Voice cracking. Trying to contort my face into something that suggests affability. "These allergies are killing me. I'm out of tissues. I've got to blow my nose."

"Still got to sign out."

"I'm just getting some fucking tissues. I'm not signing out."

"Anytime you leave this room you have to sign out."

I take the pen and sign and mark my time, letting my fucking snot drip down onto the sheet. "You fucking happy?"

"That isn't necessary, Ezra."

I just walk away, out of the dialing room, down the hall to the men's room.

The stall furthest from the door—*my* stall—is occupied, so I go in the one at the other end and sit on the seat. Sometimes I'll just stare into the grey of the metal stall door—imagine it was the world and the world was nothing. That I was nothing, melted down into warm soft grey.

Down the row at the end stall (my stall), I hear Ricardo Boston grunting through clenched teeth. "Fuck I've got a dirty butt. I've got a very dirty butt."

The illusion breaks. I'm here. I'm something, and so is the world. I'm here and so is everybody else.

I wad up like twenty plies of toilet paper and stuff them into my pocket, then head back to the dialing hall, to my row and there—there right in front me: Dante Paris bending over my station, lifting my bag.

"Hey," I shout at him, passing the supervisor desk, Dennis gesturing at me, telling me to sign back in. "*Hey*."

Dante looks up, dropping my bag to the floor. "Sorry, I was just moving it."

"Don't touch my fucking bag." I get in his face. He falls backward into my station, knocking the computer monitor with his elbow, pressing his hand into my pile of kleenex.

"Hey hey *hey*," Dennis shouts, coming over. "What's the problem?"

"Nothing," I say.

"Yeah, nothing," Dante says.

Dennis points at me and gestures toward the break room. "Come talk with me a minute."

"Nothing happened."

"I know, but let's talk. Real quick."

Fuck. It's fucked. It's all fucked. I somehow fucked my spot at the one place where you can get away with anything.

I follow him.

Dennis leans against a vending machine and looks me in the eye with that I'm-not-mad-I'm-disappointed wannabe father shit. "I think you should head home for the day."

"*God*." Bones and blood pushing through my skin. "I said nothing happened. *He* said nothing happened."

"Dude, I fucking saw you. You can't be pushing and intimidating people, man. I'm not writing you up or anything but you have to leave. Just for tonight."

I storm back to my station, grab my bag—leaving my

headset and tissue pile—and exit out the building. It's already night. The only thing to go right today. I get in my car and take the backroads because I'm in no rush to be home.

∿

A long straight corridor unfurls before me and it's beautiful. Plowing a tunnel through the night, past the blur of trees and hills beside me. A droning bass rattling my speakers—vague music from one of the college stations, intermingling with the engine's dull thrum and it feels like fingers adjusting my spine. I move like a cell through vessel. Alone in the body of the world.

A ropey strand catches in my throat. I grab a handful of toilet paper and hock into it. Like egg, like cum. I toss it to the passenger side floor, a floor you can't see for the tissues.

A pair of lights creep out from around a bend and into my rearview, rending the illusion of isolation. Only seconds and they're growing, gaining, and then the car's right on my ass, practically tonguing my bumper. High beams flash. I wait. They flash again, and the driver lays on the horn.

A rule of mine: when I've got some guy behind me, and they're honking or flashing trying to get me to speed up—*especially* when I'm already going the limit—I'll drop my speed by five MPH. They flash or honk again, they lose another five. Do it again, they lose another. See how they like *that*. Once I get down to thirty or twenty-five MPH, they usually pass, and I'm left wishing they'd followed me home instead.

Maybe tonight.

So I let my foot off the gas. The Camry moans and

drags down to forty-five MPH. The car behind clutches closer to my ass, less than half a car's length between us.

You like that?

The lights flash again. A double honk. I drop down to forty MPH.

The centerlines change from solid to broken. If they had any sense they'd pass, but the car honks and flashes its brights again. *I can go all fucking night, bitch.* I drop it down to thirty MPH. More honking, more flashing. Half a mile later and the centerlines return from broken to solid.

There: the headlights veer left toward the oncoming lane. *Now* the car's trying to pass. Fucking idiot.

Nope. Smashing the gas, I tug the wheel left to stay ahead. *You lost your chance buddy.* The engine growls, shuddering to keep pace. *Now you're stuck with me.* My eyes flick back and forth between the rearview and the road. The headlights behind glide right. I fucking stand on the gas and swing back into the right lane, engine rumbling up through the floorboards into my anus. The Camry glides too far, front tire grazing the shoulder. I wrestle it back into lane, still flooring it, climbing to fifty-five, sixty, pushing all the way to seventy MPH, seventy-five, eighty. The headlights in the rearview slowly shrink. My eyes click back to the road and

Four legs. Mottled fur. Glowing marble eyes. Broad beautiful antlers.

I nudge the wheel and slam the brakes, but my right foot is still on the gas. The Camry slides, slides past the deer, tires squealing, branding blacktop. Spinning out. Releasing the gas, the Camry bucks to a halt at the end of a perfect one-eighty arc. Headlights resting back on the stationary deer. My headlights blending with the other car's headlights. The deer between. And then

It sounds like buckshot into a beer keg. The car—a piss-yellow Volkswagen Golf—swerves too late, smashing the animal's hind. The deer spins like a wet nickel, spitting meat and fur, half-annihilating across the roadway. The VW passes, shifting the air pressure, rocking my Camry. Brakes squealing, burning deeper blacks into the asphalt. It skids right, breaches the breakdown lane, tries to correct but loses purchase, and plows the guardrail—a second round of buckshot—before flipping through to the ravine below.

Heave in. Heave out. My heart in my throat, my fist pulling at my chest. I tear the seatbelt off. Put the car in park but keep it running, and let my foot off the brake. Pull my bag from the back into the front seat. Unzip it and remove the knife. Step out into night. Blend into it.

What do you see?

There's red, and there's red twisted red, smashed into blacktop and smeared. Fetid heat and perfect moon grey and the filthiest dead shit reek you can imagine. An impossible stench, like rotting already, like bags of shit left in the sun. Logs of shit in ruptured intestine. Unwashed fur on burst flesh. Unwashed red stench, unwashed fur hot guts. The stench of bones. Unwashed red.

An insane scream. Sustained. Like the way babies scream forever, never blowing out their voices. It isn't coming from the car in the ravine, but from the road still. Behind me. Turn to it. It's a shape, moving jagged in the grey light. A maw and antlers stretched toward sky. Two legs, a pair of hoofs trying to stand. Only its front two legs exist now, the rear vanished into ripped red. It keeps trying to stand, unable to comprehend its predicament. All it understands is hurt and wanting to get away from it. To run away on legs that no longer exist. It screams. A scream that would end the world if the world made any sense, but here we are so what does that mean?

Another stench wafting through heat. Exhaust stench. Sickly brown syrup sucked through tubes, burned in engines, burned and exhaled grey and black. Follow it. See it hissing up from the ravine. The glow of headlights producing a faint halo at the lip.

Tracing the black skids to the flattened guardrail, I peer down the ravine. It's a miniature tornado's wake—leveled trees and brush, a path carved down to the Volkswagen. It rests on its side, nuzzled between ancient firs and the ravine's incline. Coolant spitting. Billowing dense miasma.

I keep the knife folded and stick it in my back pocket, sliding down to the car on damp grass and earth. Stepping onto the driver side door, feeling the ruptured engine's vibration through my foot. Peering through the open window. A stink of beer and filth rising through. A gurgling down there, distinct from the radiator spitting. Sounds a body makes.

I take out my phone and shine a light into the crushed compartment. The driver—a rag-dolled bloody frat boy— appears beneath the light, crumpled into the dashboard, resting atop the passenger window (now a floor to him). Head split, maybe—not sure whether the ragged red of his face is only ruined skin or that the bone is cracked, too. "*What the fuck,*" he froths and gurgles.

"Hey," I say. "You alright?"

"*No. No,*" he shrieks. "*I'm—I'm fucking hurt.*"

"Can you get up?"

"I don't know. I don't know."

I reach for my knife, hold it tight inside my pocket, then release. "You really shouldn't've done that back there," I say.

The boy just moans.

"Running your fucking brights on me. Fucking drinking." I'm so angry I'm almost crying. "What the fuck did you think was going to happen?"

"You—" the boy gurgles. "You fucking—" And I can see him putting it all together in his damaged brain. He realizes who I am. "*You fucking*—" He wants to blame me.

Completely disgusting. Refusing to take even the slightest bit of responsibility. I switch off the light and turn from him, scaling the grass and dirt back up to the road.

"*Wait*," he screams. "*Wait. Please.*" Again and again, then it isn't even words, just screaming, a counterpoint to the doomed deer's bellows above. Two jagged tones, sometimes in harmony but mostly not.

Years back, before we were married, when we still shared a bed—more than a decade now—I was driving Lynn home, in her car (she was drunk), late from one of her aunt's parties. I didn't want to go, and I was right to resist it—none of her family took me seriously. They'd look at me and they wouldn't even see an ape—not even a living thing. Just a weight fastened to Lynn's ankles. They were disgusting people then and still are, those who've survived.

We wound around the hills cutting from Westfield to Easthampton, silent in our seats, not even music on. I wanted her to hear the simmer.

It doesn't matter how closely I was watching the road. It was inevitable. Rounding a bend, a deer appeared beneath my headlights, stopped stupid in the middle of the lane.

It pulverized the moment we touched it. A burst of meat and stench. I stomped the brakes. We caught our breaths, examined each other's bodies and finally got out. That identical rotten meat shit stench.

The bumper smashed; a crack in the windshield; a crater in the hood. Red freckled all over. Tufty chunks of hide. Lynn beginning to cry, me holding her tight, no longer craving her guilt.

I told her that the car could probably make it home, so we got back in and continued on, new internal rumbles accompanying the standard engine growl. Lynn slipped her hand onto the top of my thigh. I placed my own over and squeezed it tight.

At home we showered and fucked, harder and with more love than even our first days of courting. A fresh knot in the rope of us. We fell asleep, a strange peaceful slumber, clutching each other, her head on my chest, breathing in sync.

Thank God Lynn is asleep when I get home. I remove my shoes, tiptoe to the spare room, and lie down on the cot. I think that I won't be able to sleep, but I do. My eyes blink closed and I'm inside a container falling through space, falling through the atmosphere, falling through oxygen and steam, landing on a black gelatinous planet, a planet of endless swamps in every direction and trees like razorwire.

I dig crabs from sunken marshes, tearing them open with bare hands, sucking their insides from carapace for sustenance. No sun—just a silver moon straining through fog and ropey vines. Voidal brush shivering. No sound but my breath and my jaw clicking and sloppy skittering at my feet.

I wake behind the wheel, smashing through a guardrail, my body tearing through the seatbelt, launching through the windshield, my weight flying forward. Flying through trees and the windows of houses. I break my arms, legs, and neck on branches and doorframes. Still flying, flying higher and higher, up through the clouds and atmosphere, past gravity. I fly through the zero of space, past the sun, the rest of our system. Flying past our galaxy to the end of the universe, and break through the wall of that, to whatever lies after. Then I wake up for real.

⌄

Driving to work means running the Route 9 gash through Hadley. A scar of malls and strip malls. Malls always growing. Malls in front of malls in front of beautiful shrinking farmlands that fill the air with cattle shit heat stench.

Constant redundancy, at least twice of everything. Three supermarkets and a Trader Joes, a Barnes & Noble and Bed, Bath & Beyond; a Walmart a Lowes and a Home Depot; a Michael's and a Joann Fabrics; a JC Penny's an H&M an Old Navy a TJ Maxx and a Marshalls. So compressed you could stand atop a utility pole and see it all.

The Russell and Maple Street intersection divides the main malls. Just take a left onto Maple, between a Wendy's and a KFC/Taco Bell, then a right onto another artery and you're in the Venture Way office park, where MSC Data

Capture is nestled on the first floor.

Traffic's a holocaust. I see three accidents—a High-lander wrapped around a tree; a fender bender between an F-150 and a Chevy Venture; a motorcyclist being pulled onto a gurney—and it takes all of my discipline not to stop at each crash site and open my bag. But I'm almost there, I've almost made it, stuck at the Russell and Maple red light, watching a Jeep Wrangler run over a seagull. The bird just walks into traffic and stands there, doesn't even attempt to fly. The Wrangler rolls forward, front wheel smashing the gull into tar. Wings flash wide and symbolic, beak open, batting, shrieking. An SUV full of young men in tank tops and headbands—they point and laugh at it. They're watching and they're just laughing, all of them.

I become extremely aware of my bag.

A loud fucking bang across the street. A bang and a scrape, like a shovel dragged across steel. I look just in time to catch this coupe—this huge white boat—swinging left out of lane into oncoming traffic, scraping against the car in front of it. It weaves over the centerline and bucks, like the driver's tapping the gas and releasing, over and over. Oncoming traffic honks and swerves over the breakdown lane, cutting around while the coupe pushes forward in vi-olent heaves. Finally, the boat just guns it, shooting ahead through the intersection, swaying back and forth across all lanes while everyone else scatters to the roadside.

Squinting through the coupe's windows, I can't see anyone. Like no one's driving. Phantasm.

I wait for the green. One second, two, three, four, five. It doesn't come so I check left, then right, and smash the gas, whipping the wheel left and pushing through onto Maple, horns caterwauling all around. I reach my turn and blow past Venture Way, keeping the coupe in sight, gaining on it.

The coupe sways and staggers like a drunk, slowing suddenly, before taking off again, tearing all over the road. We're into farmlands now with thankfully less traffic, and the two cars that do pass expertly swerve out of the way. It's only seven or eight miles before the coupe finally wags all the way across the road, departing asphalt, hopping a runoff ditch and smashing forward into a utility pole. Halted.

Letting my foot off the gas, I drift into the shoulder. Park it but keep it running. I pull my bag into the front seat and remove the knife.

Crossing the street, squinting through terrible sunlight into the coupe. I still can't make out a driver, or a passenger—no one. It's not that the windows are tinted—I can see into the car just fine. I just don't see anybody.

Approach the way cops do—from the rear left taillight, hugging the body. Keep checking for anyone who might spring out. Even if they've schemed up an ambush, they'll still need to turn around to get at me. This provides some advantage. I glance back at the road—left and right. No cars, for now. I unfold the knife.

A squeal. A squeal from inside the coupe.

Through the rear window and passenger windows— still no one, just empty seats. Stepping forward, I peer through the driver side.

Another squeal. A raspy inhuman grunt.

Movement. Movement in the driver seat. Naked flesh, folded over. Hairy and pale. A large nub of flesh, shaking and bucking.

I breathe in. Knife secure in hand, I grab the door with the other, yanking it open. The driver falls out. Pink skin. White hairs. Squealing pink blubber, falling from the driver seat into the grass.

A pig. A hundred or so pound hog snorting and squealing. It hops up on its trotters and scampers away through the brush, popping out the other end onto farmland, shrinking away toward somewhere, away from something.

Jerking back to the coupe's interior, I scan for an attacker, for *someone else*. Ducking my head inside, scanning the seats, the floors. No one there.

Folding the knife, I head back to the Camry. I sit and stare at the wheel for five minutes. Humming a song, one from my childhood. I've forgotten the name but the melody holds tremendous relevance. Then I put the car in drive and steer it back toward work.

ᐱ

They seat me by the supervisor desk and I have to listen to them all bitch and chatter the whole shift. *My father hates my husband. My wife hates my sister. I hate my daughter's preschool teacher.* Fucking narcissists, all of them.

Then the droolings coalesce into something familiar. Something with terrible potential. "It's gotta be just one guy, right?"

"Yeah, or like a few of them. A gang, maybe."

"It legit happened to my sister's neighbor. Just last week. She came out and there was this guy by her car. All her tires slashed."

"Yeah, we've got a group going on NextDoor. We're gonna get this guy. I mean, like, tires are freaking *expensive*."

ᐱ

I never eat before my shift's over. I just can't before then. It'll ruin my day. Food is an enemy. The floods of anxious nausea. The way ulcers tear me open from the inside out. The way fibrous foods turn to liquid shit the moment they hit my pancreas, leaking out my anus. Work exacerbates it. People's voices exacerbate it. I just can't do it. Not until the day's finally over and I can be alone. Real alone.

I know Lynn is worried. Everything about me worries Lynn, but this one particular thing—this I can hide, somewhat. I tell her I eat at home while she's at work. I tell her I eat again before my shift. I tell her I'm eating three square meals a day, vegetables and protein and all the essential vitamins and nutrients. It would be wonderful, but I can't do it. I can't.

I clock out at 11:00 and call in an order. Domino's pizza—ground beef, black olives, onions and peppers. Every time. I've got the timing perfect so it's fresh out the oven and into the box when I roll up. Then I drive to a parking space downtown to ingest it in solitude. Stomach twisted, walls squeezed together, begging for its first and only meal of the day.

I slide the first greasy slice into my mouth and scan the block. Lines of darkened storefronts—what used to be a Korean restaurant, what used to be a bookstore. A mom and pop café being converted into a Dunkin'. The streets empty. Empty aside from a man—this one man I always see.

I've seen him for years, as long as I can remember. Long gray hair, ripped jeans, never in a shirt. Scrawny frame but not without power—taught, stringy muscles beneath tanned flesh. Homeless—an always-was, I'm sure. A stray, a true lifer.

I'm jealous of him, sometimes.

He's always picking trash off the road. Nothing to sell or trade. Just cleaning his space—our space. Work that no one else will do.

He never begs. He never asks for anything.

He fears God. I'm sure of it. Some god—maybe not anyone else's but his. At crosswalks he'll get on his hands and knees and slowly crawl across, muttering prayer. Before I had a car, I'd see him on the bus, climbing up the steps hand over hand, crawling up and down the aisle, between people's legs, praying under his breath.

Now he's here, in the dead vacant heat, setting down on his hands and knees at the foot of the crosswalk. He begins crawling across, one hand after the other, whispering prayer, unaware that I or anyone else is watching. That's true faith, true commitment. Performance not for anyone else but him and his god. One hand after the other, crawling to appease.

A roar from behind, chewing up the quiet. Rubbernecking, I catch a pair of headlights scythe around the bend, tearing toward us. I press on my horn to warn the man in the road, but he ignores it, continuing his slow scuttle. I honk again as the headlights gain, glowing at my back, pushing out in front of me, setting the man aglow, pulling at his shadow and stretching it far up the street like putty.

The car—a wine-red Scion—growls past me and collides.

The bumper flips the man on his back, pressing him down into the street. His body twists, tires and undercarriage wringing him. The rear wheels hump over his arms and legs and only then does the Scion brake.

The driver side opens. A man—a boy—steps out. Tufts of blonde hair poking out the bottom of a Patriots cap. White muscled forearms. Cheekbones with baby fat hanging off.

I know him. From the call center. The piece of shit. I dialed beside him earlier in the week. Spent his entire shift hitting on Mackenzie Russo. Zero completes. Piece of fucking shit. I can't remember his name. But now I know his face. And his car.

The boy's face conveys nothing. Just a mouth hung agape. Void inside. I watch him glance side to side, up and down the road. A panicked animal. Looking all over for witnesses but never glimpsing me.

I wait for him to approach the body in the street. To see if the man still breathes. I wait for him to look at what he did. But it never happens. He gets back in his car and tears off.

I toss the pizza box off my lap, crank the ignition and stomp the gas. The Camry heaves after him, rattling down empty Pleasant Street. He's far ahead but I can maybe stop him at the next intersection.

Like a miracle, the traffic light flips yellow, then red. *Stop, you fucker.* But true to his nature, the Scion pushes through, over the hump, down the hill through the colleges. I lean on the gas, eyes on the red light. *The streets are dead*, I tell myself. *No one's coming through the intersection. I can just jet through, just this once. It'll be fine.*

I slam the brake just ahead of the light.

I was right. The intersection's clear. I could've run it with no consequence. Too late now. The Scion is gone.

The light switches green and I swing a uey, back toward the body in the street. Twisted, swollen all over. No breathing. Blood spat from lips and nose, already congealing. Limbs crushed into pavement. I get out of the car and scream for help but nobody answers. I call 911 and nobody comes.

The body's still in the street the next day, blackened with flies. People walk by, they drive by, but they don't look. They pretend it isn't there.

I make it to work early. First time in a long while—longer than I can remember. I walk the parking lot, chaining butts, looking for the Scion. Watching as everyone rolls in for their shift. I wait fifteen minutes for that stupid red Scion but it never arrives so I go inside to sign in.

"What took you?" Dennis says. "I saw you get here like an hour ago."

"Had an emergency," I say. "I had to, like, check on something."

"Oh. You okay?"

"False alarm."

"Okay. I won't mark you. Sit down and get dialing."

I sit between Raul Vargas and Nashra Dar. I ask Nashra if she knows the young blonde kid who works here. "Drives the red Scion," I specify. She shakes her head. I wait for Raul to get off his call and ask him. He scrunches his face weird, like a whiff of halitosis, and says "No, why?"

"Haven't seen him today."

"You two are pals?"

"There's something I want to talk with him about."

On break, I go out for a butt and see Tony and Chelle by the smoker's pole. I ask if they know the kid. "Why?" Chelle asks. "Is he selling?"

"So you don't know him?"

"Not really," Tony says. "I've sat next to him a couple times. He uses the name Dustin Callahan when he dials if it's the guy you're talking about."

"Does he drive a red Scion?"

"I don't know, man."

I head back to Dennis at the supervisor desk. "Hey, was Dustin Callahan scheduled for today?"

"Excuse me?"

"Was he on the schedule? Or is it his day off or something?"

He narrows his eyes on me. "I don't think that's any of your business."

"Did he call in sick?"

"What did I just say? Get back to dialing."

Back at my station, Raul eyes me from the side. "Did you find out about your buddy?"

"Yeah, it's fine. Forget it." And I get back to dialing.

◆

In the spare room, on the cot, I wait for sleep. Fits and starts. Miniature images flitting beneath eyelids. Castles hammered out of torn steel. Burned bodies growing swollen in lakes. An enormous hand, the size of Providence, smashing down to soil and concrete, dragging across Earth's surface, wiping out all in its way.

Then it hits.

Dustin got caught. That's why he wasn't at work. The cops found him, easily. There're cameras everywhere. There's no privacy. That has to be it—a CCTV camera captured the crash, the kill, his face, his plates. There it is. It's so obvious. I'll be reading about him in tomorrow's paper.

And with that, the visions slip away into warm darkness. My muscles unwind and I sink into mattress. The night wraps around me and I'm gone.

He's at work the next day. Smiling. He's smiling. Bullshit blonde hair under that stupid fucking Pats hat, bopping along, smiling. Just hanging out, chatty with the other teen wastes.

I take my first break early and go investigate his car. It's been washed. What a piece of shit. The only evidence is a cracked front bumper. No problem there. You can explain something like that away easy.

Hit a wall in the parking garage.

Hit a dog on the way home. Nothing I could do, it ran right out.

I don't know what happened, I just came back out and found it like that.

A fucking demon. Ruiner of life.

Back at my station, I barely dial. All I can think about is what I'm going to do. What I'm going to say. The words don't come together in my head. Only a vision of light and undefeatable justice. A brilliant white flame erupting from my throat, to lick the wickedness from the whole of his being.

Clock hits 9:59. I'm scheduled till 12:00 but the college kids never work late shifts so I switch off my dialer and watch the supe desk, waiting for him to sign out.

"Hey. Ezra." Dennis stares right at me. "What are you looking at?"

I ignore him.

"I have you down for 12:00, Ezra. Keep dialing."

I stare the biggest fucking knife at him. "I'm resting my eyes."

"That's what breaks are for."

And here he comes. Dustin bopping up to the sign-out sheet, one of the first in line. I get out of my chair and jog past the queue. "*Hey.*"

He turns and sees me. He tenses. Maybe recognizing something in my expression. Understanding fury and fate. He drops the pen on the sign-out sheet and speeds toward the door.

"Ezra." Dennis stands, coming at me. "You gotta stay dialing your whole shift. Man, you know this."

"I have to take a fucking dump, Dennis." And I rush past him, to the main lobby. Empty except the security guard. I jog through the sliding doors into a wall of slumbering heat, just as the bloody Scion rips past, out of the lot into another violent night.

⌄

I wait in the doorframe for Barb from HR to look up. Hunched over her desk in a scoliotic curve, running a pen down triplicate forms. I stand there for minutes, waiting for her to notice. Cherishing each second, running through my spiel in my head.

Finally, she looks up. "Jeez." Her head rolls—a small startle—but her eyes stay dead empty. "Yeah? What is it?"

I step forward, wiping sweat from my forehead. "I'm sorry. I wouldn't normally do this." Words I've been practicing the past half hour, steeling up, staring at my reflection in the computer's screen. "It's Bruno. Do you know

Bruno?"

She places her pen on the desk and rests her chin on her palm. "I might know Bruno."

"He's got drugs out at his station."

She nods and looks back down at her papers. "Lots of people got prescriptions. They got to take them at certain times."

"He's rolling a joint."

She stops. Closes her eyes, exhaling the entirety of her.

"And I think he has a gun." An embellishment on my part, possibly. One time on a smoke break, I overheard him bragging about carrying. Never saw any evidence to confirm, but none of that matters. All I need is for Barb to leave this room.

She opens her eyes, resting them back on me. "Alright." She stands, grinding stained teeth beneath bloodhound jowls. "Where is he?"

We head down the hallway, toward the dialing hall, stopping at the door. I point out the row where I'd seen Bruno earlier. "Alright," Barb says. "I'll take care of it. Go back to your seat."

"I need to use the restroom."

"Alright, go ahead. Then get back to it."

Barb follows me to the lobby, stopping to talk with the security guard. I continue around the corner to the men's room and stand outside the door.

"Hope you didn't think it'd be a quiet night," Barb says, and tells the guard everything I told her. He gets up and follows her into the dialing room.

I jog back to the HR office and hit the filing cabinets, yanking open the top drawer. *A-D*. Fingering through the files—*Cabello. Cafferty. Cahill.* There—*Callahan.* I pull it, flip through, find his address and snap a picture, then return it to the cabinet and head back down the hallway.

"What the fuck are you talking about?" Bruno's voice shouts out from the dialing hall. "What the fuck?" Passing the doorway, I catch him swinging at the seventy-one-year-old security guard. I take the corner, through the lobby, through the sliding doors, to my car.

᠕

No music. Just a voice on the stereo instructing me where to go, through winding bends to suburban hills. "Go through this light. Then take the first right." I swing a right onto Snowberry Court. "Your destination will be on your right." Cruising past identical pre-fab saltbox houses, windows lit like jack o' lantern sockets.

And there it is—the Scion settled in its driveway.

"Reach your destination."

I roll on further and take the first right onto Trumble Lane. Slow it to a park beside a row of arborvitae. I open my bag and remove what I need. The hoodie slips over my torso and the knife grip into my palm. The crowbar slips behind my waistline, down my leg, obscured.

Heading up the street, the crowbar gives me a stiff gait. Trying to make it look natural as cars pass, it occurs how obvious I look. Especially in this neighborhood. The type of place where they call cops on dogs barking. But I keep on, half-expecting each oncoming car to light up white and blue the moment they clock me.

But they just drive by. No one stops me, cop or otherwise.

The Scion and its house sharpen into view. Waiting for

one last car to pass, I pull out the crowbar so I can really move. Crouching low against the bushes, scuttling in fast, breaching the driveway. The Scion just ahead, beneath a lit up house. I toss the crowbar to the grass and creep to the vehicle's rear, watching for movement, inside or out.

The knife unfolds. The tires deflate with familiar gasp. I wait a beat between each one—for a motion detector to flash on, for a figure to run past a window, for the front door to swing open. Some kind of confrontation. But it never comes—just a long empty ellipsis between each stab. A coma of a house. When the final tire deflates, I collect the crowbar from the grass and climb the steps to the entrance.

First try the knob. It doesn't turn, the lock catching on the latch. Then pound the door. Give him one last shot to do the right thing. "*Hey,*" I yell. "*I know you're in there.*"

Only quiet. No scrambling. Not even the lightest footfalls.

"*I just want to talk.*"

Nothing.

The crowbar's tip presses between the door and frame as though it were crafted for this precise purpose. I wedge it in tight and push. The pressure warps wood, bends it. Press harder. *Snap.* One last shove. It's like teeth breaking. The wood cracks deep around the lock, and the door wrenches open and the crowbar clatters to my feet.

The doorframe explodes beside my head. A shower of soil, clay, leaves and root systems. A clay pot thrown, at me. A miss. Dustin stands ahead, doubled-over, wide-eyed— first at me, then the knife in my hand. Twisting on his feet, he bolts toward the stairs. I head in after him, past vases and photos of smiling families and amusement parks. He's halfway up the stairs, whimpering and grunting, when I reach him. I climb quick, three stairs at a time. He's shouting something. Maybe just noise.

Reaching, I grasp ankle and pull.

Dustin falls forward, going horizontal. Chin meets hardwood. A sick crack. A break. A scream, a spit of rust. I yank him down to the ground floor, his head and chest thumping off the stairs like a falling ball, and drag him into the hallway.

The look on his face when I flip him over. A coward's face. Already given up. A stupid fucking gape. Stupid young green eyes.

"I just wanted to talk," I whisper, kneeling down, straddling the crease between his belly and chest.

"Please," I think he says. He kicks his knees up, lightly striking my lower back. He pushes at me weakly. Posing no threat.

I raise the knife. He's already wincing (coward), squeezing his eyes closed, throwing his hands in front of his face.

The blade rains down through his fingers, splaying them red and white. Down between his cheek and eye, glancing off bone into his eye socket. Slipping in like through a melon. Barely any give, a light *pop*—silent, only felt—and the blade is inside him and he's screaming. Nothing like a tire. No glass or plastic, no armor to hide behind. It slips in and I hate the sensation, feeling his insides through the steel. Chills and gooseflesh—a button being pounded inside me that's supposed to make me stop, an evolutionary measure to repulse me from homicide, but he's flailing and a bastard and my own will toward justice and preservation wins out.

The blade rises out of him, a plume of red, and he's still throwing out what used to be his hands, guarding an already ruined face. The blade descends, into his mouth, splitting teeth from gum, splaying a tongue. Splaying throat, scratching spine. Again, blade rising and falling, a machine on its own accord now, repeating until the mangled hands fall aside, until the face stops shaking, until the face is no longer a face, just something, something that was and now is not.

I'm covered in him. The him of him all over my knife, my hands, spattered across my chest. Hot wet soaking the crotch of his jeans, touching my jeans, soaking the crotch of my jeans. He pisses my pants. He soaks me in blood. An evil thing. His him on me. All over me. Sticky. Tacky on my skin. Disgusting. I hate it.

Head to the kitchen, the sink. Twist on the water, running it over the blade, my hands. It comes off easily, easier than you'd think, easier than it has any right to be. It becomes gone like it had never been there, like it was imaginary, a game we'd been playing.

The window above the sink looks out onto his car. If he'd only been looking, watching me crouch at his tires, he could have maybe seen me and prevented this. He could have changed it all if only he'd paid attention.

And like that a pair of headlights splashes over the road, swinging right, up the driveway, flashing over my face.

Oh no.

I duck behind the sink. This new car beeps, its door clicks open. Peeking over the windowsill, I glimpse a woman—somewhere in her fifties, in clothes too young for her, long grey hair curled into ribbons—exiting the car. She gapes at the doorway and runs toward it.

I reach the entranceway just as she steps through the doorframe. She jolts upon seeing me—such shock—and I steal the moment to grab her hair and swing her head into the wall. The plaster dents. She loses balance. My fist pulls back, full of thin silver strands.

I don't give her a chance.

The knife slams her shoulder. A plume when removed. Again. She makes no noise but gasps, air escaping. Familiar. I kick her to the floor and drag the knife across her throat, then her wrists, trying to make it quick because I don't want her to feel this. She doesn't deserve this, probably.

Finally she stops moving and I feel the warmth of her on my hands. The tackiness, congealing, on my hands, on my clothes. Jesus fucking Christ get it off me. Back to the kitchen, twisting on the sink, running it scalding over my hands, over the arms of my hoodie, over the front. It's all fucking over me. It's in the fabric. It's still in my clothes.

Okay.

How do you get it off?

Rushing down the hall, pushing open doors—bathroom? Where's the fucking bathroom.

A living room. A closet. Stairs to the basement.

Finally, at the ass end of the hall, a bathroom. A bath.

I tear off the shower curtain, kick on the water, and step beneath the rain fully dressed. My clothes soak instantly, accruing weight, sticking to my skin, chafing. Grab some fancy body wash, drizzle it over me. Scrub at my arms, at my chest. Rose blooms swirling from my feet, drifting across the floor, slipping down the drain. Scrub until it's all the way clear again, and step out, leaving the water running.

Tracking puddles through the hall, stepping over the woman's body, through the front door, back into the night. Halfway down the driveway, something clicks in my head and I turn around, head back up the steps, and collect the crowbar (covered in my prints. The house, everywhere I've been—covered in my prints). I slip it behind my waist-band, down my leg, and hobble back down the driveway, down the block, to my car.

Cops. Cruisers everywhere, driving home. Cruisers at the intersections, cruisers parked on the roadsides, cruis-ers blowing past me. Then, passing Venture Way toward Route 9, I look toward the office park. Flaring blue. The whole lot lit up with flashing blue light.

I drive till early morning. Carving a tunnel through the night, moon high silver and sharp as a knife. Black woods rolling out all around. Waiting for cruisers, for flashing blue lights, but they never come for me. At 3:00 AM I head home, strip naked in the backyard and burn my clothes in the BBQ grille.

I wake at 2:00. Throw on some cleanish clothes, head to the living room. Lynn stares at the TV, fist to mouth.

"What's wrong?" I ask.

She points at the screen. "Home invasion. Last night. Over in Sunderland. Whole family killed."

The screen shows a still photo, Dustin and the wom-an—his mother—alive in the past, smiling beside a Christmas tree. I look away. "Does two people really constitute a whole family?"

"What the fuck is that even supposed to mean? That's not the point, like, at all."

"This stuff happens all the time."

"Not around here."

The screen snaps to a news anchor. "— and Dustin, who worked for a local data research company."

Lynn looks at me, wordless. I shrug and go out to the garage.

⌣

I never find out what happened with Bruno. Dustin overshadows all of it. About half of work uses his death as an excuse to skip shifts. I'm utterly certain they don't actually care, but good for them. Everyone needs a break now and again.

Then two days later, the cops come by. Four or five of them—the moment I see blue and silver I turn to my monitor and stare at my reflection staring back. Watching my skin grow wet.

The guy next to me leans into my station. "You think this is about Dustin?"

"Don't know." But of course it is. I steal a quick glance as one of the cops leads Dennis into the training room. I stare back into my monitor, pretending to dial. Waiting for them to go down the lines of dialers, pulling each aside. No, they won't need to do that. They already know. They're asking Dennis to tell them everything he knows about me. Asking if he's seen me with any weapons. I had the foresight to leave my bag in the car, but I should have left it at home. The first thing they'll do is lead me out to my car for a full search. They'll find my bag, and the knife inside, which will be sent to a forensics lab where they will identify latent bloodstains, because I was an idiot and didn't bleach it or chuck it into the Connecticut River. They'll find my fingerprints, my hair, on everything. And fuck, I still have the photo of his address on my phone.

The rest of my life is easily foreseeable. I'll be put in a cage where men with werewolf physiques will split me from belly outward and sleep inside my skin. I will be less than alive. The inverse, in fact.

"You okay man?" Raul's voice beside me, snapping me out of premonition. I didn't realize I'd been weeping. I turn and the entire room is looking at me, including the massive troopers standing over the supervisor desk.

Raul holds out his palm. "Don't worry, I'll take care of it." He gets up and heads toward the troopers. He points me out and says something to them. The cops nod and say something back. Raul returns. "I told them you were very good friends," he says, and returns to dialing.

About an hour passes and the cops leave, never once speaking to me. The entire world feels like a trap.

Everything sounds like a footstep when it's late enough. Falling acorns. Wind pattering against grass. The quiet is most violent in summer because there is no real quiet—it's all animals and insects and flora scraping in the wind.

And on top of that, there are still people. As much as I want to block them out. Cars and mail delivery. And fucking helicopters. Thrusting above, flashing spotlights down, seeking something. Always seeking something. Always certain it's me, but it never is. Clawing through the sky, above our house, but always moving on. I don't know what to make of that.

◄

Dustin Callahan and his mother vanish from the news as quickly as they arrived. At work, it's like it never happened, like he never existed to begin with. A good month later, no one speaks of him. We just keep dialing.

This is how you'll be mourned here.

Moreover: no difference was made. I pushed against the world and the world wouldn't budge. The commute is still a holocaust—steel-wrapped phone poles and bodies through windshields and babies on asphalt. Nothing earned, nothing accomplished. A death amounting to nothing.

But scale. It's a matter of scale. Minor actions culminate. Culmination is key. Patterns are established. I've seen it. Stab one set of tires and you're a nuisance easily forgotten. Stab enough of them and a militia forms against you.

Patterns move people. Patterns weave the world together. Something exists only ever as an act of repetition. Anything that does not repeat cannot exist. An objective fundamental truth, and all that matters is whether you act in accord.

◄

The backroads are dead to me. The nighttime is dead. Dead empty worlds. When I'm the only car on the road, everything beneath my skin feels empty, like cold silver wind blowing through. It's all dead and I feel dead with it.

The highways. That's where I am. It's where the world happens. Life packed in, a hundred thousand vessels a day. Plastic and metal weaving together, holding space till they can no longer maintain. Collision, departure. That's the pattern and it happens here.

So I'll hop on I-91 from Northampton and drive it all the way south till I hit Connecticut. Then I'll get off, swing back around and gun it all the way to Vermont. Watching the traffic, the drivers' faces. Their maneuvers. Finding the repetition, where people push their luck.

There it is.

On that stretch in Holyoke, passing the soldier's home, a pale green Ford Focus rises out of the onramp, slashing across the lanes between me and a tractor trailer. It slides into the inside lane and leaps past. I flip my blinkers and follow.

The highway splits into three lanes, each packed with rush hour, and the Focus weaves through, gliding from the leftmost lane to right and back again, only inches between other vehicles. I follow its invisible wake, holding ground at four car lengths, finding breaks in the congestion and moving in. Gas to the floor and the Camry groans, roaring with upward inflection, catching purchase and advancing, hurling past the mall, now only two cars away. The Ford slashes diagonal again, from left lane to middle.

A Harley rises out from the onramp.

The Ford slashes middle to right.

I see it in my head before it happens: the Ford clipping the cycle's front wheel, the cycle wobbling, then tipping. And then it's happening for real in front of me, trailing behind the ghost of my premonition. The Harley tips, throwing the rider, and both disappear beneath a truck following behind.

The Ford keeps driving.

I slam the gas and weave through, threading needles, gaining. The Focus stays in the far right lane, and it's perfect, there's a ravine to the side, no guardrail. I haul up in the middle lane, matching speed. Through the window, I see the driver—a young woman, younger than me, lips moving, singing or mouthing a song. Big round sunglasses like insect eyes. Oblivious.

I yank the wheel.

She turns her head to see me just before our vehicles kiss. Just enough time to see her recognize what's about to happen. The opening of a scream. Then the shove, the *bang*, like a gunshot. The impact pushes me away but I wrench the wheel, staying on top of her. She pulls away, leaving the roadway, launching down the shallow ravine.

Another *bang*—a blast just beneath me. My right front tire blowing out. The rim hits blacktop, an anchor by mistake, swinging me in an arc, hurling me, flipping me into the ravine as well.

Rolling. Body yanking against the seat belt, swinging around, losing gravity, hanged from ceiling, smashing knees and fingers on objects, the walls of the compartment, my head on the steering wheel, then back around, until I'm sitting right side up again, awake and alive. The airbag never deploys.

It's a sick heat, a flu in a sleeping bag—either the air around me or just my body, I don't know anymore. I'm almost sick enough to puke and can't find my glasses. The world's a blur unless I squint. There may be blood in my hair. My neck won't turn all the way. Din in my head, a thick sharp *eeeeeeeeeeeeee*. Fire in my collarbone. A throb in my kneecap. I picture a cracked geode.

I look at my hands. Blurry stupid hands. I close them and my left hand closes. My right begins to close but the middle finger, I try to close it and it starts to close but it's like a rod's been shoved up inside. It tries to bend but instead it's all shrieking agony.

Feel along the crumpled flesh of the Camry. The imploded roof. The smashed windows. The engine shaking like a trapped animal until I switch it off.

It will never be driven again. My old steed. I begin to cry. Then I fish my bag out from the rear window, remove the crowbar and head back toward the other vehicle.

The green Ford Focus, crumpled all the way around, at rest on its roof. Engine still growling, tappets clanging, puffing grey clouds from the hood. *What the fuck did you do*, I say to her, wordlessly.

Another noise. A piercing squeal, other than the one inside my head. An organic alarm. A needle, a fist full of needles in my ear, harmonizing with my tinnitus. A voice. Real screaming. A child screaming.

I call out. "*Hello?*"

No reply but the scream, the engine, the scream, the hiss of coolant splattering and misting off hot metal. Wailing.

"*You okay?*" Toward the driver side window (broken out, candy-sized pieces scattered in the grass), a lump rests on the inverted ceiling. "Hello?" Resting the crowbar on my shoulder, I kneel to peer in. "Hello?"

The lump twists. A face reveals, in and out of focus—the driver. Bloody swollen lilac lips, front teeth all punched in. A twisted anus mouth. Her fist rises and points at me. A burst of mist into my chest.

Reel backward, almost losing footing. A sting, an abrasion in the air, crawling up my chest, into my mouth, up my nostrils, licking my eyes. Pepper spray fuck. Eyes going wet and blurry, with the woman crawling forward.

I wait for it. To go all the way blind. That scratchy fire dancing in my eyes—it persists, but my vision holds. And that's the thing: most civilian pepper sprays are little more than an irritant. No real stopping power. And here's a real life example. She made a mistake.

I move in.

Her neck snaps sideways under the crowbar's heel. Gurgle and wail. Bring it down again in a wet crack. Again. Again. Until she cannot drive, she cannot speak, she cannot sing. Until her only movement is twitching, until she can't even do that. I hit her until she shits her pants, a long wet fart, and I smell it past the pepper spray. I hate it disgusting *how could you fucking do this*. I hit her again, though she's already motionless. I hit her again for no reason, with no purpose. I hit her until I'm no longer compelled to.

◆

I feel along the Ford's inverted ceiling, covered in trash, fast food wrappers, small toys. There has to be something. A half-survived coffee cup. A can of soda. God forbid water. Anything to rinse out my eyes.

A flailing lump hangs from the rear. Flailing and screaming. An infant strapped in a car seat, locked in this hell, hanged upside down, screaming and screaming. A drill on a nerve. Pitch a rising arc, a dart swung up toward heaven, to fall and pierce me entirely. I look at the blur, the squirming blur, pink and yellow and green, the wailing blur just wailing, wailing unstoppable.

I squeeze my palms over my ears and scream back at it. I scream to drown out its scream, but my scream is identical, just more of the same scream, so I stop. I put my hands back to the ceiling/floor and grope.

There. Fucking there. When all hope is gone, my hand wraps a bottle. A baby bottle sloshing white.

◆

Back at my car, my poor beautiful car. Choking back the reek of almost sour milk poured over my face, rinsing my eyes. Slumped down to the grass against the driver side door. Looking up at the freeway, traffic blowing by. Truly impossible to appreciate just how fast unless you're standing still, watching.

Wiping away the milk. Waiting, in the sound of the traffic and wind and the screaming yards away. Waiting for the screaming to stop, to be overcome by sirens. Waiting for red boxy vehicles, muscular blue SUVs that could knock over trees, tearing over the lip to bring obliteration. Waiting for tear gas and bullets to fill my body. Waiting for war. I wait for the sirens but they don't come. They won't, not ever. No one to take me. No one to save me.

Balloon

if i pushed the tip of a knife through my belly you would hear a tight invisible hiss. a stovetop clicking over to light & the pilot's out. you would watch my skin shrink & wrinkle like facsimile & so little of me would be left a box would be a waste.

you will find the pornography & hints within binding but my terror is tucked in strangers littered throughout fifty mile radii. shaking in bed & sweat my words peeking from the collage of their abuse & my legacy.

you can only re-read so many times before stories become chapters & chapters become paragraphs & paragraphs become sentences & sentences become words & words become letters & letters become stalks & circles & clusters of ink or pixel.

& you could never believe the emptiness in my chest & head or the white filling my retina & wind so fast to pop eardrums & it's like water filled with salt or oxygen twisting into your heart & the lack of space between being here and being in everything & there's no way you could grasp it but it's okay & i'm okay & the world only grew that much more gentle & soft & calm & it's all okay. it's so okay.

The Roman Soldier

We did it as a joke. Renting the Westfield Econo Lodge jacuzzi room. A joke, but not really.

I'd mentioned it to Brian on a bowl ride maybe a month earlier. "I'm gonna rent a jacuzzi room for my birthday."

He laughed. "What?"

"At the Westfield Econo Lodge. We can, like, drink and smoke in there. No one will bother us. It'll be funny." Giving a jester grin. "It's a jacuzzi room."

He laughed again. "Okay, dude."

I told Efrim my plan later that week, over at his dad's place. I pushed open his door and he looked up from his computer, cracked lips and sinkhole eyes. He hadn't slept in days, obliterating his father's liquor cabinet and recording songs about the Jordanian Civil War.

"I'm renting a jacuzzi room for my birthday."

His eyes went live. He smiled the way a mask smiles. "A jacuzzi room?"

"Yeah, at the Westfield Econo Lodge."

He stomped out his cigarette on the hardwood, giggling, making a goblin face. "That's so fucking stupid."

Then Seth called the day of, while me and Efrim were coming out of Liquors 44 with the supplies. "Dennis, what's good?"

"I'm with Efrim," I said. "It's my birthday."

"That's delightful. Happy birthday. What're you jerks up to? You need any buttsex?" Our codeword for weed ("Soapy buttsex" if it was good shit). We told everyone the reason we called it that was because cops are less likely to follow you into the woods if they overhear you talking about "getting into some sketchy buttsex," but obviously that's a lie. We did it because it was stupid. It was funny.

"Yeah, absolutely. I'm renting a jacuzzi room. We've got some liquor."

"You're renting a jacuzzi room?"

"At the Westfield Econo Lodge. You want in?"

Silence, then laughter. "Okay, sure. I'm in. Pick me up at my place."

Everything I'd ever done was for someone else's enjoyment. In third grade, I stuffed my fingers down my throat, forcing a stream of puke (leftover hot and sour soup from Chinese takeout) onto the lunch table. The cafeteria came to life with disgust and awe. When I was twelve, I told the drama club I jacked off ten times a day (a lie—I hadn't once successfully masturbated, still unsure of the mechanics, of the necessary vigor to let the white out). It was a gift to them—something for them to joke about. Two years later, I'd tell my closest circle about the watermelon I hollowed out and fucked (another fabrication—I still didn't understand masturbation, and wouldn't until after high school). They gleefully tormented me about this for years.

This was my purpose. All I had to offer. I was sure of it. People won't keep you close out of love. But destroying yourself, letting others destroy you—it keeps them from hating you completely.

∧

The sign evoked a hospital, or a barbershop—words and bars in red and white. Centuries ago, hospitals and barbershops were the same thing, more or less—you'd go to the barber for shaves and cuts, but also bloodletting and amputation. That's why the poles look like candy canes.

The structure below was beige stucco and deep green roofing. Sickly trees clawing out from mulch. It sat between the I-90 off ramp and a Wendy's, overlooking Westfield—a gasping town, a murdered town, with streets and avenues full of feral dogs and monsters dressed in people's skin. An apocalypse happened there, was still happening, and no one quite knew what to do. So they climbed the tallest hill they could find and built an Econo Lodge on top. A retreat, an oasis you could afford.

We tore into the parking lot, sliding into a spot between a Humvee and a Pontiac station wagon. Efrim wanted to come in with me to register. He hated the idea of me doing anything without him. I told Seth to stay in the car.

"Why?"

"It's sketchy if it's three people."

"How is three sketchier than two?"

"If they see three guys renting a one-bed jacuzzi room, they're gonna think it's sketchy."

"Anyone who rents a jacuzzi room at the fucking Westfield Econo Lodge is gonna look sketchy."

"Just stay in the car. We'll be right back."

A grey weed miasma poured from our doors, quickly

diluting in the hot garbage air, and we headed in. The reception reeked of bleach, stabbing up my nose and scraping at my throat. The woman at the desk looked like Peter Cook but prettier. "Can I help you?" A voice that'd been choked. A collapsed voice—one that knew, deeply knew the world was ending, but you still got to pay bills. You still have to show up. We weren't old enough to understand, to recognize how much we had in common with this woman. We still thought our lack of franchise was temporary, that our best days were still in our futures. Genuinely believing that one day, if we played our cards right, each day would be as carefree and joyous as this one.

"Yeah, do you have any jacuzzi rooms?" I held in my laughter, but Efrim giggled at my side, gently bucking forward and back.

The woman's face stayed iced. "Let me look." Dried apricot hands tapped across the keyboard. "Do you want the square jacuzzi or the heart-shaped one?"

Efrim cackled. "Oh, you gotta get the heart-shaped one."

"Yeah, I'll take the heart-shaped." She copied my ID and took my cash.

❦

It was exactly what you'd expect: creamy, mold-speckled wallpaper peeling where the walls and ceiling met. A charcoal carpet with grey and wine accents. A bed and two chairs. And wedged into the corner, set before two streaked wall-length mirrors: a concave, dog-dick-red heart, encased in concrete and tile. Its bottom coated in chalky grey stains.

"Whooaaa," Seth said. "This is pretty, pretty, pretty

grimy."

"No." Efrim ran his hands over the tub's lip. "It's per-fect." He twisted the jacuzzi knobs and steaming grey wa-ter thundered out.

I flipped on the bedside lamp—the shade runny with weird amber resin—and punched the A/C down to sixty de-grees. The unit shuddered and gasped. I filled the bathroom sink with ice and stuck the Smirnoff and Bloody Mary mix in. The OJ wouldn't fit, so I took off the top of the toilet tank, poured down some ice and lay the bottle on top.

It's easy to get drunk fast if you want it to be. Orange juice neutralizes the choke of vodka, so you can down at least three Solo cups of the stuff in under five minutes. You won't gag, it won't twist your stomach. That's how clean it tastes. You can drink and drink and it'll only taste better the more you drink. Still young in our abuse, years before our guts would be ravaged by ulcer and abscess. I don't miss those days (I can't, it's impossible), but I know Efrim does.

Three screwdrivers and two bowls and the steaming grey water rose to the tub's lip. I shut off the faucet and got the bottles from the bathroom, placing them atop the jacuzzi's tiled edge. We stripped. Efrim's wire body practically hair-less, all sallow skin, tight starved muscles clinging to bone. Seth wrapped his waist with a towel before disrobing. We turned on the jets and slipped in.

Efrim and I sunk into each of the heart's butt cheeks,

while Seth sat at the point. Cramped, but as long as we clung to our corners we wouldn't touch. Any touching would need to be deliberate and ironic. "It isn't gay if people are watching," I'd told Efrim once, wobbling drunk at some dance night (no, I know the precise one), before sucking on his disgusting tobacco-resined lips. Everyone around us laughed.

I poured another round. The heat climbed into my skin, mixing with the liquor, strengthening its power. Water pounded at my vertebrae, punching gently at my discs. I touched myself beneath the murk of the jets, where no one could see.

"Shit, I'm fucked up." I pointed to Seth. "Is tonight gonna be a bad night?"

Seth looked down and away.

I nudged Efrim's elbow. "Seth and I get fucking *bad* when we drink together."

"We don't need to talk about that," Seth said.

"Like two years back? We got this bum to buy us growlers. Fucking plowed through them shits like nothing, so quick we didn't even know we were wasted until we stood up. Like *whoooaaaa*. We go outside, smoke some butts, and end up tossing half his dad's firewood into the road."

"Hold on," Seth said. "It was like five pieces of wood."

"Like fifteen. At least fifteen. Like twenty pieces. Then we spend the whole night waiting to see if cars will run them over." I laughed. The only one laughing.

"Nothing happened though. I knew nothing was gonna happen."

"Or how 'bout that night at Gianni's? So they used to have this bartender, and he never carded us. So one night we go in there and pound three Long Island Iced Teas. Like one after another. I give this guy a look and we head down to the bathroom, like this shitty basement bathroom, and we do a little coke. Next thing we know, we're *fucking that place up*. I'm talking smashing the goddamn mirror, I'm puking in the air dryers, just out of fucking control. It was like fucking Fallujah."

"Come on man."

I slapped Seth on his shoulder. "This guy's a fucking monster when he drinks. At least when he drinks with me."

"Stop."

"What? These are classics. It's fun. This is fun."

Efrim frowned, eyes away from us. Looking at himself through the fog in the mirrors. Not disgusted. He didn't care about strangers' tires popping over splintered wood, or the poor bar-back who'd have to clean up me and Seth's wrath. He didn't care about those things. He was only jealous. He always was jealous, of any world existing without him. He still is, and will always be.

Eight months back at Seth's twenty-first birthday, he dropped acid and sliced a cigarette out of his girlfriend's mouth with a katana. Weeks ago, he saved an elderly woman who'd collapsed face-first in the Stop & Shop parking lot. Her glasses snapped apart, wire frames sticking in her retina. I didn't tell those stories. Those were hero stories, and I didn't care if Efrim knew them.

We drank another round, smoked another bowl, ripped around three more butts, just ashing over the side onto the carpet. Seth's head lolled, nodding forward before snapping back. "I feel like I'm gonna pass out." He stood, wobbly, lifting one leg over the side of the red heart and tile, dropping his foot down on the blackened carpet. Glistening thick thighs, belly and ass. He pulled a towel from the floor and wrapped himself quick.

I swigged from my cup. Head swimming and throat ached, cracked. "Yeah, not a bad idea." I stood up.

"You fucking *pussy*." Efrim put on a faggy lisp, like he always did when we were drunk and around other people. "Come back here and stop being *such a fucking pussy*." He grabbed my wrist and gave it a yank.

My feet skidded, my knees buckled, but they didn't fall out. "I'm gonna crack my *fucking head*," I snarled, pulling away, my wrist slipping from his fingers, nearly toppling backward over the rim.

Efrim squinted, cutting his mouth into a frown. He'd given me the same look the last time we'd done mushrooms, when he grabbed a kitchen knife and jokingly waved it at me, before winking and returning it to the drawer. He raised his fists and leaned forward.

"Don't." I put my hands up in front of me.

Giggling through creased frown, he pushed forward, swinging a long stringy arm, slapping me just between my crotch and belly.

"*No*. Fucking stop. Knock it off." But this was what drew us to each other's orbits. The constant push and pull. Always competing for the room. Gobbling up each other's oxygen, just sucking it out of every space we occupied.

"Maybe we should be a little more quiet?" Seth said.

Efrim splashed water toward him and the bed. "Sweetie, the only people here are lawyers and their whores. It's fine."

I stepped down to the carpet (soaked and slimy, like something alive), grey churning against my skin, space pulsing against my eyes (the vodka in my blood circulating through me, top to bottom, limb to limb, over and over). I grabbed a washcloth from the floor and tied it around my balls and outer thigh, so only the side of my sack was visible. I asked Seth (sprawled across the bed, a round leg peeking through his bath towel, like a gutter Frazetta cheesecake piece) if he wanted another drink.

He grimaced, but then: "Yeah, sure. A Bloody Mary. I didn't eat today."

Grabbing the bottles, I filled half his Solo cup with vodka and the other half with Bloody Mary mix. I dug into a grocery bag and tossed him a bag of potato chips. Then I grabbed the disposable camera. Dew beads clung to it, like it'd been sweating.

Seth ignored the drink and tore open the chips, scooping fistfuls into his mouth. Lifting the camera to my face, I framed his sprawled wet body in a tiny black box—a diorama. Something unreal. He stopped eating. "What are you doing?"

"Documenting our *love*," I said, misquoting a movie I otherwise couldn't remember. I wound the advance. *Click. Flash*. Captured.

"Don't let him have all the fun." Efrim rose from the tub, still in that raging queen affect. He lifted his leg, standing his foot on the jacuzzi's lip, like Teddy Roosevelt perched on a bear carcass. The heat dragged his ball sack toward his knee. An old man's sack. I turned the camera toward him. *Click click click.* Lifting his palm to just beneath his chin, he blew a kiss. Through the black box of the viewfinder, he looked doused in blood.

⌁

Brian and Roy swang by. I answered the door in my washcloth loin cloth and Brian's face melted with equal parts inspiration and disgust. Looking past me, over our wreckage. "Jesus Christ." Roy just stared down at his shoes, clenching and unclenching his jaw.

Efrim flung a thin knobby finger at Brian. "Why don't you get more comfortable." Pushing past me, rushing him, grasping his belt.

"*No. No no no.*" Brian pushed back at Efrim's hands, laughing but some real panic there too.

I went for Roy, hands outstretched toward his crotch. He grimaced, almost smiling, but mostly grit teeth, shaking his head. "If you touch me, I'll fucking belt you."

Efrim made a few more lazy gropes at Brian before slapping his ass, hard and loud. He teetered backward in the heat, face turned slick and lazy, sloshing, rapist eyes. Lumbering into me, pushing his belly into mine, gyrating sweaty and slick. I pressed further into him, my belly slipping off and around his starved concave pelvis. "Oh here's the real man," he said. Humping. A joke. Blood rushing to my shaft. My balls slipping out from the washcloth, slapping the inside of his thigh. A joke.

"Jesus Christ." Brian laughed and clapped, red-faced, pushing past us, looking away and then looking back. "You should just give him the Roman Soldier and get it over with."

Efrim stopped and squeezed my shoulders (those enormous neanderthal hands), like he could yank my flesh right off the muscle. His mouth became a circle, an O, a perfect round void punched through his face. Eyes wild like when I first told him about the jacuzzi room. "Dude."

I didn't say anything.

"Dude," he repeated. "We have to."

"I don't know man."

"We have to. Don't be a bitch."

"Let me piss first." I slipped out of Efrim's hands and into the bathroom. My piss sputtered toxic orange into the pristine pool, so dehydrated. Through the walls, I could hear them all talking, then laughing. Someone—Efrim— hushing them. Then bad stage whispers. Laughing again. I flushed and came back out and they all stopped and stared at me, smiling.

◢

We found it online. No pics, just a .txt file. This collection of sex positions. At least half were fake, like ones no one could've possibly done. Like the Disrespectful Winston— you fist a girl (or a guy, I guess) in the ass, get a fistful of shit and rub it in her (or his) face, like *Look what you did. You should be ashamed of yourself.* Or the Teleporter: you bang a girl (or a guy, I guess) doggystyle, facing a window, and you swap out with a different guy with the same sized dick. Then you creep outside, go around to the window and wave while the other guy keeps plowing her (or him). Probably no one's ever done that either.

But Efrim's favorite was simple and entirely plausible. When he first read it off to me, the image snapped together in my head like one of those cheap 3D animations. *Click*. The Roman Soldier.

I cackled. Efrim cackled with me. We told it to our other friends, who cackled too. Simple and perfect, like an orchid, or a scalpel. Like all the best jokes.

᭡

I laid down on the floor, the whole carpet saturated, soaked and slimy and cold. Brian wound the disposable camera's advance. *Click click click.*

Roy leaned over me. "You sure you want to do this dude?"

I sat up. "Can I get another swig?"

Efrim handed me the vodka. Even though it was almost gone, the bottle felt heavier now than when I'd bought it. I took my swig. I could barely even taste the burn at that point. I handed it back. "Alright," he said. Face scrunched, shaking giddy. "You ready?"

"Yeah, sure. I guess."

"You heard'em." He stood over my face. A strange inverted valley between his legs. A sacred mountain. All my futures. He unbuckled his knees and began descending.

"Jesus Christ," Brian said. "Holy shit."

Efrim lifted and held his cock. His hips descended lower, lower, closer, closer, until they almost smothered the light. I closed my eyes.

Warmth. Insane warmth. One sac over one eye, and then the other. Soft loose flesh like a grandmother's throat. A weird reek—of shit and sweat, but also beyond those scents. But it was the warmth, this fleshy sticky fucking warmth on my face. Warmth like heaven. A pink pig draped over my face.

"Holy shit," Seth said.

Then down, draped down my nose. A pungent tube. Hot as a stroke. A thimble's worth of sticky fluid dribbled from its end, down my septum.

It was done. A ball over each eye. His cock down my nose. A flesh helmet. A mask. I became the Roman Soldier.

The shutter clicked. The room screamed and laughed. The flesh jiggled on my face, but didn't let up. I could hear Efrim hushing everyone. He whispered. "So ... lift ... hold ... I'll —"

"What's going on?" I said. His crotch reek slipped into my mouth, sour like mold.

"Nothing," Efrim said. "Just a second." More whispering. "Don't let ... the rest —"

"Yo I think I'm done here."

"Okay, okay." The flesh lifted off my face. Opening my eyes, black became brown became the room, the mold-speckled ceiling. Efrim stared down, bloody eyes, teeth locked in gaping crescent. "Happy birthday." Raising the Smirnoff bottle above his head. Bringing it down.

Crack.

The world goes hot. Hot and wet. *Crack.* The world becomes slick and hot and gaping. *Crack.* Throwing my limbs up in front of me. Trying to scream. A thick round knee dropping to my throat. *Crack.* The world as two sets of hands holding me down. *Crack.* The world as glass against skin and hair, as glass against bone. *Crack.* The world as my nose plunging down into face. Teeth snapping against glass. *Crack.* Booted feet stomping ribs and crotch. The world as grunts and laughter. *Crack*. The world as caved-in ribs and burst testicles. *Crack*. My skull breaks before the glass does. And when the bottle finally falls to splinters, Efrim yanks the phone off the nightstand and pounds my face till it's no longer a face, until it's no longer anything. They stand there, heaving, inhaling the mist, the reek of mold and piss and shit and brains, they huddle over my body, they hug and they laugh.

⌃

It's something they'll always remember. Something for when they're old, a reminder of what it's like to be young. Brian and Roy finally strip, they hold their dicks and piss on my body, into the broken hole that used to be my face. They'll pose with my body, snapping pictures, knowing they'll never be developed, that the camera will be burned in the bedside trash can. They'll watch the sunrise from the balcony, streaked with blood, smoking cigarettes and the last of Seth's buttsex, telling each other secrets they'd never shared with anyone and never will again, laughing and crying, holding each other, kissing each other's foreheads and cheeks with dry, ripped up lips. Saying how much they love each other. They will pull my body onto the bed, fill the sheets with toilet paper and towels and set it alight. They'll leave, loading into Roy's car and setting off onto the highway, dropping everyone at their respective homes. They will sleep the rest of the day, wrapped in cotton cocoons while the A/C flushes out the summer fever. Or maybe they won't sleep at all, shivering, replaying the night over and over, sometimes giggling, sometimes completely still.

It bursts, blooms and is no more.

He wakes up.

Film
Making

It was five years and two weeks when we filmed. She was the dead woman and I played her husband.

I tip the Ziplock and drizzle a shotgun-red halo around her forehead's perimeter. Only a little makes it into her hair. She slipped—cracked her head on the hardwood, the bottom of her boots caked with ice and slick. (What we already shot).

The aperture shifts and it's behind my shoulders and I mock tears over her body. Later, I'll make her spirit rise with opacity adjustments and overlays. She will move through her kitchen (my parents', really) and hesitate over a picture of her and her husband (a photo of us—the real us—from a year before, holding half-sour pickles at the Brimfield Flea Market). She will walk through the house and through plate glass into snow (freshly fallen—not in the storyboard but it works). She will walk through the snow and lie between two maples, holding in a quiet place—all quiet and grey. She will lie and close her eyes and fade and drift apart from This Place and be gone and be quiet and grey.

Everything preserved I see, in milky plastic video. Milky like thin disgusting milk. Everything more or less how I envisioned.

The dead woman laughs and I wash strings of blood from her hair. We kiss and eat leftover mashed potatoes and stuffing. We depart the house she died in and drive back to our apartment, studded tires gripping iced concrete.

BURNED
ASFUCK
▬
SO
ALIVE ⬡

Acknowledgements

"Waxing Moon" originally appeared in *Gravel Magazine*.

"The Young People" image courtesy of Nick Verdi and Isidorah Germain.

"Where We Breathe" was edited by Mike Corrao and Andrew J. Wilt, and originally appeared in *Collected Voices in the Expanded Field* (11:11 Press). The title and lyric excerpt are taken from the Boys Night Out song of the same name.

"Burn You the Fuck Alive" was edited by Maggie Siebert, and originally appeared in *HARSH*.

"The Buried Man" was edited by Ian Kappos and Karter Mycroft, and previously appeared as part of *Los Suelos, CA* (Surface Dweller Studios), a multimedia project consisting of short fiction, visual art, a video game, and a goddamn skramz band, with all proceeds benefiting the California Rural Legal Assistance Foundation. Check it out at lossuelos.com

"Poison Nurse" was edited by Charlene Elsby, Alisa Leigh, and Lindsay Lerman.

A portion of "In the Shadow of Penis House" originally appeared in *Witch Craft Magazine* and was edited by Elle

Nash. Another portion originally appeared in *Acéphale and Autobiographical Philosophy in the 21st Century* (Schism Press), and was edited by Gary J. Shipley and Edia Connole.

"Puppy Milk" was edited by Justin A. Burnett and originally appeared in *Hymns of Abomination: Secret Songs of Leeds* (Silent Motorist Media), a celebration of the work of Matthew M. Bartlett. As such, "Puppy Milk" borrows several elements from Bartlett's oeuvre, such as the town of Leeds, a sinister radio station, and goats.

"Highway Wars" and its title (a misheard Smashing Pumpkins lyric) originates with my very good friend Justin Davis Jacobs, who brought the concept to me several years ago. Many of his ideas made it into this final version.

"Balloon" originally appeared in *decomP Magazine*.

"The Roman Soldier" was edited by Maggie Siebert and Caitlin Forst, and originally appeared in *NDA: An Autofiction Anthology* (Archway Editions).

"Film Making" originally appeared in *Unbroken Journal*.

Final edits completed by Ben DeVos and B.R. Yeager.

BEHIND THE MASK

ANOTHER MASK